Everything He Thought He Knew

Also by Marcus Lopés

The Flowers Need Watering

Everything He Thought He Knew

Marcus Lopés

TORONTO, CANADA

Marcus Lopés
Toronto, Ontario
Canada

Publisher's Note: This is a work of fiction. Names, characters, places, and incidents are a product of the author's imagination. Locales and public names are sometimes used for atmospheric purposes. Any resemblance to actual people, living or dead, or to businesses, companies, events, institutions, or locales is completely coincidental.

First Edition

Book Layout © 2017 BookDesignTemplates.com
Cover Design: Lieu Pham
                www.covertopia.com

A previous version of this novel, entitled *Freestyle Love,* was publshed by Lazy Day Publishing in 2011.

Everything He Thought He Knew / Marcus Lopés

Issued in print and electronic formats.

ISBN 978-0-9958294-3-5 (softcover).--ISBN 978-0-9958294-2-8 (PDF)

To J. R. Fortier,
who taught me what love is all about.

For the people I love
who make this world shine bright.

Preface

I didn't always want to be a writer.

Actually, that's not true. I didn't always know that I wanted to be a writer. Growing up in a fairly religious household (staunch is, perhaps, the more apt word) and possessing a natural talent for the piano, I was *encouraged* to use my gift for the 'Glory of God.' So, I did … use my 'gift,' and spent my childhood and adolescence playing in church. And much to the dismay of the church elders! When I sat down at the piano, I could almost hear their moans and groans of disapproval before my fingers touched the keys. I had a penchant for doing the unthinkable: rearranging classic hymns like 'How Great Thou Art,' 'Amazing Grace' or 'There's Power in the Blood.' I was doing something that — to my parents' chagrin — came naturally to me. I was breaking the rules.

Although music dominated my formative years, I was a closeted writer. I wrote stories in notebooks and journals, which I hid under my bed. Returning to Canada after studying for eight months in Nice, France, that was when I realized writing — more than music — was my passion. And I gave myself over to it.

I quickly discovered that writing is a messy affair and that the road to success is paved with many obstacles (and rejection letters) along the way. But I wouldn't be dissuaded. Despite how daunting the writing life could be, I knew it was my calling. And I had to heed the call.

So, I wasn't surprised when, in the early part of 2005, I sat down and wrote a story about rules that mirrored my own life. My late teens to early twenties were turbulent years, and I needed rules to govern my daily life and to ground me. Those rules were ... unbreakable. And that story, published in September 2005 and entitled, "Malachi and Cole," later became my first published novel, *Freestyle Love.*

When *Freestyle Love* hit the electronic bookstores in 2011, I hoped for a bestseller. That didn't happen. And that disappointed. I thought I'd written a good book. After all, I'd worked hard on the manuscript — editing, reediting and editing some more. The publisher told me they loved the story and asked for very few changes. The reviews — some good, some (many) not so good — had me doubting my talent as a writer. The book limped to a slow death, and was pulled from online when the rights reverted back to me five years later.

During those five years I kept writing, working to hone my skills. I read books on writing to find anything of value to help me become a better writer. I had also written another novel, and began researching what it would take to self-publish. I decided to go the self-publishing route with *The Flowers Need Watering*, which is available on Amazon.

I learned a hard lesson with *Freestyle Love*, one that I wouldn't repeat with *The Flowers Need Watering:* the importance of a professional editor. In reviewing the manuscript for *The Flowers Need Watering*, my editor hit on all the big-ticket items — character and plot development, structure, continuity, story arc, theme development, repetition and plot holes. He didn't only point out what wasn't working, but also what worked well. Through that process I realized something else. Maybe *Freestyle Love*, despite what I thought at the time, wasn't my best effort. Now I knew I could do better. So, I decided to try.

What follows is a complete rewrite of *Freestyle Love* that has been through two rounds of vigorous editing by Dave Taylor of thEditors.com. I am eternally grateful for his insights and wisdom.

Throughout my writing journey, I've often felt 'caught' (*Caught* was the original title of *Freestyle Love* before publication) between the life expected of me and the one I imagined. Malachi Bishop and Cole Malcolm may or may not be caught by something more sinister: the idea of true love and its sure path. Malachi, a writer and professor of creative writing, is a rigid — even awful — man paralyzed by a long-held grief knotted around his heart. He is, perhaps, not the most likeable protagonist, but it's my sincere hope that he is a real one. Cole, a successful management consultant, is older and unafraid of the things that love is all about. *Everything He Thought He Knew* tells a story of two men caught by love and betrayed by it. It is a journey of self-discovery that forces Malachi and Cole to confront their present and their past, bringing into question the larger fantasies of home and their place in the world.

Everything He Thought He Knew doesn't guarantee the normative happily ever after ending of the romance genre. My hope is that it transcends it.

– Marcus Lopés, 2018

Everything He Thought He Knew

Prologue

THIS WAS IT. THE moment he'd been preparing for his entire life. The end of introspection and self-flagellation. Yet it felt … surreal. He still didn't believe it was happening, despite the evidence around him. The boxes stacked around the room. The walls stripped bare, dotted with holes where the IKEA print of New York taxi cabs, and framed photos of Toni Morrison and his other celebrity friends used to hang.

He remembered every moment that had played out here. He remembered the laughter. He remembered collapsing onto the chocolate-brown leather sofa as he read, and reread, the letter confirming his first novel had been accepted for publication. He remembered the sweaty, breathless sex on the sofa, the floor, in the shower. Rarely the bed. A past he'd carry close and into the future.

Yes, this was it. The moment when he felt, finally, like he'd become a man.

The commotion outside broke his reverie. Malachi Bishop bounced off the sofa, crossed the room and pushed open the balcony doors. The thumping music, the shouting and the skunky smell of burnt leaves rushed at him. Proof that it was

Friday night and all bets were off. He couldn't wait to be free from it all.

Jenna, Malachi's silver-haired neighbour, leaned over her railing. "I'm tired of you druggies acting like you're the only ones who live here!" she barked. "You need to learn the meaning of respect."

"Respect this!" a guy with blue hair shouted back from the balcony below and flipped her the bird.

"Oh, no you didn't…" Jenna stood up straight. "That's the final straw. Now I'm calling the police." She turned to go inside but froze when she spotted Malachi. "Do you believe those two?"

Malachi, watching the scene unfold below, stepped back from his balcony's railing and raised his hands defensively. His message was clear: leave me out of it.

"This is a good, family-oriented neighbourhood," she lamented. "Or at least it was until those jackals moved in."

"We're on our balcony," the blue-haired guy spat. "We can do as we fucking please."

"And the language," she said, indignant.

His fellow 'jackal' turned around slowly, blew out a large cloud of smoke and looked up. "Hey, Malachi! You wanna come down for a drink?"

Malachi bristled. They'd never been introduced, so how did the guy know his name? Despite how 'liberal' Malachi considered himself to be, he didn't voluntarily associate with guys who had tattoos covering their arms and multiple piercings. *Did he read my book? Is that how he knows me?* Not really knowing what to say, Malachi swallowed hard. When he caught the woman's accusatory look, as if he were in collusion with their free-spirited neighbours, he grimaced. "No.

No, thanks. I've got some work to do." He raced back inside, sliding the balcony doors closed with an unintentional bang.

He returned to the sofa and chuckled. He could still hear his disgruntled neighbour repeating her threat to call the police, that was until the music was cranked up even louder. He tried to block it out as he packed up the DVDs piled on the coffee table. Just then the phone rang and he jumped. He raised himself up slightly and reached for the phone wedged between the DVDs and a stack of literary journals. "Hello," he said, falling back into the sofa.

"I'm running late," Taylor Blanchard said.

"Where are you?" Malachi asked.

"Still at the office. I started reading your book after my last class and I haven't been able to put it down. God, Damien is a freakin' prick. I don't understand why Ryan hasn't left his sorry ass."

They laughed.

"Hurry," Malachi said.

"I will. I'm almost done with this chapter. I should be home in about twenty minutes. But is everything all right?"

"Yes. I just can't wait to see you." Even after three years of dating, they still acted like new lovers who couldn't get enough of each other. That first kiss when Taylor arrived home from work set off an atomic explosion of passion that had them naked almost instantly. They talked with an intimacy that, in many ways, scared them because neither of them had felt so connected to anyone else before.

"I'll hurry," Taylor said.

That made Malachi laugh. Ever since their first date, Taylor was always running late. It turned out to be a good thing. Malachi learned to practice patience.

"Should I pick something up for dinner?" Taylor asked.

"No. Well, maybe." Malachi paused. "It depends..."

"Depends on what?" Taylor sounded concerned.

"Your mother called," Malachi said quickly, as if expelling some evil force.

"What's the crisis this time?"

"No crisis. She's invited us over for dinner."

"Tonight?" Taylor sighed. "I'll call her. I'll say we already have plans."

"That's what you told her last week," Malachi said, curbing his urge to laugh.

"You want to have dinner with my mother? Fine. But we're not telling her we bought a house."

"You and your mother have too many secrets."

"You've met the woman, right? I didn't imagine that." There was a brief silence. "You know what she's like, and I'm not in the mood for the great inquisition. 'A house? How can you afford a house? What bank would give you a mortgage? I still don't know how you afford the car...' Christ, my ears are already ringing."

Malachi grinned. "She might surprise you."

"God, you're cute." Taylor chuckled. "And I love you."

"Now you're changing the subject," Malachi said coolly.

"Yes, I am. I'll be home soon. We can talk about it then."

"Yes, we will."

"See you soon, beautiful man." Taylor hung up.

Malachi tossed the phone back onto the coffee table. It was a week after the publication of his second novel, and they were excited about their recent home purchase. It took them five months to find the perfect house. Some were too small, most were too expensive, and the rest were too far from the city. And then they struck gold — a three-bedroom house on Regent Street in the section of town known as the Glebe. Immediately they saw themselves laughing and sharing Malachi's famous veal scaloppini and sweet potato gnocchi with their friends in the cosy dining room. It'd be so easy for them to manoeuvre about the airy kitchen as they cooked together. Then every evening wrapped up in each other on the sofa in the spacious living room. They'd each have their own office, and everything else they'd need — banks, coffee shops, grocery stores — were just minutes away on foot. Perfect. It was just perfect.

He smiled as he thought about Taylor and how he'd let himself be swept off his feet. He loved the way Taylor searched him out when he came home, taking him into his arms in a crushing embrace. His protector. His strength. His refuge. Malachi loved the way Taylor looked at him as though he was the only person in the world who mattered. He loved the tenderness of Taylor's touch, his spirit of generosity, his patience.

When it came to Evelyn Blanchard, Malachi thought Taylor needed to engage some of that patience. He'd lost his own mother even before she died. He let go of her without making any attempt at reconciliation. Taylor, if he were open to it, had the chance to be better than him, to not let silly misunderstandings separate him and his mother. Then again, perhaps Malachi would have been just as annoyed if his mother had doted over him the way Evelyn did Taylor. What would it be like to be the sole, and beloved, prodigal son? Malachi cringed.

His eyes roamed the books, stacked on the floor next to the coffee table, which he'd yet to pack. Sometimes it felt like a dream, but he knew this was real. He'd been caught up in his studies when Taylor came into his life and turned his world upside-down. Living in Ottawa, Malachi did what everyone else did. He joined the civil service and tried to shape a career he wasn't sure he wanted. All the while he kept writing, and Taylor championed his work. As he searched for meaning in a world filled with competing priorities, Taylor let him know what was truly important. When he was paralysed by long periods of self-doubt, Taylor reminded him of his worth. He needed that gentle handling now, especially after reading Jason Miller's harsh review of his novel in the local paper: *Bishop's rushed follow-up to his greatly overrated one-hit wonder,* All I Do Not Know is True, *is little more than a pretentious, predictable money grab. Clearly, Bishop is more concerned with proving how smart he is than in telling a good story.* He longed for Taylor to walk through the door and take him into his arms, hold him safe … and maybe even track down Jason Miller and slash his tires.

This apartment … it was where his adult life began on that humid August day when they'd moved in and built a home together. Sweaty and exhausted from hauling furniture up three flights of stairs, they sat on the sofa eating a Domino's pizza and sharing a bottle of Black Tower riesling. They were nervous, like on their first date, and uncertain as to what the future would bring.

"I love you very much," Taylor had said and reached for Malachi's hand.

The declaration stunned Malachi into silence, but not because he didn't believe it. It wasn't the first time Taylor had said that, but this time it was how he said it — with absolute conviction. He meant it. That was the moment Malachi realized he'd never love another man. "I love you, too," he said, the words coming easily. From that moment came a simple truth: Taylor was his life. All that mattered was making Taylor happy. He didn't care if that meant always doing the laundry or getting up at four in the morning to write so they could spend as much time as possible together.

Malachi realized that the blaring music had stopped. He sat up straight and glanced at his watch. It was quarter to seven, and Taylor should have been home by now. He picked up the phone and dialled Taylor's office number at the university. No answer. Then he called Taylor's cell. Again, no answer. He moved off the sofa and crossed to the window. He looked down into the street and saw a police cruiser pulling up to the curb. He smirked. Jenna finally had the nerve to call them. He watched the officers get out of their vehicle and enter the building. He looked up and down the street. It was empty. Where was Taylor?

He jumped at the knock on the door. Had Taylor forgotten his keys again? He rushed to the door and opened it. "I was beginning to worry…" He froze. Two grim-looking men — the police officers who he'd seen just moments before — gave their names and asked to enter the apartment.

Inside, the shorter man spoke first. "How are you acquainted with…" He paused to look at his black notebook. "Taylor Blanchard?"

"He's my fiancé," Malachi said with a slight edge. They'd talked about getting married, but neither of them had proposed.

"There's no easy way to do this," the officer continued. "There's been an accident…"

Malachi heard the words but they instantly fell away. Something about Elgin Street, a car and two pedestrians.

Investigators were still on the scene. Taylor had been hit first and succumbed to his injuries on the way to the hospital.

"I don't understand," Malachi said, feeling himself trembling. "I just talked to him … not even an hour ago. He was on his way home…" Tears filled his eyes and raced down his cheeks.

"I'm sorry for your loss," the other officer said.

"He lost consciousness almost immediately," the first officer said. "The pain … he wouldn't have suffered long."

"You're mistaken. I mean…" Malachi could feel his legs about to give out on him, and before he could move to the sofa he collapsed to the floor. When he woke up, one officer was kneeling over him, the other radioing for an ambulance.

"Don't move. Help's on the way."

He couldn't move as he thought about the plans they'd made for the future. They'd talked about hosting Taylor's family at Christmas in their new home, and visiting Paris the following summer. Suddenly, the man who was his saving force — a champion of his writing, his confidant, his best friend — had been plucked from his grasp.

How was he supposed to live without the man who'd taught him what love was all about?

Freestyle Love

(Present Day)

ONE

THE DARKNESS PROVIDED COVER and kept him hidden from the piranhas circling around him. Well, not exactly hidden, but at least slightly concealed. Cole was pensive as he dodged hungry looks whenever the strobe lights flared. He inched backwards, the square pillar now obscuring him from view. He just wanted to be left alone, to fade into the darkness that shielded him from the pain in his heart.

Maybe that was only partly true. That he wanted to be left alone. Or maybe Cole was looking for some type of connection, no matter how limited. Why else would he have wandered into Groove? If he'd really wanted to 'fade into the darkness,' he'd have gone to any other drinking establishment instead of the city's lone gay bar. Perhaps he just didn't know what he wanted, and that shouldn't have surprised him.

Cole gulped the last mouthful of his beer and, with his head down, edged towards the bar. He wasn't sure how much more of the thundering music he could take, yet there he was handing over a ten-dollar bill to the bartender. It was the only way for him to escape his present as much as his past. He couldn't do that when he was sober. Sober, he couldn't take down the beast running roughshod over his life. Drunk was better, drunk was safe.

"Oh, sorry," Cole said, his words somewhat slurred, when he bumped into the guy next to him. When their gazes met, his body went rigid. He stood there for a moment, eyes wide open and not blinking, and then extended his hand. "Cole Malcolm." He sensed the guy's hesitation but stopped himself from walking away. For once in his life, he wasn't going to be someone else's doormat. "What? Can't a guy say hello?"

"Malachi Bishop," was the barely audible reply, which was followed by a flimsy handshake.

"May I buy you a drink?" Cole was surprised to hear himself ask.

"Actually…" Malachi shoved his hands in his pockets. "I'm just heading out. Not really in the mood for this tonight."

"Me, either." Cole took a swig of his beer. "Why do we do it?"

Malachi raised an eyebrow. "Do what?"

"Suffer temporary hearing loss, get stupidly drunk and hop into bed with random strangers."

"Wow. Maybe that's your goal —"

"I know you don't know me well," Cole interrupted, "but I was being sarcastic."

Malachi pulled his hands out of his pockets and checked the time. "Like I said, I'm just on my way out. Enjoy the rest of your night." He walked away.

"That went well," Cole mumbled, his eyes glued to the man's back as he disappeared into the darkness.

Cole took another swig of his beer, which lodged in his throat, and then shoved his way through the crowd. He set his unfinished drink on an empty table and headed for the restroom. When he emerged a few minutes later, the deafening music made him stagger. This was a mistake. Whatever he needed, whatever he was looking for … this wasn't it. He shot blindly towards the exit, stepping on the heels of the guy in front of him and nearly tripping. He stumbled forward and, reaching to push open the door, crashed into the guy on his right. It was Malachi Bishop. They exchanged curious looks but didn't say anything. Cole sighed, pushed open the door and let Malachi pass through ahead of him.

Outside, Cole followed Malachi down the stairs and onto the sidewalk. "Malachi…" He grabbed him by the arm, then moved to block his path. "If you won't let me buy you a drink, could we maybe walk for a bit?"

Malachi peeled Cole's hand off his arm, waited a moment, then said, "Sure."

They walked in silence, avoiding looking at each other as the street noises held them hostage. Cole opened his mouth to speak a few times, but no words came. He didn't know what to say. He didn't know why he'd even wanted to walk with Malachi. What was he hoping to achieve? What did he think this stranger could offer him? They came to a stop in front of a 7-Eleven, which was doing a brisk business. Their eyes finally met, the light from the store's sign revealing their tired faces.

"I didn't think it'd be this hard," Cole said after clearing his throat.

Malachi covered his mouth as he yawned. "I don't really know what you mean."

"I came out tonight because I thought I needed…" Cole ran his hand down the left side of his face. "I don't know, I…" His voice cut out and, at a loss, he turned to walk away. He felt the firm hand on his shoulder holding him in place.

He wouldn't look at Malachi, didn't want him to see the tears banking in his eyes.

"You've lost someone you care about," Malachi said, his voice rumbling low, softer even. He pulled his hand away.

Cole spun around and didn't bother wiping the tears off his face. "My brother, Paul, but how did you know?"

Malachi clasped his hands together behind his back. "I know the look. I see it every morning when I shave." He bit down on his lower lip. "What happened to Paul?"

"He took his own life a month ago," Cole said quickly. "I tried to be there for him. I mean, I knew how much he struggled, but I didn't know just how bad it was. He didn't like to talk about it, as if that didn't make it real." He paused. "Paul was my best friend, and now he's gone."

"I'm sorry."

"There's this void, this gaping hole in my life and I don't know what I'm supposed to do. I try to remember what his voice sounds like, his laugh..." Cole rolled his shoulders. "It gets harder with each day. I'm afraid that one day I'm going to forget everything about him."

"You won't forget him," Malachi said, his voice scratchy and raw, unable to camouflage his own torment. "You'll hold onto the memories you have of him, remember what you meant to each other."

"I hope you're right."

"It gets easier. Right now, because you're still in shock, you don't think that it can get easier, but it does." Malachi rubbed his eye before a tear could escape. "And you'll always remember the sound of his voice and his laugh. It's what gets you through each day."

Cole trained his gaze on Malachi, whose eyes seemed moist. The change in the man was remarkable, no longer a mysterious and distant stranger, but someone who actually seemed to care. "Are you okay?"

"I'm fine." Malachi took a step forward. "It's late. I should really head home."

Cole took a matching step backwards, blocking Malachi's path. "You've lost someone, too, right?"

"Half a lifetime ago."

"And it still hurts?"

"Always," Malachi said. "Listen, it's been a long day and I —"

"If you're not able to talk about it, then how am I supposed to believe that it gets easier?"

"With faith," Malachi said with an unexpected surge of conviction. "You have to believe."

"I don't think that I have that kind of faith," Cole said.

"You do. We all do." Malachi offered a reassuring smile. "Don't dwell on what you didn't do for Paul, or how you think you failed him."

"In high school, we rowed together and won the provincial championship twice. Then after university, we met up for drinks a couple of times a week. Sometimes I'd just look at him and knew he understood. That drove our brother and sister crazy." Cole chuckled. "I could tell him anything and he never judged me."

"Look, if you need to talk…" Malachi pursed his lips and pushed them from side to side. "My place isn't far."

"Are you sure?" Cole regretted the question as soon as it crossed his lips. He wasn't ready to say goodbye, to let go of the hopeful feeling he felt for the first time since his brother's death.

"I'm sure." Malachi began to move off.

Cole waited a moment, uncertain if what was happening was real or a dream. He knew by the ache that was beginning to rise that it was real and not one of his many unfulfilled fantasies. He jogged to catch up to Malachi, who led the way in silence. When they arrived at Malachi's condo five minutes later, Cole felt himself trembling. Why was he so nervous?

"Here, have a drink," Malachi said as he came into the living room. He handed Cole a glass, then sat down on the sofa.

"Thanks." Cole made himself comfortable on the other end of the sofa and sipped his drink. "I'm sorry about earlier. I didn't mean to dump all my baggage on you."

Malachi didn't say anything, just stared blankly into his glass.

"Sometimes I think it's easier to talk to a stranger," Cole continued. "I'm not close with my siblings, but by the way they hid at Paul's funeral… They seemed more concerned with how his death made them look. I mean, why is it that we still can't talk openly about suicide and mental illness? Fuck…"

"Look, I —"

"I'm doing it again, aren't I? I'm sorry, I don't mean to rattle on." Cole drained his drink in one gulp. He had to stop talking about Paul and find a way to move on. Talking about his dead brother wasn't going to get him laid. He set his empty glass on the coffee table. "It's my first night out since Paul's death. God, you must think I'm a loser since he's all I talk about." He stood. "Maybe I should go."

"I don't think you're a loser," Malachi said, watching Cole cross the room. "I think you're like everyone else who struggles to get over the death of someone they loved. You're trying to figure out how to grieve, how to go forward. There aren't any hard and fast rules. If there were, I'd have had them mastered by now."

Cole lowered himself into the matching club chair. "What was their name?"

Malachi polished off his drink, stood and left the room. He returned with a bottle of scotch and poured generous amounts into their glasses. He placed the bottle on the coffee table, handed Cole his glass, then made himself comfortable in his earlier position on the sofa.

Cole saw the blankness in Malachi's eyes and wanted to call back his question. He really didn't need to know their name. And maybe Malachi couldn't say that name. Maybe saying it would open up old wounds that he wasn't sure would heal again. Maybe he wasn't ready for that. "You don't have to tell me their name," Cole said ruefully. "I didn't mean to pry."

"His name..." Malachi's chin dropped to his chest. "He was my best friend. Actually, he was more than that. He was the guy I thought I'd spend the rest of my life with." His voice was unsteady, cracking with every third word. "I never even got to say goodbye, or tell him again how much I loved him. And, Christ, I don't even know why I'm telling you this. I mean, we don't even know each other."

"It's like I said." Cole lifted his glass to his mouth. "Sometimes it's easier to talk to a stranger."

"His name..." Malachi, wiping away the tear rolling down his cheek, looked up. "His name was Taylor. He was the first guy I had fallen in love with, and it was just so easy to be myself with him. Do you know what I mean? We just... Everything was so easy. There was never a great debate about who should take out the garbage. If I had a long day at the office, I'd walk through the door and dinner would be on the table. And vice versa. Then the house..." His voice broke off, the words catching in the back of his throat. "We bought a house together and he never... I had to move in there by myself. I had all of his things in boxes and I ... I couldn't stay in that house. Not without him."

Cole moved out of the chair and sat down on the sofa next to Malachi. "I'm sorry."

"Don't be sorry," Malachi said with an edge. "I told you it gets easier, but it doesn't. Look at me. Taylor's been dead almost six years and I'm a wreck talking to a fucking stranger about him." He locked his gaze on Cole. "It doesn't get better. At some point, you start convincing yourself that it hurts less." He sighed. "And maybe that's true, that it hurts less."

There was a long silence. They sat there, their legs sometimes touching, and let their eyes rove the room as they finished their drinks. In the short time they'd been together, there had been a shift. First, Malachi had listened to Cole, let him tell his story. Cole wasn't sure what he had said, but then Malachi opened up to him. That had to mean something. They'd established some sort of connection, right?

Cole slid to the edge of the sofa and placed his hand on Malachi's knee. "Thanks for sharing. I don't think this was the type of night either of us imagined."

"Kind of makes us look pathetic, right?" Malachi rose, causing Cole's hand to fall off his knee. He collected the empty glasses and scotch, and again disappeared.

Cole, meanwhile, moved off the sofa and crossed to the fireplace. He picked up the silver picture frame and studied the photo of the smiling brunette. The guy was hot. *If that's Malachi's type, I should just leave now. I mean, if we were to start dating it might be hard to compete with a ghost.* At the clearing of a throat, Cole returned the frame to the mantelpiece. Then he turned into the room and, unable to dodge Malachi's questioning look, gave a nervous laugh. "I was just..." He shoved his hands into his pockets. "That photo ... that's Taylor?"

"Yes."

Cole didn't know what to say as a new silence crept in. Them standing there and not saying anything made it seem like they didn't share a bond. But Cole was convinced that they did, and he wanted to hang on to that connection, as if his life depended on it. Or more than that. If he wanted to change his life he had to be bold. He took a step forward, pulled his hands out of his pockets and cupped them to Malachi's shoulders. Their eyes met, the stare intent and wild, and in it some semblance of truth. Or was it understanding?

He leaned in and pressed his lips to Malachi's. They stood there, not moving, with their eyes open. Cole expected Malachi to pull away, but that didn't happen. So, he gently pushed his tongue out, sliding it across Malachi's wet lips. He let out a soft groan as he glided his hands down Malachi's arms. The moment his tongue touched Malachi's, the kiss took on a life of its own, both men giving themselves over to it. Cole wrapped his arms around Malachi's waist and held him close. Now, with their eyes closed tight, they were panting and running their hands over each other's bodies as they struggled to keep their balance. Giddy laughter escaped as their bodies jostled into position.

Malachi suddenly pulled out of the kiss and ran his hand across his mouth. "I'm sorry, I —"

Cole leaned in and kissed Malachi again. He pulled away, offered a seductive smile, then rested his forehead against Malachi's. "I'll go if you want me to," he said, trying to quell that all-consuming ache. "But I don't want to be alone tonight. I don't think you do, either. God, I have to stop cutting myself off from the world. Maybe you do, too. I know being alone isn't the answer. Maybe I'm naïve, but I don't believe we're made for a solitary life."

"Maybe some of us are," Malachi said, "made for a solitary life."

"I don't think you believe that. Everyone deserves to be loved."

"I don't have any more love to give."

"Malachi…" Cole searched for Malachi's hands and held them tightly. Immured in another silence, his heart surged when he caught the sweet scent of Malachi's breath. Was Malachi the type of person he could fall in love with? He applied a little pressure and then, against his will, let go. He started to walk away.

"Cole, please," Malachi said, making an urgent play for Cole's hand. "Stay."

Cole's lips curled into a smile and his knees went weak as he thought about what was happening. He was trying not to give it too much meaning, yet he found himself already imagining a happy future. The kind that fairy tales were made of.

His heart raced as Malachi, still holding his hand, led him down the hall. They undressed in the darkness and climbed onto the bed. Cole had never believed in love at first sight, not until now as they surrendered to each other. He knew he was getting ahead of himself, and maybe it was even creepy, but he couldn't stop himself from wondering if he'd found 'the one.'

One thing was certain: in that moment, he'd found absolute bliss.

HE'D BROKEN THE RULES. Not just any rules. His rules. And the 'golden rule' at that. He knew as much when the tall, lean figure emerged from the bedroom and came towards him. *Fuck!* He reached for his half-empty cup of coffee. *This isn't going to end well.*

Malachi winced after gulping the lukewarm liquid, returning the black mug to the table with a loud clank. He sat back in his chair and yawned, his mouth opened wide revealing his uneven teeth. Then he flinched, his gaze fixed on the hairy bronze cyclist's legs in the dining room archway. Now they were face-to-face, and him unexpectedly eyeballing the naked man who stood with his arms folded across his chest and seemingly unaware, or unconcerned, about his obvious state of arousal. The morning after was never easy. Why did he think this would be different? Ogling the man's waist, Malachi felt his cock twitch and then the heat burn in his cheeks. He dropped his head. There was only one way this could end. Badly. He should have known better.

"Do you mind … if I … take a shower?"

Malachi levelled his gaze at the man, who now stood with his legs spread slightly apart like a model posing for a photo shoot. *Maybe it's just a dream. I'll wake up soon and be alone. Like always.*

"Malachi —"

"Oh…" *Not a dream. Damn!* "Sure." He stood, unable to take his eyes off his guest. Leaving the room, he watched as the guy unfolded his arms and ran his hands through his dark hair. The ungraceful movements reminded Malachi of their rough and almost violently passionate sex, and made the hair on his neck stand up. And something more heartbreaking. It reminded him of Taylor, and how he used to sweep the hair out of his face whenever he was about to say something he thought would set Malachi on edge.

Malachi retrieved a towel and facecloth from the hall closet, then returned to the dining room. He purposely walked light-footed to go undetected, and locked his gaze on the handsome figure's pale backside. *Oh, God…* He swallowed hard, his excitement building again as he remembered, with a mixed sense of pleasure and dread, having had his face between that firm ass for most of the night. *You were stupid. Don't be stupid again.* He cleared his throat.

The man spun around, took the linens from Malachi and held them in front of his crotch. "You haven't forgotten my name, have you?" he asked, sidling his eyes at Malachi. "It's —"

"I haven't forgotten your name, Cole," Malachi said, cutthroat, and then drew in a deep breath. "I didn't mean to snap. Just go take your shower." Yet his tone — harsh and dismissive — hadn't changed. It was a message, one he hoped Cole understood.

Cole sucked his teeth and disappeared down the hallway towards the bedroom.

Malachi went into the living room filled with bright morning sunlight. It was a day to feel hopeful, yet a familiar heaviness pressed down on his chest. He sat on the worn brown leather sofa and stared blindly at the hardwood floor. That heaviness had him choking back a metallic taste in his mouth. It was the usual side effect of the morning after: guilt.

He'd imagined spending his entire life with Taylor. There wasn't supposed to be anyone else. Just the two of them. Forever. But he never got a chance at happily ever after. And at Taylor's funeral, he promised to love him eternally. He'd never let another man into his heart … not like that. It was a foolish thing to say, yet in the moment he meant it. He'd never let himself betray Taylor or his memory.

But he was a man … with needs. He longed to be touched, longed to be loved, but there wasn't any love in what happened last night. Like the occasional one-night stands he'd had with random pretty boys when he was horny, it wasn't supposed to mean anything. Just good, clean sex. A way to satisfy a fix. He wouldn't let meaningless and crude sex create a bond. No, he wouldn't let anyone or anything soil the love he and Taylor had shared.

This … this was different. Malachi felt it. Something was happening, stirring his insides. But he couldn't let it take hold. He had learned that love hurt, happiness didn't last, and the only thing guaranteed was a lifetime of pain. He could not — would not — go through that again.

Yet he felt his lips curling into a smile. He had not forgotten Cole's name. It carried a certain presence and authority that was both attractive and intimidating. A tingling sensation swarmed over his body as he pulled up the image of Cole standing in front of him, naked and nonchalant. He loved the way Cole's short, pointed nose drew attention to the runnel above his thin red lips and the dimple in his chin. *God, those eyes!* Those eyes expressed unremitting desire, hopeful friendship. He could almost feel again the warmth of Cole's body pressed against his and the joy that swelled within him as they held each other.

For everything he thought about one-night stands, waking up with Cole beside him didn't summon the outrage he'd expected. Why not? After all, Malachi had ignored the rules that governed one-night stands. His rules. A covenant he'd signed his name to, secured by the whole of his being. That covenant had been broken the moment Cole approached him at Groove. He introduced himself as Malachi Bishop, breaking the cardinal rule of first names only. He tried to ignore the significance of that because, in his mind, he had no intention of hooking up with Cole or anyone else. He was at Groove because of Shane Martin, his best friend, whose week-long nagging about going out dancing had worn him down. Besides, it briefly took his mind off Zach Brennan, one of his students who hadn't been to class lately. He was worried about Zach ... for all the wrong reasons. And drinking and dancing to the early morning hours wasn't Malachi's scene. Not anymore. He'd done enough of that during university, suffering through the next-day hangover and piecing together the fragments of memory. Yet there he was reliving those chaotic, sleepless nights of his youth and, surprisingly, having a good time.

And Cole ... Cole surprised him. He didn't ply on the platitudes about how beautiful and sexy he was. He talked intimately about his dead brother, and that resuscitated a pain Malachi had worked hard to keep suppressed. Malachi almost wished that he'd met a normal guy, one who'd ask where he was from or complain about the weather before asking what he was into. He knew that the moment he talked about Taylor that his defenses had shut down. And that first kiss had awakened a deep ache that he thought he'd never feel again. But it wasn't having sex that upset him. It was that he'd allowed Cole to sleep over. Another rule broken.

He'd always, *always*, stuck to his rules. Almost immediately after orgasm, he'd shepherd his 'guest' out of the condo. No pillow talk. No revealing of unnecessary details about himself. No planning a future hook-up. Sometimes he'd let them catch their breath, clean up a bit or even shower. But as soon as they were dressed, he escorted them to the door, accompanied by an awkward silence. And the scene always played out the same. "Do you have everything?" he'd ask. "Wallet? Keys?" He didn't want them coming back, didn't want to face them again. It made it easier to accept the overpowering role desire played in his life.

He listened. Nothing. He hadn't noticed that the shower had stopped. He rose from the sofa and made his way to the bedroom. His gaze fell on the sheets and duvet bunched near the footboard and half hanging off the bed. His throat clenched. He was, one more time, fighting that metallic taste in his mouth. He went over to the bed and frantically started to strip it, as if that would wipe out its history. He'd just stuffed the bedding into the laundry hamper when Cole appeared from the bathroom. Their eyes locked, and it seemed like they were each probing to find some hidden truth. *What does he expect me to say?* Malachi wondered as he watched Cole brush his wet hair out of his eyes. *Why do we have to say anything? Why can't we just walk away?* He gestured Cole out of the bedroom, then followed him down the hall and into the foyer.

"This is awkward," Cole said, stepping into his shoes. "I mean, it seems more awkward than it should after everything we talked about."

"At the end of the day, we're still strangers, so I don't think we could expect it to be otherwise." Malachi waited until Cole had retrieved his black leather jacket from the closet before adding, "Do you have everything?"

"I think so." Cole slipped on his jacket. "Actually, I'd … I'd like to see you again."

Malachi raised an eyebrow. "Let's not complicate this."

"Complicate what? Am I the only one who remembers what happened last night?"

"Cole…"

"What? Did you enjoy last night?" Cole crossed to Malachi. "You said you told me things that you haven't told anyone."

"That's not the point." Malachi's tone was sharp. *He can't see what's happening. We're two grown men trying to romance the notion of love into perfect firsts. The first glances exchanged. The first hellos. That first touch. It doesn't work. It never does.* "Last night was fun. Let's leave it like that."

"I don't get it." Cole touched his hand to Malachi's face. "If you thought last night was fun, why don't you want to see me again?"

"Last night was a mistake," Malachi said, almost shouting.

"A mistake?" Cole, his eyes on fire, withdrew his hand. "Where did that come from?"

"Well, what do you expect?" Malachi stepped around Cole and stood near the living room entryway. "Do you really expect us to fall in love after spending one night together or because we shared a few silly details about ourselves? Do you think that we could actually have some type of meaningful relationship?"

"It's not impossible," Cole snapped. "It happens all the time."

"Not with me," Malachi shot back.

"It could … if you let it."

Malachi looked down. He thought about the crudeness he associated with one-night stands, and suddenly everything about his current situation felt disgusting and immoral. He wasn't sure why, but perhaps with any other guy he wouldn't be making such a big deal about it. He could let sex be sex and not overthink it. Cole was different. He felt that. And his life was complicated enough. He didn't need Cole adding to the mix. He raised his head, he and Cole staring at each other with wild, lusting eyes. But Malachi, who let logic and reason guide him more than his heart, foresaw that the scene had only one ending. "You should just go."

"All right." Cole let out a low, exasperated sigh. As he walked to the door, he reached into an inside pocket, pulled out a taupe-coloured business card and set it on the occasional table next to the closet door. "I'm in town a few more days. If you change your mind, you can reach me at the number on —"

"Oh, I see," Malachi broke in, the harshness back in his voice. Then came the disparaging chuckle. "Seeing me again is less work for you."

"Malachi, that's not —"

"Just another quick fuck."

Cole bristled. "You know what? Just forget it." He grunted as he pulled open the door. He was about to step into the hall when he turned and looked critically at Malachi. "I thought..." He bit down on his lower lip. "I thought we had a connection. I felt something, but maybe I was wrong." He rolled his eyes. "How long do we wait on happiness before it completely escapes us?" He didn't wait for an answer. He turned and rushed down the corridor.

At the sound of the soft thud of the door hitting the metal doorframe, Malachi went over to the black baby grand — the second-hand Schimmel he'd bought four years ago — parked in the corner of the living room and sat down. His heart was in his throat as he played a few random chords, his thoughts shifting between images from his past and visions of his future. That was the moment he knew nothing would ever be the same.

***

Under the bright blue sky tainted with a reddish-orange hue, Cole walked southward along George Street North towards downtown Claredon. He was on the shaded side of the street, a gentle breeze blowing against his skin.

He sighed as a torn section of the *Claredon Times* lifted up off the sidewalk and blew onto the road. The morning brought the resurgence of an inner peace, a quiet settling down of self-doubt that had plagued him since his youth.

There was something about being in a strange city, a 'visitor,' that temporarily allowed him to be free of himself. Or free from the part he was used to playing. He surveyed the people as they walked towards him and eventually passed by, imagining that their lives had a perfect symmetry to them, that they were fully integrated into this town they called home. He had spent so many years searching for that symmetry, and then waiting for it, like the religious waiting for Christ's second coming. He thought he had found it once, but it disappeared as quickly as night folded into day.

He felt disconcerted and unfocused, the self-doubt that had been squashed earlier resuming its dominance over him. The quietness of the town, in the early morning, was both calming and disturbing since he could hear himself think. His thoughts troubled him and he tried, unsuccessfully, to wish them away. He came across a small park and sat down on a bench. When the sun came into his eyes he felt about his body for his sunglasses, which he usually kept in his inside jacket pocket. Had he left them at the hotel? *Oh, Christ! Maybe they fell out of my pocket at Malachi's when I took out my business card?* He replayed the scene at the door over and over in his mind, trying to assess his approach and if there had been any other way of handling it. Had he given up too quickly? He could see that Malachi might be difficult to handle, the type of guy who makes the rest of the world uneasy around him — not a *diva*, just a man used to having everything his way. *Why do I want to see him again? Maybe it* is *just about sex.* That admission made him feel, for better or for worse, a little more at ease with himself.

He raised his hand above his eyes to block out the sun and saw a man on the other side of the park. The man had his back to him and stood in such a way to suggest that he was urinating into the bushes next to another bench. It was the type of thing he expected to see in Toronto but not Claredon, which he'd been enjoying now for five days. He had attended a conference on corporate governance and decided to stay on over the weekend. He had another meeting there Monday morning with a client, and was then heading to meet with his colleagues in the company's Ottawa office. It was a city that kept throwing surprises at him. The advertisement for Groove, in the hotel's directory of local attractions, had caught his attention. The ad sold Groove as the hotspot for local talent because of its Thursday night karaoke contest, and the top-name DJs brought in from Montreal and Toronto on the weekend. That was what made him go there in the first place.

That night he'd just wanted to forget Jeremy Turner, not pick up a random stranger. Although he relished the wild energy Jeremy brought to lovemaking, Cole didn't see a future with him. That was partly why he ended their seven-month affair. Paul's death had taught him that life was too short to be with someone he didn't love just so he wasn't alone. He'd arrived at a point in his life where he longed for something more than sex. He wanted to feel some greater force stir inside him, move him, compel him to act. Something about Malachi had stirred him. And when he thought about Malachi now, he thought about how they had come together honestly, humbly, without pretence, and how — despite the circumstances of their meeting — it had felt so *right*.

Leaning forward slightly, his moist lips opened as he breathed deeply. He held his in-drawn breath until he gasped, then blew it out forcefully through his nose. Cole stood, walked to the intersection and, squinting, gazed in the direction of Malachi's condo building, now off in the distance and indiscernible to him. His heart thumped. *He did the right thing,* Cole thought of Malachi restricting their love to one moment in history, closing it off from the possibility of something enduring. *I'd have done the same thing if it had been me staring down an out-of-town visitor.* Why, by doing the right thing, did it feel so wrong to him? What was Cole looking for and whatever it was, why was he convinced that Malachi held the key?

"Is it any wonder we're always in search of happiness?" he said aloud to himself, and shoved his hands in his jacket pockets. Was it possible that he just didn't understand the concept of happiness? *God, I'm pathetic. 'Concept of happiness.' What the fuck is that?* He turned around and headed towards his hotel. *What if I'm not any better than him? What if I've been waiting on happiness so long that it's eluded me?*

He stopped walking, his heart pounding in his chest. Did he have the courage to *do* something, to be a man? He spun around and, in a trance-like state, stared again in the direction of Malachi's condo building. He thought about his past, and how he had somehow managed to always lose control. He wasn't sure if he believed in fate, but for once in his life he wanted to act as though he was in charge, that his present and his future were in his hands. With Malachi, he'd been daring, put himself on the line to live in the moment, fuck the consequences. In a way, he was still dangling, searching for something he knew to be completely abstract. He could see how pathetic — or worse, desperate — he must have looked, like he was clinging to a fairy tale.

After a time of just standing there, unaware that people were looking at him oddly and wondering if he was okay, he started to move. Where was he headed? He didn't know. And at the moment, he didn't really care.

THREE

"ON A CLEAR DAY I bet you can see Toronto," Shane Martin said as he pushed open the sliding glass doors. He stepped onto the balcony and inhaled the warm, humid air.

"Not quite," Malachi drawled from the kitchen. He poured out two glasses of the Cave Spring cabernet he knew Shane liked. He joined his friend outside and handed off one of the wineglasses. "The only thing that way is Chemong Lake."

"Still, from up here, it would be a spectacular view of the city." Shane tasted his wine.

Both men leaned against the brown-painted metal railing but didn't look at each other. Instead, they stared up into the dull blue-grey sky and the new band of thick dark clouds approaching from the west. The rain had fallen in hard, pounding sheets until mid-afternoon, holding everyone hostage inside. Now it seemed like just a matter of time before the city would drown under another downpour.

"Have you ever thought about buying a unit on the other side of the building?" Shane asked.

"What for?"

"The view, silly," Shane said, exasperated.

"No." Malachi shook his head and sat down at the square oak-stained table to the right of the patio doors. "I'm fine with this view. I'm not going to bankrupt myself just to have a view of Toronto. Besides, if I did that you'd be here all the time."

"Ha-ha." Shane sat down across from Malachi. "You certainly wouldn't be bankrupt."

Malachi rolled his eyes, something he tried to control but was a natural reflex whenever he was bored by Shane's silly talk. His best friend was a romantic, always high on fairy dust with his gaze held squarely to life's most beautiful moments. Malachi, a self-declared realist, envied that. His experiences made it hard for him to see life's greener pastures. And he hadn't invited Shane over for an after-work drink to discuss the view from his balcony. He had something else to get off his chest, but was still hesitant to confide in anyone, even Shane.

They sat in silence for a time, their eyes roaming each other as they listened to the faint sound of cars rolling down the street below, the occasional horn honking, or some other unnameable street noise. They could be in each other's company for hours and not say much, like a long-time married couple who were no longer in love but who stayed together because staying was easier. From the first day they'd met at Claredon College, where they both taught, the intensity of their bond made it so words weren't always necessary. Sometimes Malachi caught Shane's lingering look that reminded him of how he used to check out Taylor. Was that Shane's way of saying he wanted more? Maybe, but Malachi felt their friendship was too important to risk some type of amorous liaison.

"So, what happened to you the other night?" Shane asked.

Malachi shrugged. "I was tired, so I went home."

"You could've let me know."

"You seemed preoccupied." Malachi chuckled. "Sucking face with that guy —"

"Fuck off." Shane tried not to smirk, but Malachi's laugh was contagious. "Anyways, it didn't amount to much. He turned out to be bi."

"Ew…"

Shane, holding Malachi's gaze, lifted his wineglass to his lips. He pulled it back without taking a sip. "Have you … met someone?"

"Don't be absurd." Malachi dropped his gaze and felt the change occurring inside of him, like he was losing control. And he had lost control. He knew that when he saw himself in the mirror in the morning. The air of conceited confidence he wore — that Shane once told him he admired — had been replaced by adolescent curiosity. He felt flustered, insecure and, in an odd way, common. *What's happening to me?*

"You *have* met someone," Shane insisted. "It's about freakin' time. What's his name?"

Malachi, with an eyebrow raised, levelled his eyes at Shane. Although eager to free himself from the obsession that immured him, there was something still holding him back. Fear. He didn't want to end up looking like one of those desperate men vying for love on one of those reality TV dating shows. No, he wasn't the type to get married at first sight. He thought he had more self-respect than that. "I hardly think you have to know his name."

"Aha!" Shane let out a soft chuckle. "That's what that is."

"What? What are you talking about?"

"The wonder lust dancing in your eyes," Shane said, matter-of-fact. "You're right. I don't have to know his name to see he's succeeded at penetrating your body armor, piercing your heart. That must be difficult for you, and one inconvenient truth. Malachi Bishop, bitten by the love bug." This time he lifted his wineglass and took a sip. "How long has this been going on?"

"Not long at all," Malachi spat. "And for the record, I haven't been 'bitten' by anything."

That was only partly true.

The whole truth was Malachi felt disconnected from a world obsessed with love and its sure path. Like it was necessary to be with someone, perhaps anyone, because being happy depended on it. Was that some type of new moral code? Was that now the nature of the human condition? After Taylor died, he had let go of that grand mysticism. He'd met his one true love and the universe had played the cruelest of jokes on him by taking Taylor away. But it wasn't a joke. His soul mate was gone and there couldn't be another one out there for him now. No, he couldn't believe in enduring love. That, to him, was nothing but a great white mythology, like religion. Deep down, he did want to find love again. Yet even six years on, it still seemed too soon to start searching. Really, he'd only ever dreamed of promising to 'love and honour' one man. Taylor. He couldn't imagine shackling himself to another guy forever because he might have desired him in the now. He learned the hard way that such desires didn't last and could easily be snatched away. Maybe those types of promises would make sense if he were more like Shane and dreamed of settling down, building a home. Malachi had no interest in such things anymore, right? He needed to be free. He needed to live. Or...

Malachi felt his cheeks burn when he suddenly found himself thinking about Cole's hot mint-scented breath, the wet kisses and the gentleness of his touch. Oh, for fuck's sake, he thought, avoiding eye contact with Shane. Maybe he's right. Maybe I have been bitten by the love bug. He raised his hand to his mouth, feeling like he was going to be sick.

Naked and wrapped up in each other, Malachi couldn't remember the last time he'd felt that type of peace of mind, healing of a broken spirit. He was used to crawling into bed at night with his usual companions: loneliness and disappointment. They tackled him, wrestled him to the ground, defeated. He remembered Cole lying there beside him and listening to his even-tempered, low-pitched snore filling the air. He didn't feel alone then. Shane was right. Cole got past his defenses when no one else could. He was losing himself in the quagmire of Cole Malcolm in the most unexpected way. And that struck at the core of his happiness, at the solitary life that he'd come to depend on.

And he was happy, wasn't he? He was a respected professor of English literature and creative writing. His fourth novel, *No More Time*, had made the national bestseller list in the *Globe and Mail*, remaining there for twenty-two weeks. It had also been short-listed for the Man Booker International Prize for fiction. Even Jason Miller had grudgingly admitted it was an 'absorbing work of fiction.' But would Cole Malcolm be the force that would upend him and his life? And would it be for better or for worse?

"Tell me about him," Shane said with a hint of suspicion. The slight edge in his voice suggested that he really did not want to know.

"Tell you about him?" Malachi laughed. "What can I tell you? I've only seen him once."

While they were close, best friends, there were certain topics that Malachi had made clear he never wanted to talk about. The big one was their sexual exploits. He wasn't remotely interested in hearing about what Shane did and with whom. Claredon was too small for that. Besides, there were better ways to get off. That didn't stop Malachi from sometimes imagining what Shane was like in bed. It often made him laugh because he could see Shane as being vocal, grunting and twitching with each touch of pleasure. Or that maybe he got off on dirty talk. He wasn't sure why, either, but he had a strange feeling that Shane liked to be humiliated. At that thought, his lips curled into a smile.

"What's so funny?" Shane asked.

"Nothing." Malachi sat up straight in his chair.

"You're not going to tell me anything about him?"

Malachi shrugged. *I should be able to tell him something. Christ, Cole's all I think about.* His lectures the last two days were scattered and incongruent. At home writing, he'd spent much of the time staring at the blank page as he relived in his mind how Cole suckled his nipples and left him breathless. "He's a senior consultant with Borden Management Consultants," he said. "I'm not really sure what he does exactly. And he's a great kisser." *Why did I say that?*

"I see."

"I also told him I couldn't see him again."

Shane scrunched his eyebrows. "Why did you say that?"

"He lives in Toronto."

"So?"

"It wouldn't work."

"So you say." Shane lifted his wineglass in the air as if he were about to make a toast. He sipped his wine, and then surprised himself by asking, "Did you fuck him?"

Malachi's eyes widened, filled with a sort of contemptuous angst. His look softened when the image of Cole standing naked before him in the dining room archway flooded his mind. "I know where his birthmark is, if that's what you mean." He settled back into his chair.

He had to stop talking about Cole. He was hard and embarrassed because of the angled erection bulging in his pants, even though Shane couldn't see it. He wondered if Shane believed him about how it couldn't work between him and Cole? Did he believe it himself? *He believes in true love,* he thought of Shane, who looked humourlessly at him. *And fate. He'd try to see the goddamn silver lining.*

"It's true," Shane said, "that you barely know him."

"A complete stranger."

"And heaven forbid that Malachi Bishop let anyone or thing disrupt his routine." There was a silence. "I mean, really ... after a few hours of mediocre sex —"

"The sex was anything but mediocre." *Why am I saying these things?*

"Oh!"

Malachi, catching the surprise in Shane's contralto voice, smiled thinly. What did his friend expect? That he and Cole had never found their rhythm? Or that they'd made out in some washroom stall? Malachi didn't like to rush. Maybe that was Shane's scene, but it wasn't his. He wasn't the type to hole up in some dark alley with a stranger who he'd let yank his pants down between his thighs.

"You're smitten."

Malachi smirked. "Nothing so romantic."

"How does he feel?" Shane asked nervously.

"I don't think it matters," Malachi said. "You know me. I'm good at screwing things up."

Shane stood, moved to the railing and spun around.

Malachi didn't like the way Shane looked at him. He imagined he saw a hint of jealousy, or disdain even, in his eyes. But why? He held Shane's gaze a moment longer, then looked away. He understood. Shane was afraid. He was the last of Shane's friends who was single. *He can call me and say, "Let's go to Montreal this weekend," and I don't have to get permission from anyone.*

"Then I don't understand why it's 'impossible,'" Shane said.

"Well, whether it was or wasn't, it is now." Malachi stood, picked up their empty wineglasses and went inside. He heard the balcony doors slide closed as he poured the remainder of the wine between their glasses. He set the bottle down with a hard clank. He turned to his right and held out Shane's glass. "Do you think I'm waiting on happiness?"

"I don't know what that means." Shane chugged his wine as if taking up a frat house dare. "Is that what he said when you told him you wouldn't see him again?"

"Yes."

Shane laughed. "And do you think he's right? That you're waiting on happiness?"

"No." Malachi grabbed his wineglass and headed into the living room. He sat down on the sofa, his gaze held to the burgundy liquid.

"You don't sound too sure," Shane said as he came into the room. He lowered himself into one of the brown leather club chairs opposite the sofa.

"It's just that…" Malachi looked up. "When you think about how we met and —"

"Because it was a one-night stand," Shane cut in.

"Yes." Malachi placed his wineglass on the coffee table. Talking about Cole was supposed to bring a finality to it, render it truly impossible. Why was it that the opposite was happening? "It just seems —"

"Too good to be true?"

"Exactly."

"Because he's interested?"

"Yes," Malachi said askance. He bounced off the sofa, shaking his head as he paced the area in front of the entryway to the dining room. "But beyond that —"

"You'd say beyond that there is truth."

Malachi sighed in frustration. He cupped his hands to the sides of his head and dragged them down his face. He stopped pacing and looked at Shane. "Truth … that's what makes it so —"

"So, what?"

"Immoral."

"Immoral?" Shane let out a straight-from-the-stomach laugh. He set his drink down on the coffee table as he rocked back and forth, clenching his stomach, but he could not control the repeated convulsions of laughter that tackled his body.

"Stop that!" Malachi, leaning against the entertainment centre, sat back down on the sofa, his nostrils flaring.

Shane's mouth and eyes were moist, and through his blurred vision he could see Malachi staring at him with cold hateful eyes. "Immoral..." Shane chuckled again. "What pray tell does that mean, Father Bishop?"

Malachi, biting down on his dry lip, looked away. "That everything is out there, running ahead of us, beyond —"

"Stop!" Shane shook his head. "Do you hear yourself? You can overanalyze it if you want, but all this talk about truth is bullshit. I get it... Taylor was the love of your life, and a drunk driver took him away from you. And because of that, you don't want to get hurt again. Maybe you don't believe in true love anymore either, but admit that. Deal with that instead of trying to intellectualize the immorality of falling in love from a one-night stand. Christ, no one gives a fuck."

Malachi sat there for a moment, stunned by the forcefulness of his friend's words. And the silence that followed seemed to prove that there was even more incongruence in his life than before.

"Early day tomorrow." Shane gulped the last mouthful of his wine, then fixed his gaze on Malachi. "This doesn't have anything to do with Zach, does it?"

Malachi's eyes went wide. "Zach? Why would Zach —"

Shane raised a hand. "Fine. If it has nothing to do with Zach, then you should call the guy."

"I don't know why you're bringing up Zach," Malachi said askance. That was a lie. Zach Brennan was his most talented student, and maybe he coddled him more than anyone else.

He saw Zach's potential and wanted to nurture it. And despite the rumours, they'd never been more than student and teacher.

Shane rolled his eyes, lifted himself out of the club chair and made his way towards the door.

Malachi came into the front hall and fingered the bronze horse statue. "So, I call him. And say what?"

"He at least deserves an apology for how you treated him."

"Fuck off!"

Shane smirked. "You know, you can fall in love again. It doesn't mean you'd be betraying Taylor or what you had together. You'd simply be living in the now. And I think Taylor would want you to be happy. Don't you?" Silence. "Call him," he said with an impassioned emphasis. He opened the door and waved as he strutted into the corridor.

Malachi returned to the sofa and stretched out, his legs crossed and his hands cupped to the back of his head. He stared dreamily at the stark white ceiling, held hostage by the fragments of his conversation with Shane. When it came to Cole Malcolm, he kept waiting for the revelation, some great truth that would reveal itself — provide some justification for him to displace or undermine the possibility of happiness. After what he'd been through with Taylor, he didn't believe that he could be happy again, or even that he wanted to be. Yet it had been so long since he last felt that rush of emotion, or let that absolute giddiness seize hold of him. It made him 'irrational,' and he didn't like that. A familiar question popped into his mind. *How can love be a saving force if it's constantly absent from my life?*

He reached for the remote control for the TV and caught a glimpse of the envelope with 'Holiday Inn' stamped in the upper-left corner. He sat up and stared at his name, printed in neat block letters, before lifting the envelope off the coffee table. He held it delicately, as if weighing its contents. It had been slipped under his door a couple of hours after he'd kicked Cole out. He wasn't sure if Cole had somehow made it back into his building or if one of his neighbours had found the envelope in the foyer and decided to deliver it. He pulled out the folded piece of paper, unfolded it, and glared at the text.

> Malachi,
>
> I am confident you will think me *mad*, but my heart is so certain, and for me to not say anything would make me a fraud. I want to see you again because I think you're amazing. You're the type of guy I can see myself falling for. Hard. It's not as crazy as it sounds. What I say to you now is real. Consider your own feelings and how it felt when we were together. If there's a chance you may some day feel the same, contact me.
>
> I hope to hear from you.
>
> > Cole

Malachi had read and reread the note, trying to make sense of it all, to see beyond. *I'm the type of guy he could fall for,* he thought, smirking. *But that's just silly. He doesn't even know me.* He stood and, carrying the note to his office, remembered that warm flurry of emotion that had invaded his body when he woke up that morning to find Cole there beside him. Yet he was still suspicious about any type of love evolving from a one-night stand. How could it be real and endure?

At that moment, it all felt complicated and embarrassing. The responsibility of some possible future rested squarely with him. He felt a nagging grey weight in his chest. It held both the promise of something new and wonderful, as well as the fear of opening old wounds. The faint sound of footsteps from the unit above his echoed through the room. Occasionally he could discern a chair being dragged across the floor. These were only temporary distractions from the dilemma of Cole Malcolm and what he was inclined to do about it. He glanced at Cole's business card, propped up against the photo of his grandmother next to the computer monitor, and sighed loudly.

He sat down at his desk and stared blankly at the screen for a moment before his fingers began dancing across the keyboard. He drafted several versions of his message, deleting them because he felt they made it sound like he was either too desperate or too expressive when he wanted to remain somewhat aloof. He wasn't trying to play at something, but to, in a small way, keep his dignity intact. He settled on the following short missive:

> Cole,
>
> Let's get together for dinner. My treat! (Call it an apology for my appalling behaviour the other day.) This week's a bit hairy, but what about next weekend or the following week? Let me know what works for you and we'll take it from there.
>
> Malachi

After staring at the text for some time, he dragged the cursor across the computer screen and clicked on the 'Send' button. *Maybe I'm the one who's mad.* In sending the e-mail, he felt a sense of relief, the release of some great burden.

He shut down the computer and laid out his papers for the morning before heading to his bedroom. After stepping out of his blue jeans, which he tossed on the chair in the corner of the room, he sat down on the bed and pulled off his socks and T-shirt. Feeling a certain anxiousness, Malachi climbed under the bedcovers and turned off the lamp next to the bed. He lay there thinking about Cole. *What if he doesn't respond?* He felt sick, a metallic taste in his mouth. He swallowed several times to wash it away but it loitered. *It's not the response that matters.* But it did matter and he knew it.

He spent the next hour rolling from side to side. He thought about getting up and doing something but concentrating on *anything* would be impossible. Then he sat up abruptly in his bed and turned on the lamp. He reached for the pen and black hardcover notebook that he kept on the nightstand. His hand sped across the page. Then, as brusquely as he'd begun, he closed the notebook, returned it and the pen to the nightstand, and switched off the lamp.

He slid down in the bed and stared into the darkness. Something didn't feel right but he wasn't sure why. He closed his eyes and counted backwards from one hundred. That seemed to calm him somewhat. And before long he was fast asleep, swept up in the happy life that came to him each night in his dreams and gave him hope again.

FOUR

MALACHI PUSHED THE ROUND white button for a third time and waited. He took a step back and looked up at the red-brick building. His eyes roamed from window to window, hoping to see some type of movement, but against the bright afternoon sun he couldn't see much of anything. He checked the time. Twelve minutes to three. *Where the hell is he?* He pressed the button again. There was another long silence. He started to walk away when he heard the crackling sound through the intercom speaker and spun around.

"What?" The voice sounded groggy, like it belonged to someone trapped inside a drug-induced hallucination.

"It's me," Malachi said, leaning into the intercom.

"Me, who?" This time the response was slurred and barely audible.

"Zach…" Malachi drawled. "Let me in." Another silence. Then came the buzzing sound, and he moved quickly to open the door.

Inside, he heard the tumble of the dryer coming from the basement that was accompanied by a soft humming. Someone was happy, and he wished it was him. He mounted the stairs, loosely gripping the railing, until he reached the third floor. He made his way down the narrow, dimly lit corridor and turned his nose up at the smell — bacon, curry and cigarette smoke — that made his eyes water. He stopped in front of the door with the number twelve on it in brass lettering and rapped on it. First there was the sound of the chain lock scraping across the door and then the clunk of the deadbolt turning over. The door opened wide, and a shadowy figure stood in the darkness of the space behind.

"Welcome to paradise," Zach said. He let go of the door and disappeared into the darkness.

Malachi stuck out his arm to prevent the door from closing in his face and entered the apartment. He coughed, the smell of cigarette smoke filling his lungs. The apartment was stuffy and silent. He heard the thud of the door closing behind him and waited for his eyes to adjust to the dark. Then he moved towards the small dot of reddish-orange light that flared every time Zach dragged on his cigarette. He went into the living room and made a beeline for the window. He drew back the curtains, the sun streaming into his eyes and making him squint. He opened the window and pressed his face to the screen, drawing in long, deep breaths. Street sounds bounced into the room — a dog barking, the rev of a motorcycle engine, the whistling of the wind. After he felt like he'd expelled the smoke from his lungs, Malachi turned to Zach. "Mind if I turn on a light?"

Zach, seated on the sofa, screwed out his cigarette in the near-full ashtray on the coffee table. He switched on the lamp on the end table to his left and, levelling his gaze at Malachi, flicked his eyebrows.

Now with the illuminated lamp and the sun lighting up the room, Malachi took in the space before him. The TV was in the corner opposite Zach. There was a worn blue wool-upholstered chair to his left angled perfectly for watching TV.

Behind the chair was a silver floor lamp. Wherever there was space, books were piled against the white walls, some of the stacks as tall as him. On the wall above the sofa was a poster of Canaletto's *Venice: The Piazzetta from the Molo,* the lone piece of art in the room.

"Something to drink?" Zach asked and picked up the empty glass from off the coffee table as he stood.

"Sure. Water." Malachi's gaze followed Zach out of the room, then he ran his hand over his face. He could have used a stiff drink to calm his nerves. *Why am I so nervous?* he wondered and sat down in the chair. *There's nothing to be nervous about. There's nothing wrong with me being here. I just need to make it clear that there can never be anything between us.* "Oh, thanks," he said after Zach returned and handed him a short glass filled halfway with a golden liquid. He brought the glass up to his nose and smelled the smoky aroma. Scotch. He took a sip and almost instantly began to relax.

As soon as he looked at Zach again, Malachi felt himself trembling. Something about being in this apartment for the first time, and the way he and Zach were constantly dodging the other's gaze, made it seem like he was on a silly blind date with someone he'd met off the internet. It was scandalous, more so than the one-night stand he had had with Cole Malcolm. That was because Zach Brennan was his student. Like the others enrolled in the advanced writing workshop, Zach was in the final semester of the certificate program in creative writing. Malachi taught the course and Zach, perhaps for the most insidious of reasons, was his favourite pupil: the dreaminess of those narrow greenish-brown eyes reminded him of Taylor. That was what easily threw him off his game, and maybe even explained the awkwardness between them now. Still, he was never sure why he felt both compassion and pity for the young man he strangely admired.

Seated across from Zach, Malachi wasn't sure what he felt now as he studied him. Maybe that was because it reminded him of that awkward moment with Cole. He wasn't looking for just another quick fuck. Christ, he wasn't 'looking' for anything except to avoid the hurt that would prevail if he crossed the line with Zach. Their eyes met and Malachi squirmed as he tried to unwrap the mystery, tear down the wall. Zach's short-trimmed beard concealed the boyish looks of his usually clean-shaven face, a look that often had Malachi pushing down desire, pushing down any shot at happiness. Perhaps it was the light, but Zach's face seemed grave and drawn, made him look haggard. His eyes … Malachi could see the dead in them, the nothingness. He recognized the message in the look, that he didn't feel part of this world. There, Malachi could relate all too well. The grey jogging pants were baggy on Zach. *Has he lost weight?* Maybe it was just the style of the pants since Zach's white T-shirt somewhat hid the evidence of his proud, beer belly.

"Why are you here?" Zach asked harshly.

Malachi gave a nervous laugh. "Well, you see…" *Calm down. Just tell him the truth.* "You've missed the last two classes, and you haven't handed in the last assignment." He looked intently at Zach. "I'm concerned."

"Concerned?" Zach picked up the package of Du Maurier Signature next to the ashtray.

Malachi held his breath. There it was, in the gracefulness of Zach's movements, the thing that stirred something inside of him. *Oh, God. Why him?* He focused on the cigarette dangling between Zach's thin pink lips, surprised by how much he wanted to then, at that moment, kiss him. Then as Zach fingered the silver lighter with his initials, Malachi could almost feel the touch of Zach's fingers dragging over his body. It was torture. Absolute torture.

"I didn't think you'd notice." Zach lit the cigarette and took a couple of deep drags.

"I noticed." Malachi placed his hand over his mouth and pointed at the ashtray.

Zach rolled his eyes and screwed out the cigarette. He picked up his drink and gulped it until it was gone. He set the glass back down on the coffee table, the catchall for everything — newspapers, magazines, his wallet, the open package of condoms. He lifted up the *Claredon Times*, and whatever he was looking for wasn't there. He sighed, tossed the paper onto the floor and sat back in the sofa. "Well, there's no need to be 'concerned.' As you can see, I'm all right."

The phone rang. They stared at each other until the ringing stopped. Zach was the first to look away. He stood, crossed to the window Malachi had opened earlier and closed it. With the street noises cut off, they were held hostage by the silence that had them lost in their own thoughts.

Malachi's eyes were glued to Zach, who remained at the window with his back to him. The way Zach's grey jogging pants were wedged in the crack of his buttocks, showcasing the roundness of his backside, sent a tingling sensation racing over Malachi's body. He found himself imagining what it would feel like to hold Zach in a clenching embrace, and how eager Zach might be to submit to his will. Zach spinning around brought the daydream to an end, and Malachi could see just how much the situation seemed impossible. They were trapped in their roles of teacher and student, and unable to *talk* to each other in a meaningful way. He stood and went to Zach. "Are you sure you're all right?" He cupped his hand to Zach's shoulder, a gesture of reassurance as much as it was a way to steady himself. Zach's eyes were wild and, delving deep into his core, made him weak in the knees.

"A little tired perhaps," Zach said with a hint of annoyance. He rolled his shoulders, forcing Malachi's hand away.

"All right." Malachi took a step back. *He's not really there. He's gone off to some other world.* Not knowing what to do, he shoved his hands in his pockets. Malachi wasn't naïve. He was keenly aware of the repressed affinity they shared, and that pained him because he could not — would not — name it. It couldn't be love because they really didn't know each other. But there was something deep and metaphysical between them, like an unnameable communion that involuntarily committed them to each other. *Could it ... could I ... do I really love him?* People noticed the intensity of their stares, feeding the college gossip mill that had their 'clandestine affair' at full throttle. While they were never planned, Malachi frequently found himself having coffee with Zach at the café on campus. Their public, and animated, debates were rippled with laughter and drew even more attention to them. It all conspired, bore witness to their 'closeness' that kept people talking about them. And the worst and most confusing part for Malachi was that Cole Malcolm was now somewhere in the middle of it all.

Zach stretched his arms above his head, his hands clasped together, and rose up on the tips of his toes. He held the position for a moment, his smooth navel exposed. He brought his arms back down to his sides and offered a coy smile. "Did you really just come here to make sure that I'm all right?"

"Yes." Malachi pulled his hands out of his pockets and took up his earlier position in the chair. "Lately your writing's been, well ... rather black."

"Black?" Zach returned to the sofa, cupped his hands to the back of his head, and stared at the ceiling.

"Yes, you know..." Malachi switched to his disciplinary teacher's tone. "Your writing's macabre, morbid ... preoccupied with death and dying."

"What's wrong with that?" Zach brought his head forward.

"It seems like it might be a red flag, like a ... a ... call for help." *Christ, that was stupid.*

Zach burst out laughing. "A call for help. Really? That's the best you've got?" He wiped the tears from his eyes. "Somebody dies every day, yet we still treat death like it's taboo. Heaven forbid we talk or write about it because that raises red flags. Jesus!"

"All right." Malachi raised his hands briefly in the air, like he was surrendering to the enemy. "Calm down."

Zach stretched out his legs, resting his bare feet on the coffee table. "I think writing about death will make it easier when it comes. It will come one day, and we should be ready to embrace it like it'll embrace us. Death completes the circle, releases us from this ... this hell."

"Hell?" Malachi sat up straight. He held his gaze on Zach's feet, and then slowly dragged his eyes up the long legs to

Zach's large hands covering his crotch. His heart raced and, in that instant, he knew he had to go. If he stayed, he'd be risking everything. He lifted himself up from the chair, but a will far greater than his own held him there. After a few moments, he moved to the sofa and sat down next to Zach. "Hell?"

"Yes." Zach removed his feet from the coffee table. He reached for the cigarette that he'd screwed out earlier, relit it, and turned his head away from Malachi as he blew smoke across the room after a long drag. "Hell is living in a world that doesn't give a damn," he said, his voice filled with a sense of urgency. "Have you ever asked yourself what you're doing here, what any of us are doing here? If you died to-morrow, would it make the slightest bit of difference to the world? Would the world even notice?" He held the cigarette over the ashtray, tapped it twice and, after the ashes dropped away, took another drag. "We shuffle from one place to the next without really being aware of where we are. We're on autopilot, and call it living but we're not really present. We're not ... we're not doing anything. We're just passing the time. Do you know what I mean?"

Malachi looked down. "No, not —"

"I think you do know what I mean," Zach broke in, then coughed. "I think you feel it, too. That there has to be, just has to be, something real beyond this life."

Malachi stiffened and raised his head. "I believe there's something real *in* this life." He relaxed and settled more com-fortably into the sofa, shifting his body sideways to study Zach. *I do feel it. I feel like something's missing, that in a way I'm missing.* It was a feeling he couldn't shake and made him feel like he didn't belong. In his own life he was still searching for that something real, waiting for it to be let loose.

Zach stubbed out the cigarette and shifted his body to face Malachi. "How can it be real when we strangle desire because of some corrupt notion of good?"

"I'm not sure I follow."

"You're not a very good liar."

"This life is real," Malachi said, businesslike, "like this moment because you and I are here right now. I'm not imagining that, am I?" He tapped Zach's foot with his. "You seem real to me." There was a silence. "And you know … we can't always do what we want. There are consequences. People can get hurt."

"You're making excuses," Zach spat.

"No, I'm not. I'm being a realist." Malachi ran his hand across his mouth. "Life is complicated at times. Not everything is black and white."

"That's why nothing's real. When our true desires —"

"Stop!" Malachi shook his head. "You're confusing good with virtue. The two aren't the same."

"That's not what I'm doing."

Malachi had the control to censor himself. There was no sense debating the issue with Zach, who didn't seem open to his point of view.

"Maybe I'm not so virtuous and that's why I don't understand what I'm doing here," Zach said. "Or what any of us are doing here for that matter. Why do we have such desires if we can't act on them? Why, if there's an all-powerful god, would He make us suffer like that? What's the goddamn fucking point?"

Malachi didn't know how to respond to that, not without antagonizing Zach even more. Maybe it was too late to hold himself back. Maybe this conversation was long overdue. "I don't know what we're all doing here," he said with a slight edge. "And maybe we're not supposed to know. Maybe we can't know until we know who we really are."

"But that's what I mean." Zach slammed his fist into the arm of the sofa. "It's like we're on this perpetual quest, always searching for something that our lives depend on. Happiness, wealth, fame ... love. I'm tired of searching and waiting. Fuck, man, I'm tired of being absolutely false."

Malachi drew in a deep breath. *Christ, Zach's right again. There's always something to search out, something we're trying to grab onto and make our own. And for what?* It was almost a game, and Malachi was caught in it, too. He was trying to find happiness within, to live consciously and *be* in the present without distraction. Was that impossible? "Get outside your thoughts. Don't let them determine what's good or bad or corrupt." *Do you hear yourself?* "Feel what's good and right here," he continued, placing his hand to his heart. "Feel it for yourself."

They searched each other's eyes, as if they'd finally understood that they'd arrived at a place they both longed to be. Malachi didn't resist when Zach made a play for his hand, their fingers intertwined like their lives depended on it. The handholding had him reliving a night from a couple of months ago when he had gone out for drinks with his students.

It was two o'clock in the morning when he'd found himself alone with Zach at the Red Lantern, the more popular of the two pubs closest to campus. Alone for almost two hours, they talked about books, debated politics and religion, and unexpectedly revealed the secret dreams neither of them had shared with anyone else. Malachi, when he was twenty, had applied to CSIS and still longed for that covert life. Zach didn't just want to write. He wanted to travel the world and teach English in remote mountain communities. There was a natural flow to their interactions, like two people who had known each other all their lives. Their quips and jabs were accepted with laughter and the rolling of eyes that were more dramatic than any real suggestion of displeasure. This was different from any of their other meetups because no one was around to watch them. There was the bartender, but he was too busy wiping down the other tables and not paying attention to them. But when the bartender disappeared into some back room, Zach reached across the table and placed his hand on Malachi's. The touch made Malachi feel buttery inside and willing to let desire have dominion over him. He was on the verge of losing control, and that would have been disastrous.

He blinked rapidly when he heard a child scream, somewhere distant, and then nothing. He was on the edge again but he couldn't let desire win. He had to be strong, do what he knew to be right. He applied pressured to Zach's hand, released his grip and stood. "If you're all right like you say, then I should go."

Before he could take a step, Zach had bounced off the sofa and blocked his path. The next thing he felt was Zach's lips against his, and then Zach's tongue prodding his mouth. He kept his eyes open as they kissed, perhaps the shock preventing them from closing. The kiss gained an unexpected momentum, and Malachi wrapped his arms around Zach's body and drew him into a crushing embrace.

Malachi slid his hands underneath Zach's T-shirt, his hands running up and down the smooth back. He glided his hands around to Zach's chest to the hard nipples and squeezed them. When Zach groaned, Malachi pulled out of the kiss. They rested their foreheads together and closed their eyes, a moment of peace that allowed them to catch their breath.

This is crazy, Malachi thought, once again eager to lap up the bitterness of Zach's taste. Malachi couldn't believe that he was actually playing out one of his secret fantasies. At the end of class, as Zach packed up his books and notebooks, he always tried to discreetly study him. Zach's tanned skin, his coy smile, or the tight jeans showcasing his round clenched ass as he walked out of the classroom … Malachi had often fantasized about rushing over to him just before he disappeared and kissing him. He'd never do such a thing because he knew it was wrong. *And this is wrong. He's my student. This could cost me, us, everything.* He took a step backwards, releasing his hold on Zach and offered a rueful smile. "I have to go."

"Please, don't go," Zach said as a tear rolled down his cheek. "This is what's real to me."

Malachi's throat constricted. He didn't know if what he felt was love or desire, or some odd mix of the two. Yet it was what he'd felt that night when Cole held him. It was deep, swirling inside of him, and untamed. He looked down, spun around and made a beeline for the door. He hesitated. He wanted one more look at Zach, but if he turned around he knew the battle would be lost. "I'm sorry," he said in a whisper, opened the door and left.

COLE MALCOLM SET THE empty tumbler on the wooden tabletop with a loud clank and then buried his face in his hands. He was at Trends, the restaurant where he and Malachi had agreed to meet. He'd been too nervous to eat anything all day and, as the effects of his second grasshopper began to manifest, his head felt heavy. *I'm such a fool.* He uncovered his face and sat back in his chair. He'd given up hope of seeing Malachi again, chalking up their one-night stand to another night of meaningless sex. Then came Malachi's e-mail. It not only surprised him but sparked something inside of him, made him twitch. It had him thinking that maybe he hadn't imagined their connection after all.

It took a little back and forth to find a day that worked for both of them, but once a date had been set, Cole staggered through life in a daze. Each day he kept building up hope that something would unfold between them that would change his life forever. He couldn't wait for the next time he stared into Malachi's dark brown eyes, heard him laugh, held him — felt Malachi deep inside him.

He sighed and checked the time. Twenty-four minutes past seven, and Malachi had still not shown up for their dinner date, which was set for six thirty. He had tried Malachi's home and cell phone numbers, but each time the call cut straight to voicemail. *He's not going to show, and that's what makes me a fool.* The giddy hopefulness he felt when he arrived at the restaurant was at its bleakest ebb. It felt like he was always surrendering himself to fate and the wretched misfortunes that plagued his life. Was anyone else being fucked over like him?

He saw the thin-faced brunette coming towards his table and reached for his wallet. "Just the bill," he snapped before she could say anything. He looked around the restaurant, which he hadn't expected to be so busy on a Thursday evening, and slouched down in his chair. All around him were couples, friends or colleagues talking and laughing about their lives. He was alone, quietly wondering if those around him were judging him the way he did others when he saw them eating by themselves. He was always curious to know if they were waiting for someone, or had they been stood up. *God, I'm a horrible man.*

He wasn't a horrible man. He'd never stood anyone up, never toyed with someone's emotions the way Malachi toyed with his. He could never be that cruel. He shrugged, as if accepting this perpetual state of unhappiness as his destiny. "I guess it wasn't meant to be," he said aloud to himself, too willingly resigning himself to fate's fury, as if it were all beyond him and his control.

Cole pulled three five-dollar bills from his wallet and placed them inside the leatherette cheque presenter. Then he pushed his chair back from the table and stood, shoving his wallet into his back pocket. He headed for the exit, holding his gaze to the ceramic tile floor as if he'd just been publicly shamed. *Why didn't he show up? What made him change his mind?* Cole staggered and leaned against the wall in the reception area. *Was there an accident?* The thought of Malachi being in an accident made him nauseous. That would be a different type of blow and utterly unbearable. He took several deep breaths and left the restaurant.

Outside, he stood motionless for a moment beside his car. The June evening air was hot and sticky, the bright sky rapidly darkening as thick grey storm clouds rushed across Claredon. At the first drop of rain, he scrambled to unlock his car and climbed in. The rain fell in torrents, and he stared blankly at the windshield but sheets of water obscured his view. When the rain let up, he inserted the key into the ignition and flipped the engine. He sat there for a time with the car running, still uncertain as to what to do, and slowly becoming convinced that there was nothing he could do without appearing desperate. "Why the fuck didn't he show?" he said through gritted teeth and pounded his fists against the steering wheel. When he calmed down, he backed the car out of the parking spot and drove towards the exit where he faced two options. Turn right, and head to Malachi's to make his case for them. Or turn left, and gun it towards the 401 and his home. He kept his foot on the brake, and stared ahead at the dark and ominous skies. Was that a sign? Could he not see that this was the moment to become the man he dared to be?

A car rolled up behind his and honked twice. He took his foot off the brake and pressed down on the accelerator, jerking the steering wheel to the left.

***

Malachi stood in front of the floor-to-ceiling windows in his living room and watched as the dark storm clouds edged their way eastward. His unit, located below the penthouse level, offered a view of the west side of Claredon. Like he'd told

Shane, on a clear day he could see Chemong Lake. Today, his focus was held to the Claredon College sign on the Administration Building only a few hundred metres away, and where the storm had already blown through and left a path of devastation.

He gulped the last mouthful of his scotch, then went into the kitchen to pour himself another. Malachi returned to the living room and sat down on the sofa. He took a couple of sips and stared absently at the TV. *This can't be real*, he thought as the day's events swirled in his mind. *It's all a dream, just a terrible, terrible dream.*

But it wasn't a dream. He had lived it.

Thursday was his busiest day at the college because he taught three of his four classes. His morning was spent teaching the three-hour long advanced writing workshop, and Zach had not shown up again. His English literature and creative writing courses were scheduled in the afternoon. He had tried to teach the literature class, slotted in right after the lunch break, but he couldn't concentrate or express his thoughts coherently. He'd stop mid-sentence, his gaze fixed on some blank spot on the wall. "I'm fine," he said defensively when a student asked if he was okay. He dismissed the class after only twenty minutes. As the students trickled out, Malachi sat down at his desk and wrote out a notice cancelling the creative writing class. He posted it on his classroom door, then went to look for Nancy, the senior instructor, to let her know what was happening. When he couldn't find her, he made for home.

He wasn't fine. He was caught up in the paralyzing, blackly saddening events of the day that had him questioning everything he thought he knew. He now saw his own life in Claredon as imaginary and formless, indeed a fabrication. It also had Zach's question poking at him: what are we really doing here?

Now he had no idea, no fucking idea.

He felt numb, and he wasn't sure if it was because of the alcohol or what had occurred over the lunch hour. The scene kept replaying in his mind and reminded him of a splinter just under the skin — painful and difficult to remove. He drained his drink and held the glass to his forehead. He closed his eyes and heard the scream as if it were real again.

It was lunchtime, and he was in his classroom eating a grilled chicken and avocado sandwich while reading the *Economist*. He didn't initially pay much attention to the scream, which was somewhat muffled, because he thought it was just some of the students horsing around. It was the mournful cry a short time later that made him get up from his desk and go to the open window. Staring down into the parking lot, he recognized the female students from his advanced writing workshop huddled together and wiping away their mascara. He couldn't make out what they were saying, the words indiscernible through the sobbing. Then came the knock on his classroom door, which he always left ajar in case a student needed to talk to him. He looked in the direction of the door and was surprised to see Shane, who was supposed to be in a meeting with the graduation committee.

"What's that all about?" Malachi asked, pointing at the window.

Shane closed the door and crossed to Malachi. He didn't look out the window. All he did was give a languid shrug. "Sit down, Malachi."

Malachi raised an eyebrow. *Of course he knows something. He's Mr. Popular with the students, their on-campus daddy.* "What's going on, Shane?" He remained standing.

"There's been an accident," Shane said in a dark tone as he moved to the desk in front of Malachi and balanced himself on the square desktop.

"Involving a student?" Malachi swung his head back to the window and down below the students were still consoling each other. "Please tell me it wasn't one of my students."

"Malachi…" Shane cleared his throat. "I think you should sit."

Malachi, leaning against the windowsill, folded his arms. "Oh, for Christ's sake, Shane … spit it out already."

"Zach," Shane blurted out.

"Zach?" Malachi stood up straight, his heart pounding. "Is he all right? At the hospital?" He started towards the door.

Shane slid off the desktop and grabbed Malachi by the arm. "Mali…"

Tears pooled in Malachi's eyes. "No, he's not —"

"Zach's dead."

"No, it can't be," Malachi spat, twisting out of Shane's grasp. "Not again."

"Malachi…" Shane cupped his hands to Malachi's shoulders. "Zach's dead. I'm sorry. I know the two of you … were close."

Malachi, blinking rapidly, didn't resist when Shane pulled him into a loose embrace. He let himself cry. As Shane held him, he was remembering how Zach tasted, the voraciousness of the kiss. It was like a great collision that couldn't be put off any longer, like the sudden ascent to heaven. Yet as much as he'd wanted to stay and lie down with Zach, he left. That act may have been noble, but now all he felt was regret.

Malachi pushed Shane away. "Do you know what happened?"

"Not really," Shane said. "I was there when Nancy left the grad committee meeting to talk to the police in the hall. I overheard one of the officers say that Zach's body was found on the ground beneath his balcony."

"Wait a minute." Malachi's body went rigid. "Did he jump or fall?"

"The police are still trying to piece it together," Shane said.

The phone rang, waking Malachi from his dream-state. His glass slipped through his fingers and hit the edge of the coffee table as it fell to the floor. He leaned forward to pick it up and, for a moment, thought he'd be sick. He went into the kitchen, set the glass in the sink and stood with both hands flat against the countertop. "Zach's dead," he said for the first time, making it real. The acknowledgment seized hold of him, filled him with a deep, searing pain.

He snatched the glass from the sink and, his hands trembling, poured more scotch into it. The moment the liquid touched his tongue his throat constricted, his chest tightened and his head started to spin. He set the glass down forcefully on the counter and bolted for the bathroom. He flicked on the light switch, dropped to his knees and held his head over the toilet. His breathing was shallow, and tears came into his eyes and dripped off his face into the water. He could see his reflection and the redness of his eyes. *Have I been crying that much?* When he thought he was okay, he leaned back and stiffened. For some reason that he couldn't explain, he suddenly had an image of Zach's body twisted and sprawled on the ground. He was involuntarily thrust forward and vomited partially into the toilet, down its front and onto the tile floor. It seemed like he wouldn't stop throwing up, but when he did he cleaned up the mess and took a shower.

Afterwards, he changed into some clean clothes, returned to the kitchen and dumped the remainder of his drink down the sink. He poured himself a tall glass of water, then made his way into the den. He sat at his desk, his heart heavy, and wiped the tears from his eyes but they kept flowing. After a while of staring blindly at his computer monitor, he opened his e-mail application. A reminder popped up on the screen: 'Dinner with Cole.'

"Fuck!"

THE DOORBELL SOUNDED JUST as Cole stepped out of the shower. He towelled himself dry, then rushed to pull on his jeans and light-blue shirt. He peeked around the stacked boxes to see the clock on the nightstand. Quarter to nine. The interior decorator was fifteen minutes early. Cole, who returned less than a half hour ago from cycling the Martin Goodman Trail along the lakeshore and second-guessing his life decisions, wasn't impressed. He needed more time to sort himself out, figure out his next move. He headed downstairs, his bare feet still wet and slippery against the hardwood staircase. He slipped on the bottom stair but managed to keep his balance. His hair wasn't completely dry, and he was annoyed as water dripped onto his shoulders and darkened his shirt. He drew in a deep breath, then opened the door.

"Come in," he said tersely and closed the door when his guest was inside.

"You must be Cole," the man said, holding a black leather portfolio in one hand and extending the other. "I'm Dean."

"Take a look around." Cole offered a quick handshake. "I'll be back in a few minutes." He sprinted back up the stairs.

Cole returned to the en suite bathroom and patted his hair dry with a towel. He combed it back from his forehead, giving himself his usual fedora hairstyle. Gazing into the mirror, he recognized the aimlessness in his eyes. *What the fuck is wrong with me?* It was a question that he asked himself almost daily but an answer never came. He felt as though his life lacked meaning, that he hadn't done much of anything. Then again, he was always comparing himself to his father, who was a doctor, and his lawyer mother. They were 'royalty' in their fields. *Am I ever going to do anything of substance?* His work as a management consultant bored him, but he'd never been passionate about anything, never felt he had a calling. That scared him. He was desperate to leave some sort of mark on the world but worried that, in the end, he'd slip away unnoticed. He once thought about running for mayor but shelved the idea after Paul's death. He could barely look after himself then … did he really think he could run a city like Toronto? He went into the bedroom, pulled on a pair of socks and sprayed on a light dosing of Joop before heading back downstairs.

In the living room, he found Dean standing near the fireplace and scribbling notes on a pad of paper. They exchanged a quick look that acknowledged the other's presence.

"Would you like a coffee?" Cole asked, following Dean into the dining room.

"That would be great," Dean said.

Cole went into the kitchen and took two mugs from a shelf underneath the island counter. As he poured the coffee, he glimpsed Dean in the dining room shaking his head as he assessed the space. He rolled his eyes. Granted, he was rarely praised for his sense of décor, but the house wasn't a dump, either. When the real estate agent had shown him the Tudor-style home in the city's Annex, it was empty. The stark white walls made the rooms appear larger until he moved in.

Settling into the new space, it felt cluttered with so many of the large antique pieces he'd inherited from his grandmother. And despite the art on the walls, the place felt static and boring. Like his life.

"This place just needs some colour," Dean said, walking into the kitchen. He set his portfolio down on the counter and reached for the mug Cole slid towards him. "I'm not talking about anything bold, like a red living room."

"I hope not," Cole said, relieved.

"Some blues, browns, maybe a grey." Dean slurped his drink. "Just enough to warm up the place, make it feel lived in."

"That makes sense." Cole gestured Dean back towards the living room. He picked up the black portfolio along the way and, when they sat down on the sofa, placed it on the cushion between them. Their eyes met and Cole offered a faint smile. He wasn't certain about Dean's abilities as an interior decorator, but one thing he could say was that the man was hot. Dean had been referred to him by a friend, and that had his guard up. Was this an attempt at matchmaking? "What about the furniture?"

"This sofa has to go," Dean said playfully, but absolutely serious about his assessment.

"I know." Cole sat back in the deep, oversized sofa that he loved.

"I don't think you need an interior decorator." Dean winked. "The detail in the woodwork is amazing. Some of the furniture is too big, but if you spread it out more throughout the house, it won't feel so cluttered and the space will open up. And remember, colour. Get rid of all this whiteness, add the right accents and, cha bang! It'll be a picture out of *Style at Home*."

Cole laughed. "You make it sound easy."

"I can pick out some paint colours for you and recommend a painter if you don't want to do it yourself."

"That'll be a big help."

They looked at each other with a hunger that both alarmed and excited Cole who, pursing his lips, glanced away first.

Dean checked the time. "I should get going." He set his mug on the coffee table and stood. He grabbed his portfolio and made for the front door.

Cole, carrying his mug, followed Dean into the front hall. "What do I owe you?"

"The initial consultation is free." Dean opened the door and stepped outside. He turned to face Cole. "But how about dinner sometime?"

"Dinner..."

"I'm free Saturday."

"Saturday..."

"Great. I'll call you Friday to set a place and time." With a smile spreading across his face, Dean quickly spun around and ambled down the walk.

Cole watched from the door as Dean climbed into his car and drove away. He closed the door and went through the house to the backyard. He sat down on the veranda steps and focused his attention on the perennials that needed pruning. That was at least something he did fairly well. A heavy weight settled over him — that feeling of hopelessness that came to him each night as he lay down alone. "Christ!" It sounded like he was crying as he ran his hand over his face.

His mind was in turmoil. He didn't know what to think about Malachi or Dean. Beyond their one-night stand, nothing else had happened between him and Malachi. So why couldn't he get the man out of his mind? And Dean, if anything, would only be a distraction, an imperfect means to an end. He couldn't imagine himself *with* Dean, not the way he did with Malachi. That was it. The only man he wanted didn't want him. Right then he couldn't imagine ever being happy. Did that make him pathetic?

It's all an illusion. He moved off the steps towards the rickety shed to collect the pruning shears. *I'm imaginary and unreal. A joke, one big practical joke.* He opened the shed door, which fell off its hinges.

He looked up at the blue sky. "You are a truly cruel, vindictive god."

***

"I forgot how much you look like your brother, so like Paul," the woman said slowly.

"Right..." Cole burped and forced down the acidic fluid that had backed up in his throat. It was later that day and he'd decided to go for a drink instead of going home. Here he was again, fighting off that beast wreaking havoc on his life. And drunk was the only way to beat it. Drunk was still safer.

"I'd give anything for one more night with him, just to be able to fall asleep one more time in his arms." She placed the change on the bar. "I hope you're not driving."

"No. I..." Cole slid his hand in his pocket and fingered his keys. "I should cab it."

"Yes, you should," the woman agreed, offering a gracious nod for the generous tip.

Cole, his head spinning, struggled to stand. "You're a good woman, Stella," he slurred, pointing his index finger at her. "And, remember ... men are pigs."

"Go home and sober up, Cole." Stella laughed. "Love you, too!"

Cole staggered out of Riley's, the Irish pub two doors down from his office on Queen Street West, and looked up and down the street. Everything was blurred, moving in and out of focus. He didn't know from one moment to the next if he'd be able to hold himself up or fall down.

"Come here, sweetie..."

He felt the arm wrap around his waist and looked down to see the redhead offering an encouraging smile as she helped him to the edge of the sidewalk. "My ... saviour..."

"Wait here," Stella said, now looking at him disapprovingly as she leaned him against the parking ticket machine. She stepped into the street and flagged down a cab. With the help of a stranger, she manoeuvred Cole into the backseat. "Kendal Avenue," she said to the driver. "Hopefully he's in a state to give you the exact number." She slammed the door closed.

As the taxi pulled away from the curb, Cole placed his hand to the window and winked at Stella. "She's my ... saviour," he said of the woman who'd almost become his sister-in-law.

"I bet she is," was the barely audible reply from the front seat.

Cole closed his eyes and tried to sit absolutely still. It seemed like the taxi driver was purposely aiming for every pothole, and each time the car dipped Cole could feel the sickness inching up his throat. Fifteen minutes later, Cole couldn't take it any longer. "I'll get out here," he said urgently. The cab came to an abrupt stop, lurching him forward. He threw a couple of twenty-dollar bills at the driver, who thanked him energetically, and rolled out of the vehicle. He walked in a zigzag for a short distance, then stopped. He stood still, trying to get his bearings. *Just hold on. You can make it.* But he couldn't. Make it. The next thing he knew, he was involuntarily bending forward and hurling a mushy, sour-smelling mix of beer, French fries and chicken fingers onto the sidewalk and his shoes. Breathing deeply, he wiped his mouth on the sleeve of his shirt, slowly brought himself upright and looked around to see if anyone was watching. Alone on the deserted street, he slipped off the pair of black Fairwood Macudam that he'd bought two days ago from Rockport and, walking home in his sock feet, tossed them into the trash bin on the corner.

A few minutes later, he arrived home and fumbled to jam the key in the lock. He finally got the door open and, loosening his tie, moved deeper into the house. The welcoming silence was the worst, like shackles holding him hostage to a lonely, insufferable existence. He turned on the lamps in the living room, revealing the open and unopened boxes scattered about the room that attested to that insufferableness, the absolute chaos framing his life. He'd woken up early to organize the mess before Dean stopped by but decided to hit the bike trail instead.

"You're a fucking disaster," he said, grunting, and eased himself down onto the sofa. Dean was the little bit of excitement that had wiggled itself into his day, which passed like so many of the days that came before it. Once he made it to the office, around twelve thirty, he spent the afternoon holed up at his desk reviewing various reports, returning client calls and attending meetings where no decisions were made.

Dean ... now there's an eager beaver. He burst out laughing, although he really didn't find Dean's late-afternoon call funny. Dean already had a list of restaurants to propose for the dinner date. Cole wished that he hadn't answered the call, that he would have had more time to come up with a reason to back out. But he felt trapped, and although it wasn't how he imagined being 'submissive,' picked a restaurant and agreed to a time.

Cole, not wanting to throw up again, didn't move quickly and took his time getting up from the sofa. He went into the dark kitchen and opened the fridge, the bright light making him squint. Now he had the munchies. He pulled out the leftover pasta salad with chicken and the glass pitcher of lemonade, setting them on the counter. Then he grabbed a fork and sat down at the island bar-counter, eating in the dark and drinking directly from the pitcher.

Everything was spinning out of control, and Cole knew it was just a matter of time before his life would blow up. It had to because he wasn't doing anything to defuse the detonator. He couldn't shake the feeling of being alone in the world or how he could possibly survive another day. *You're being an ass.* The thought wasn't his own but that of his brother, Paul, who'd always had a way of lifting him up. If only he could talk to Paul again, be encouraged by someone who believed in him.

On a night like this, when he felt stuck and didn't know how to get himself moving again, he would have called Paul. They'd have met for drinks, and Paul's infectious, from-the-stomach laugh would have cured his ills. *God, I miss him.* Tears banked in his eyes as he relived the grief of his brother's death, mourned him like he did the very first time.

He and Paul had shared the deep bond that some said belonged to twins, which they were sometimes mistaken for. They were almost the same height, although Cole was half an inch taller and the eldest of the two by eleven months. Growing up they shared a room and each other's clothes until junior high school, when their parents bought the larger house across the street and they each got their own room.

Even after they stopped rowing together and Cole left home to live closer to the University of Toronto campus, they stayed connected. When Paul followed later on to Toronto, they'd meet up for dinner or drinks a couple times a week, or attended some of the summer music festivals at Ontario Place. Cole was proud of Paul who, like their mother, had become a lawyer.

They weren't just brothers. They were best friends who told each other everything. Paul was the first person Cole, at fifteen, came out to. Cole could still hear his brother's guttural laugh when he confessed to being in love with their blond, buffed neighbour Todd. How could Paul not laugh when Todd was married with a two-year-old son and another on the way. "Good for you," Paul had said with reserved acceptance when he took in Cole's sombre look. He didn't care and that was exactly what Cole needed to hear. He remembered Paul saying that nothing had changed. Cole was his brother and all that mattered to Paul was that he was happy. Something *had* changed that day. Cole knew Paul was the most important person in his world, the person he loved and needed the most. He loved him even more because Paul just didn't care, treated him the same the day after he came out as he had the day before.

Then, a few months before his eighteenth birthday, Paul told Cole about his recent bipolar diagnosis. He showed Cole the pill bottle and flicked his eyebrows. "One a day keeps the demons away."

"Not funny," Cole spat.

"Sure it is." Paul winked.

"I hear you pacing your room at night…" Cole cupped his hand to Paul's shoulder. "Should I be worried?"

"No. I'm like Superman. I'll be here to protect you. Always."

There had been a number of 'incidents' that their parents had chalked up to adolescent rebellion. There were times when Paul talked so fast Cole couldn't understand him or make sense of what he was saying. But his brother wasn't crazy. It was just that Paul always told him he was fine, and Cole took him at his word. Perhaps, like their parents, he didn't *want* to see the truth, or didn't want to have to deal with it at the time.

He shoved another forkful of the pasta salad into his mouth, and when he swallowed it lodged in his throat. He had no time to react. His mouth opened and he sprayed the countertop with everything he'd eaten in the last ten minutes. He got up and turned on the light. The lumpy, yellowy liquid ran over the edge of the countertop, dripping onto the floor. He thought he'd be sick again just looking at it. He cleaned up the mess, throwing out the rest of the vomit-covered salad, and went upstairs to shower. Then he crawled into bed and lay there, staring blankly at the ceiling. The sour taste that lingered in his mouth — that even a one-minute rinsing with Listerine couldn't take away — had him thinking about the day that changed his life forever.

It was a Friday, the air humid and sticky, the sky a robin's-egg blue. Stopped at a red light, Cole adjusted the seat of his Devinc Hatchet Carbon bike. It was his first ride since he'd bought it a week ago. He'd just gotten back on when his cell phone rang. "Cole Malcolm." He always answered his phone like a radio host announcing a contest winner's name.

"Sorry to bother you," was the greeting.

He recognized the sultry voice immediately. "No bother at all, Stella. Just testing out my new bike. What's up?"

"I know we're supposed to have dinner tonight, it's just … I've been calling Paul for the last three hours. He hasn't answered one call. Finally, I just decided to go to his condo, but he's still not answering."

Cole opened his mouth to speak but censored himself. Paul didn't go anywhere without his phone. No matter how busy he was, he took a moment to respond to an e-mail or text message, even if it was just to say, "Work is crazy. Chat soon." Cole, his grip tightening on his phone, stiffened. He'd sent Paul a text earlier confirming their dinner plans and there had been no response. His throat clenched. Something was wrong.

"Have you tried him at work?" he asked.

"No," she said. "Paul said he was taking the day off to run errands."

"Are you still at his condo building?" Cole asked.

"Yes."

"Why don't you let yourself in?"

"I lost my key last week," Stella said. "I've been waiting for Paul to get a copy made. You know how forgetful he is."

Cole laughed. His brother only 'forgot' things when it was convenient, like his wallet when they went out to dinner. "Get the concierge to let you in."

"I tried. It's some newbie. He's being a prick."

"I'm on my way. Give me about twenty minutes."

Cole ended the call. Then he gunned it, weaving in and out of the bike lanes, and running red lights, as he sped towards Paul's Jarvis Street condo. He jumped his bike onto the sidewalk, chained it to a nearby bike rack and ran into the building. He dialled the ring code and waited. No answer. While he had the key to Paul's unit, he didn't have the swipe card for the street-level entrance to the building. He rapped on the glass door and, after a moment, the concierge buzzed him in.

"Hey!" The concierge rose from behind the desk, chasing Cole to the bank of elevators. "You can't just storm in here."

"My brother's in trouble," Cole said as he pushed the elevator button.

"Who's your brother?"

"Paul Malcolm."

"Oh, cool. He's one of the nice residents. Still, I have to call up to his unit. Procedure."

The elevator doors slid open and Cole rushed in, frantically pressing the button for the sixteenth floor.

"Hey!" The concierge, a man not much older than twenty-two, stuck out his arm to prevent the doors from closing.

"Either get in or back the fuck off!" Cole shouted.

The concierge stiffened, his gaze held to Cole, and stepped into the elevator. "There's no need for that kind of language."

A bell dinged. The elevator doors opened, and Cole sprinted down the corridor towards the redhead standing in front of Paul's unit. He hugged Stella quickly and then banged on the door. "Paul!" He drove his fist against the door three more times. Still no answer. He pulled out his keys, fumbled through them for Paul's and jammed it into the lock. He turned the key and pushed down on the door handle almost simultaneously. The door opened slightly and stopped. "Fuck!" The door chain lock was in place, preventing him from opening the door any farther. He told Stella to stand aside, then ordered the concierge to stand to the left side and hold the door open as far as it would go. Then he took a step backwards and kicked at the door.

"Hey!" The concierge let the door close. "You can't —"

"Hold the goddamn fucking door open!"

The concierge stepped back into position, and Cole kicked at the door eight more times before it finally flew open. He moved forward cautiously into the dark space, Stella holding his arm. All the blinds had been drawn and there was an odd smell that he could not discern. He searched for a light as they roamed from room to room calling out, "Paul," which bounced off the listless walls to no response.

Cole switched on the light in the bedroom. "Christ…"

"No, no, no!" Stella screamed, running to the bed.

"Oh, Jesus!" The concierge, entering the bedroom, backed up against the doorframe. He saw the empty pill bottle on the nightstand and levelled his gaze at Cole. "Is he?"

"Yes." Cole, seated on the edge of the bed, had his hand cupped to Paul's cool wrist. "He's…" He took a breath, not sure he could say the word. "He's dead. We should … call the police." He heard the patter of feet running down the hallway. He looked at Stella, her face pressed into Paul's chest as she cried, and wiped at the tears streaming down his face. His gaze fell on the nightstand. Next to the empty pill bottle were two notes. One was for him, the other for Stella. He picked up the folded piece of paper with his name on it, unfolded it and read the scrawling handwriting.

> Cole,
>
> I don't seek forgiveness but understanding. You of all people know how I've struggled. I've tried to not let this illness consume me, be me, take control. But it's been too much lately, too hard to bear. I love you all, but I can't go on like this.
>
> P.

The ringing of the phone startled Cole. He rolled onto his side and picked up the phone on the night table. "Hello."

"Sorry to bother you so late," Dean said, "but I think I may have left my sunglasses at your place this morning."

Really? He's fucking calling at this hour about sunglasses? It was ten past eleven. "You could have," Cole said with a hint of annoyance. "Hang on while I take a look." He set the phone down and went to look about downstairs. He returned a few minutes later and said quickly, "Sorry. I don't see them."

"Maybe I left them at Mrs. Callaghan's," Dean said ruefully. "I went there straight from your place and I remember having them."

"Hope you find them." Cole's voice was a little hoarse.

"Are you okay?"

"Oh, fine. Allergies."

"Terrible time of year for them."

There was a silence.

"What are you up to?" Cole asked, immediately wishing he could call back the question.

"Not much. Why? Were you —"

"It's late. I should —"

"Understood," Dean said somewhat bitterly. "Sorry to have bothered you. Goodnight."

"Night." Cole hung up, tears coming into his eyes. He felt sick with the sense that he was missing something, that he was perhaps trying too hard to create the perfect happiness of his imagination. He had to find a way to get Malachi out of his system because he simply wasn't functioning. *Is it just lust? Is that all I'm feeling? Is there any such thing as love?* Perhaps his only move now was to consign love to history.

"HERE," SHANE SAID, HANDING a square-shaped glass to Malachi. "You look like you could use this."

"I guess," Malachi said with defeat as he accepted the drink.

"You look horrible." Shane, an intimidating figure with his solid football player's build, took up a position near the gas fireplace. He stood and watched as Malachi lifted the heavy glass to his nose. He did the same, sniffing the peat-smoke scent of the golden liquid, and smirked. It was good scotch, Lagavulin, which he purposely kept on hand for Malachi. Shane's eyes widened as he watched Malachi down his drink in one gulp as if that were his regular ritual. He wanted to say something but his words kept lodging at the back of his throat. "Are ... you ... sleeping?" he eventually got out.

"Sleeping?" Malachi laughed. "Hardly. I try, but I toss and turn all night. Or at least that's what it feels like. While the rest of the city's sleeping, I'm up writing. I'd guess I'm about halfway through the first draft of a new book. That's a good thing, right?"

Shane said nothing. Instead, he stared at Malachi, who was bent forward with his elbows on his knees and his face in his hands. He studied Malachi's movements the way his high school football coach did before critiquing his technique and tried to decipher their meaning. When Malachi sat up again, it was back — the blackness in his eyes that made him look tired and deflated. Horrible! *He's suffering, and probably blames himself, but it wasn't his fault.*

Unlike Malachi, or many of the students and faculty at the college, Shane was not still mourning Zach Brennan. He never had an affinity for Zach, and was suspicious of him. He felt that, although their exchanges were limited, Zach disparaged him. Had Zach seen through him? But Shane was concerned about Malachi who, in the weeks following Zach's death, had retreated into a self-imposed exile. Maybe this was how he'd dealt with Taylor's death, too. Shane recalled Malachi saying he couldn't imagine opening his heart any time a guy showed interest in him. So, he wouldn't let Zach in and look what happened. Zach was gone along with any chance that Malachi might have had at happiness with him. *Can't he see the pattern?*

That was why Shane tried to intervene, reaching out through e-mail and phone calls, which all went unanswered. Every time Shane stopped by Malachi's classroom in between classes or at the end of the day, he found the door locked and the room empty. Shane wasn't sure why Malachi had come to him now. Yet he was happy and anxious all at once. The truth was out. Zach's death had been ruled an accident. The toxicology report showed Zach had a high level of alcohol in his blood. That suggested he hadn't intentionally jumped off the balcony, and that it was more likely that he slipped and fell. But that didn't stop the despicable and erroneous rumour — that Zach died of a broken heart because Malachi loved his job more than him — from weaving its way around the college. Shane wanted to assure his friend that he wasn't responsible, but how could he sensitively broach the subject?

Shane sat down on the sturdy coffee table. He went to place his hand on Malachi's thigh, offer a gesture of reassurance, but at the last moment pulled back. The sadness in Malachi's dark eyes made his heart sink. "It's been a terrible scandal for the college. Enrollment will probably plummet next year." *Way to go, idiot. That'll cheer him up.*

"Is that the scandal?" Malachi asked, leaning back into the sofa. "Or am I?" He looked down. "I know what people are saying. I tried to pretend like it wasn't ... obvious."

Shane smirked, but wiped it off his face when Malachi raised his head. Even Shane, like many of the other professors, couldn't hide his disapproval when he saw Malachi and Zach together. At one of the staff meetings, everyone knew it was a warning directed at Malachi when Nancy made a vague comment about the necessity of "keeping a respectable distance from students."

There was a collective consensus among students and staff that Zach was smart and talented. Zach was the most promising student and everyone believed, even Shane, that he'd succeed as a writer. A logical man by nature, Shane could easily argue that Malachi was just trying to nurture Zach, help him reach his fullest potential. It was what he wanted to believe, to reassure himself.

"You don't know how fucking hard I tried to keep it spiritual, on that higher level," Malachi said brusquely. "I'm not a fool. I knew Zach wanted more, but after Taylor..." He rolled his shoulders. "I keep pushing guys away. I *know* that. It's how I cope."

Shane raised an eyebrow. "You think you're coping?"

"But when Zach stopped coming to class I had to know that he was all right. I should never have gone to his apartment."

"You mean…" Shane threw Malachi an accusatory look, as if he personally had been betrayed. "You and Zach —"

"No, no, no," Malachi interrupted. He pushed himself off the sofa and took up the space previously occupied by Shane in front of the fireplace. "I mean, Zach kissed me and I didn't stop him. We didn't have sex, even though he asked me to stay, but I left." He levelled his gaze at Shane. "You know me. I've always been able to look beyond some momentary thrill, to see the consequences of my actions. It just seems that with Zach … I utterly failed."

Shane raised an eyebrow. "Always?"

"You know what I mean." Malachi sucked his teeth. "It was different with Zach."

"You can't always take the moral high ground. And I'm not trying to pass judgment, but you do seem to spend more time analyzing life than living it."

"Moral high ground…" Malachi shook his head. His eyes became moist and he folded his arms. "I'm not like you. I don't live ruthlessly for the moment."

Shane stiffened. "What the hell does that mean?"

"'Be happy in the now' or 'live for today' doesn't absolve you, or anyone else for that matter, of taking responsibility for your actions. If anything, they're skewed aphorisms of extreme individualism. The only thing I've ever seen come about from a 'living as if you'll die tomorrow' attitude is pain. It wreaks havoc on other people's lives and shatters relationships."

"You're being mean," Shane said.

"It doesn't bother you that you have a 'reputation' or that people are always judging you?"

"Not everyone. Just you."

Malachi rolled his eyes.

"At least I'm living," Shane protested.

"And I'm not?"

"Not really." Shane bit down on his lower lip. "And what happens between consenting adults —"

"The guy stuck at home isn't necessarily 'consenting' to you fucking his boyfriend," Malachi broke in, then looked away. "I'm sorry. I didn't mean —"

Shane waved him off. He stood, picked up Malachi's glass and headed for the kitchen. *I'm not the one guys are fawning over,* he thought, tamping down his anger and filling their glasses. *I'm the guy who settles, who only ever gets the leftovers. He doesn't see that, though. He doesn't see anyone but himself. It's all about him and fuck the rest of us. It's easier for him to wallow in misery, act the same with Cole as he did Zach than change his fucking ways.* He returned to the living room, handed Malachi his glass and sat down on the sofa. They let their eyes rove the room as the silence hung in the air between them. Shane felt the shift that had somehow changed them — how they saw themselves and each other. Was that all because of Zach? He broke the silence with, "Did you love him?"

"Zach?" Malachi sat down in the armchair near the fireplace. "Yes, maybe ... Christ, I don't know." He took a large gulp of his drink. "What the fuck does it matter now? I mean,

I couldn't say it when it mattered. Admitting it now doesn't mean anything."

"Maybe it would mean something," Shane said cautiously. "That you're finally breaking free of Taylor's grip on you."

Malachi, blinking back the tears pooling in his eyes, smiled faintly. "I did love him. God, I wish I'd told him when he was alive, when I held him. I just … couldn't bear opening myself up to a world of hurt. But then again…" He wiped his face. "Look how things ended up."

"Then I should ask…" Shane hesitated, but his curiosity got the better of him. "Whatever happened with that other guy you met?"

"Nothing."

"I don't understand. You seemed interested in him."

Malachi shrugged. "Maybe I wasn't that interested because I stood him up. I didn't mean to. We'd made plans to have dinner together on the same day … when Zach…"

"But he understood, right? When you called him to —"

"Darling, not everything is meant to be. And, really, what would I have said? 'This student and I had a thing and almost slept together. But now he's dead, so dinner's off?'"

"Malachi…" Shane's harsh tone showed a measured displeasure with Malachi's crassness and his use of 'darling.' Shane loathed the twang that lingered — its suggestion of simple-mindedness and the vulgarity of the gayness he sought to lift himself above. "Things could be different with this other guy. I mean, get out there and live instead of dissecting what went wrong with Zach. Stop thinking the worst, that you're always going to end up getting hurt. Maybe this time it's the real deal and you, and maybe someone else for that matter, stand a chance at actually being happy."

"Maybe."

"For you, that's progress." Shane tried not to smirk. "Do you even know what you want?" he asked with the insistence of a mother trying to understand the child constantly getting into trouble.

"No." Malachi drained his drink.

A new silence fell over the room and Shane sat there contemplating his dear friend who looked broken. *I wish there was some way I could help him, that he'd let me be his confidant again. He keeps cutting himself off, pushing me and the world away.* He left the room to retrieve the bottle of scotch and, before sitting down again, refilled their glasses. Drinking had a way of prompting them into conversation, and he hoped to firm up Malachi's commitment to their summer trip. They'd talked about going to New York City together, and the thought of sharing a room had Shane trying to quell the excitement racing through his body and bulging in his pants. Yet sitting across from his friend was also perfect, and lessened the isolation and separateness he felt eating away at them.

"Don't take this the wrong way." Shane leaned forward slightly. "But when you let go of Zach, and the notion that you could have saved him, then you'll start to live again." He shook his head. "Don't look at me like that. Zach's gone, and there's nothing you can do about that. Don't overanalyze it. Don't let it consume you."

"Maybe Zach was right." Malachi stared coolly at Shane. "He thought we're all living a façade and that none of this is real." He downed his scotch, set the glass on the coffee table and stood.

"Malachi…" Shane rushed to intercept Malachi, who was heading for the door, and searched for his hand. "You don't believe —"

"I don't know what to believe anymore." Malachi jerked his hand out of Shane's tight grasp, opened the door and left.

Shane turned over the deadbolt with a weighty sense of loss. He stood there for a time, his forehead pressed against the door, inhaling and exhaling. He didn't know what to think or what to do. He went back to the living room and turned on the TV to catch the news.

He knows I'm here if he needs me. I'll always be there for him.

EIGHT

MALACHI TUGGED ON THE thick manila envelope wedged into his mail slot. After trying to delicately pull it out, he gave a powerful yank and the envelope came free. His heart leapt into his throat when he saw the return address and thought he'd faint. He did not — could not — move, his legs dead weight. Then, after a time, he breathed deeply and lowered himself to the mailroom floor. Sitting cross-legged with his back against the wall, he held his gaze to the name in the top upper-left corner. Z. Brennan. He swallowed hard as tears crept into his eyes.

He poked his thumb into a hole in the envelope and tore it open. He peeked inside, sliding out the small envelope that had his name sprawled on it in Zach's angular handwriting. He pulled out the contents and, leafing through the manuscript pages, smiled wanly. Zach had written a book, something none of his other students had ever done while still in the program. He shouldn't have been surprised. After all, Zach had been his star pupil. Malachi rubbed his eye, then picked up the other envelope and flipped it over. He took in a deep breath as he lifted the flap, which wasn't sealed, and slid out the neatly folded papers. He fought to hold back his tears as he read the letter.

Dear Malachi,

You'll never know how many times I've tried to write this letter, or the number of versions that ended up balled on the floor or torn into pieces. It wasn't just that I was searching for the right words but more that I couldn't write. Every time I set pen to page, nothing happened. I froze. Some other force locked up my hand and made it so I couldn't move it. Until that day when you came to me and everything changed. I could write again, live again, and make a little sense out of this life in pieces.

You came to me, and it was like a dream to hold you, taste you, feel you close to me. I had wanted that for so long, in fact from the very first time I saw you. Do you remember when we first met? It was almost two years ago, the first day of classes at the college, and I was standing in line at Second Cup. The barista, after counting the change I'd handed over for my cappuccino, said I was fifty cents short. I searched my pockets and rummaged through my backpack, but I had no other money on me. You reached past me and gave the guy two quarters. I said, "Thank you," but you looked through me. Then you ordered an Americano and moved to the end of the counter to wait for it. I was two feet away and still you didn't look at me. I desperately wanted to say something else to you then, but you kept checking the time. Fuck, you were intimidating and so aloof.

Fifteen minutes later, I walked into my English literature class and saw you writing your name on the blackboard. My heart leapt into my throat. For a brief moment, I thought that God was real and that He was smiling down on me. You acted as though we'd never met before, like I was just like every other student. Maybe to you I was. That hurt for a long time until I finally got to know you. And getting to know you wasn't easy, either.

When you came to my apartment, I wanted you to make love to me. I wanted to fall asleep in your arms. I wanted to tell you so much more about me and learn so much more about you. After we kissed, you looked at me like no one else ever had. Like I was worthy. I wanted that moment to last forever. Just when I thought we had released the stranglehold on desire, reality hit. You walked out because of how 'wrong' it was for us to be together because of your position at the college. I didn't care about that. That day I needed you. Maybe that's because you're the first person I've truly loved. Don't ask me to explain it because I don't think I can. I know I love you, and that's the only thing that's real to me.

From the beginning, I felt like there was

some type of special connection between us. I can't explain that, either. It's just the feeling I've had, deep in my gut, that you've always understood and that we've shared the same pain. Loneliness. To feel so alone in the world, so terribly alone. You know what I mean, right? It's like I'm constantly on the outside looking in.

Maybe it's because I'm not rushing anywhere. I mean, every day I see someone jaywalking across a busy intersection, or a car speeding up as the light turns yellow. Why? Why the rush? We're so impatient, barely taking the time to savour the beauty that surrounds us until … it's too late. And, then, what's the point?

I hope I'm making sense and not just rambling, but I think you understand. I saw it in your eyes after you pulled out of the kiss — the breadth and depth of that understanding, of our love. Oh, Malachi, I don't know why I waited for you to come to me. If I had made the first move a long time ago… That's beside the point. The other day was our moment, and we let it slip away because we didn't have the courage to hang on to it.

It all feels so heavy, like I'm weighted down, like I'm sinking — like the Queen Mary's anchor plummeting to the seabed. Once in position, I cannot move. I've been fighting this heaviness for a long time. Its clinical name is depression. Maybe that's why my writing has been, to use your terminology, macabre. A couple of weeks ago, my doctor upped the dosage of my medication. God, not a good thing. I couldn't think straight, couldn't write. I had to finish my book, so I stopped taking it. The insomnia is the worst of all. It's also why I missed your classes because I've only been managing to sleep during the day. The other day you caught me literally twenty minutes after I'd dragged myself out of bed.

It's been four years since the official diagnosis, but it feels like I've been battling this demon for as long as I can remember. When I confided in my older brother, Greg, about the diagnosis, that was when the great family secret was revealed. My mother hadn't in fact run out on us like my father told me when I was fifteen. Greg didn't really seem to know or care if it was depression or bipolar disorder, but my mother tried to take her own life. My father had her committed to the Holtman Mental Health Institute in Etobicoke. According to my brother, our father wanted to 'spare' us that embarrassment and invented the story of our mother abandoning us. Why would my father do such a thing? Who did he think he was really protecting? All I knew was that I let hatred for my mother consume me because I thought she left and didn't love me anymore.

Two years ago, I went to visit her. The first thing I saw were the scars on her arms. She didn't recognize me, though. Or maybe she did. Or maybe she wouldn't have been able to recognize anyone in her state. I learned from one of the nurses that she hadn't spoken a word in seven years and that they had to keep sharp objects away from her. Do you know what was scarier? I saw my reflection in her eyes. I don't want to end up like that — completely unhinged and with no will to live.

God, it's such a pathetic existence. It's too hard, Malachi, too hard. This world … it's … hell. There has to be something beyond this life, something more meaningful. I want to find out what that something else is. That day we were finally alone together in my apartment, that was the first time I felt like there was something meaningful *in* this life. Being with you, especially when we kissed… You gave me a moment of solace, of happiness, of relief from the pain.

Don't think that you could have changed this. It was inevitable. I was never meant for this world. Then I met you. You should know that it was the thought of you that kept me alive, kept me here years longer than if I'd never met you. You gave me joy in a lifetime of pain.

Thank you for believing in me, for being my heaven on earth.

I love you, Malachi. Remember that …
always.

Zach

It wasn't an accident. If I had stayed, if I had let myself love him… Malachi felt himself trembling. He banged his head against the wall three times, unable to stop the tears streaking down his face. Through his blurry vision, he studied the pages in front of him. He held the last connection he had to Zach, the last reminder of what they never had together. As he read each word he could hear Zach's scruffy voice. The thud of each 't.' The way Zach drawled at the end of each sentence. How he cleared his throat each time he went to make a point but was unsure of his position.

Malachi remained seated on the floor until his eyes dried, then he got up and made his way to his condo. He felt remorse and then guilt. He *had* failed Zach when the clue was right there in front of him. Zach's buoyant, heart-stopping prose had turned morbid, dry and overworked. Yet he just wrote comments in the margin of assignments that Zach never came to collect. But for Malachi to have said anything would have meant acknowledging a truth that he wanted to stay clear of. That he and Zach had, from the beginning, shared a special connection. He wasn't naïve enough to believe that he actually loved Zach from the moment he first saw him at Second Cup, but there was something that drew him in. He remembered now. It was the curiosity gleaming in those greenish-brown eyes that reminded him of himself at that age.

Loneliness. That was the pain they shared. Malachi, although he never wanted to admit it, felt as alone in the world as Zach did. How could he not? He'd grown up in a stern, uncompromising home where his parents believed that being strict would keep him on the straight and narrow. He wasn't allowed to attend school dances or the parties his friends threw. His extracurricular activities couldn't prevent him from attending the Wednesday night prayer service or the great gathering on Sunday morning. He couldn't play bingo, either, when he visited his grandmother in the nursing home. They weren't Jehovah Witnesses, but some days he didn't really know what religion he belonged to or if his mother made it up as she went along.

Everything changed the day, at fifteen, when he said, "I'm gay." It was a day he tried to block from his memory, bury some place deep and inaccessible. He could still see the tears banking in his mother's eyes and how she had been crushed. On that very morning, his father's, "Have a good day, son," turned out to be the last words ever spoken between them. His coming out was the second blow to his parents. His older sister, Sarah, had had a baby when she was sixteen. She had a rambunctious toddler on her hands and no time to worry about him. As time passed, they acted like a family, sending cards to each other on their birthdays and at Christmas. But they really didn't know each other, not in a way that mattered. Malachi barely knew his nephew, Joshua, who he watched grow up in the photos his sister included in her Christmas cards.

I'm all alone, he thought, thinking about the last time he saw his sister. It was a year ago, just after Sarah's last divorce. He was in Halifax attending a symposium on George Ryga and they'd spent twenty minutes catching up over coffee. Tears were in his eyes again, and they weren't only for Zach but also for the love he'd lost long before Zach had come into his life. That seemed like a lifetime ago.

Malachi jammed the key in the door and entered the silent space that had him feeling faint. He staggered to his office, the papers slipping through his fingers and onto the desk. He took a moment to steady himself, then picked up the letter, carefully folded it along the creases, and slipped it back into the envelope. He went to the mahogany bookshelves on the other side of the room and reached up to the top shelf. He pulled down a long box made of dark cherry wood. Malachi slipped the letter into the box, which he returned to the top shelf, and then sat down at his desk. He smiled faintly as he stared at the title page of the manuscript. *This Ain't What I Signed Up For* by Zachary R. Brennan. He turned the page and blinked magnificently at the dedication:

> *To Malachi Bishop*
> *for you, because of you*

He flipped to the first chapter and began to read the final words of the young man he'd never dared to love. There was something in the writing that had Malachi cornering between sadness and joy. Zach wrote with the grace, conviction and magic that Malachi had yet to achieve.

Malachi stayed up until two in the morning devouring the words and realized something else. He wasn't sure he had the courage, or the will, to keep on trekking through, to use Zach's terminology, this hell.

But he was about to find out.

NINE

MALACHI WALKED LEISURELY ALONG Church Street with his hands shoved in his pockets. The warm and humid air did nothing to relieve the tension settling in across his knotted shoulders. *Christ, what am I doing here?* The last thing he expected to be doing on a Saturday night was jostling his way through the crowded sidewalks of Toronto's gay village. He kept swinging his head from side to side, eyeballing the men that passed by. They weren't the type of men he saw in Claredon. These men wore tight-fitting T-shirts that showcased the hard nipples of their sculpted chests and jeans that moulded to their muscular thighs and shapely buttocks. He was kind of shocked, too, at seeing the guys who went shirtless, displaying their six-pack abs. It was as though these men had stepped right out of *Genre*.

He tried not to gawk because the muscular jock-boys weren't necessarily his type, but these men were *hot!* Then he saw the dark-haired beauty walking past him and their eyes locked. He felt his cheeks burn and dropped his head. He waited a moment before cranking his head around to sneak another glimpse. The guy, who was still looking in Malachi's direction, waved. Malachi made some foolish-looking gesture with his hand and then kept walking, a smile spreading across his face.

Bars, night clubs, restaurants — all around him music spilled onto the street, colliding with the laughter and animated voices from the people who seemed truly happy. That happiness antagonized his already fragile state of mind, and the smile he wore only moments ago was gone. He couldn't shake off the tumult that he was certain would break him. He didn't believe either, as Shane had suggested, that a night of dance and drink would cure him. But maybe it would remove, temporarily or otherwise, any trace of Cole and Zach. But the images kept flooding his mind, like a slideshow projector set on automatic that he couldn't stop. Malachi remembered the feel of Zach's body against his when they kissed. Zach had slight love handles just above his waist, but they didn't take away from his athletic attractiveness. There was something about Zach's imperfections that had always aroused Malachi. Then Malachi's thoughts turned to Cole's smooth lips caressing his body and the intensity of those blue eyes. The way their bodies — first him and Cole, then him and Zach — came together as if knowing exactly how to move and how they fitted. Sometimes Malachi thought he saw one or both of them in the faces of the guys he passed on the street. Would the madness ever end?

Go home, he counselled himself as he checked the time. What would he do at home? Wait. Wait for the grief galvanizing his body to recede. Shane was right. He knew there was nothing more he could do about Zach, but it was hard for him to let go when they had, for all intents and purposes, just found each other. Cole presented a different challenge. Malachi didn't want to admit that he felt something between him and Cole the night they were together. He felt the spark, the tinder ready to ignite. *Sex can't possibly be that good without some type of connection.* Even so, he couldn't decide between finding a way to 'hook' Cole or figuring out how to flush him out of his system. And was he even capable of such careful contrivance?

Malachi, walking with Shane, slowed his pace. The distance grew between them until Shane was side by side with Cory, his long-time friend, and Eric, Cory's temperamental boyfriend. Malachi and Cory didn't get along. They were cordial to one another, but never more than that. Although there had never been an incident between them, it was more that they didn't click. Cory often talked past Malachi, avoiding direct eye contact with him while looking at Eric and Shane. It reminded Malachi of that old-school hate — the kind passed down from one generation to the next between feuding neighbours. The wounds were handed down with the inheritance, and kept active in the heart and mind. And when Cory did look at him, those wide-apart leaf-green eyes burned with the desire to strike him, wipe out a nagging menace. He stopped and stared at a poster on a lamp pole without actually reading it.

"You okay?" Shane asked as he neared and, when he was close enough, wrapped his arm around Malachi's neck.

"I'm not sure I'm up for this," Malachi said, looking past Shane to see Cory and Eric join the long line of people waiting to get into Urbane.

"Sure you are." Shane shook Malachi gently before lowering his arm. He touched his hand to the centre of Malachi's back and nudged him forward. "Get inside, have a drink, and you'll be fine."

Malachi opened his mouth to respond but censored himself. Shane, who only wanted to lift his spirits, didn't understand. Besides not being in the mood, it was late for him. Twelve minutes past ten. Most nights, and Saturday was no exception, he was in bed by now. He liked ending his day reading a chapter or two from one of the books he kept piled next to his bed. Most of the books were about writing because, despite his success, he needed reminders of the little tricks he could use to get himself writing when he didn't feel like it. On a night like this he'd rather be curled up with Dorothea Brande or Julia Cameron instead of being like everyone else and trying to get into Toronto's most popular gay bar. *Why do we do this?* The question had him thinking of Zach and their tête-à-tête. *What's the point?*

He stared straight ahead as the line inched forward, his gaze fixed to the full black mane and broad shoulders of the guy in front of him. When the line moved, Malachi took a step forward and walked on the heel of the guy's shoe.

The guy spun around, his face knotted, but his expression immediately softened. "I'm Chad," he said, extending his hand.

"Ma ... Ma ... Malachi." Malachi accepted the firm handshake of the black-haired beauty who'd caught his attention earlier. They stared at each other, both of them cognizant of how the handholding lasted longer than normal between two strangers. He pulled away first and pointed to his left. "This is Shane."

"Hi," Shane said dryly.

"We're just here for the weekend." Chad looked behind him to see if the line had moved. It had, and he followed.

"Drove in from London last night for a friend's stag." He held Malachi's gaze. "Are you from here?"

"No," Malachi said with a hint of relief. "We're from Claredon. Arrived this afternoon." He flicked his eyebrows. "This really isn't my scene. I'm not twenty-two, and standing in line —"

"I hear ya." Chad chuckled. "A quiet night at home is more my style, but every now and then … you never know who you'll meet." He winked.

Malachi, his cheeks on fire again, glanced away. The line moved forward. Just after Chad and his group of friends were let in, the rugged, mean-looking bouncer stepped in front of Malachi.

"Look for me," Chad said, almost shouting. "I'd like to buy you a drink."

"Unbelievable," Shane said, shaking his head. "It's like he has 'Fuck Me' tattooed on his forehead." He tapped Malachi on the arm. "Don't think you're kicking me out of our room for *that*."

Malachi rolled his eyes. He turned slightly to his right and, just inside the door to the club, he saw Chad holding out his hand to be stamped. His stomach flipped when Chad turned back and flashed him a generous smile before disappearing out of sight.

Finally, it was their turn, and the bouncer waved them in. Malachi held out a ten-dollar bill to pay the cover charge for both of them. As soon as they entered the main section of the club, Shane was swallowed up by the crowd. Malachi, somewhat panicked, scanned the faces around him but didn't recognize anyone. The strong stench of sweat and cologne infiltrated his nostrils, making him gag. He was ready to call it a night.

He shoved his hands in his pockets and edged his way towards the bar, hoping to stumble across Shane. He joined the mass of rowdy and horny beer-thirsty men standing in front of the bar, exchanging doubting looks with some of them. He wished that he hadn't let himself be talked into this escapade, but it did seem pathetic that he spent almost every Saturday night at home alone. There were days when he could not see himself in the world, or the world in him. This was one of those days, and locking himself away in his condo helped to ease that heaviness. And there was truth in Chad's assessment that nights like this — letting everything go while grooving to Madonna, Cher and Céline Dion — could unlock a world of possibilities, open the door to … love.

It took him about seven minutes to get a drink, then he shoved his way towards the dance floor. He surveyed the sea of men thrashing their bodies about and spotted Cory and Eric sandwiched in the middle of the mob. *They're perfect for each other*, was his silent appraisal, although he wasn't certain as to why he thought that. He navigated back towards the bar, searching for Shane, and ended up in the section known to the regulars as the Cave. It was a room at the back of the main level etched in darkness with cushioned benches lining the walls and where indiscriminate lovers gathered to 'acquaint' themselves. The chorus of moaning and slurping sent him rushing back into the main area of the bar. His head was spinning, the palms of his hands sweaty. That was it. He had to get out of there. Just then, Chad appeared in front of him.

"What happened to your friend?" Chad asked, leaning in close to ensure he was heard overtop the music.

Malachi shrugged. "I lost him as soon as we were let in."

"You're welcome to hang out with us." Chad took a swig of his beer. "Are you guys together?"

"No," Malachi said quickly. "Just friends. And thanks for the offer, but I think I'm going to head upstairs and get some air."

"We'll be over there." Chad pointed at the pool tables. "If you change your mind." He took a step forward and whispered into Malachi's ear, "You have a beautiful smile." He cupped his hand briefly to Malachi's shoulder, squeezed it gently and then moved away.

Malachi, as best as he could, tried to keep Chad in his sights but lost him almost immediately. Something was happening, a shift that he couldn't explain but that he was certain would change his life dramatically. Was he ready for whatever came next?

Absolutely not.

***

Meanwhile, Cole Malcolm had just walked into Urbane, Dean following close behind. Although going to the night club wasn't his idea, Cole saw it as the perfect escape. He was done with Dean. It didn't take him long, over the course of dinner, to realize that the guy wasn't his type. He knew exactly what the problem was, too. Dean liked to talk. Talk, talk, talk non-stop … about Dean. How his jeans, at one hundred fifty dollars, were a steal. How he talked Mrs. Callaghan into buying a three-thousand-dollar sideboard. The way other designers kept copying his style. Talk, Dean did, throughout the two-hour meal. The two bottles of wine they shared dulled Cole's contempt and made him tune out. He couldn't wait to slip away into the crowd and be free.

Cole had never gotten used to the big city club scene and stayed away from it as much as possible. The small town gay bars, like the one in Claredon where he'd met Malachi, had a homey feel to them. Guys said hello and at least tried to get acquainted without necessarily expecting sex. But by the number of intent stares of interest thrown at him after only being in the bar five minutes, it was clear that Urbane was a meat market. And he was fresh meat.

The strobe lights bounced off his face, at times blinding him, as he pushed his way through the crowd. It annoyed him that Dean had curled his fingers through his belt loops, hanging on as if his life depended on it. He worried about how that looked, like they were a couple, which they weren't. He reached behind his back and pried Dean's fingers away. He squeezed between a square pillar and a group of guys huddled in a circle. He froze, causing Dean to collide into him. *God, it can't be.* But it was. His eyes latched onto Malachi, who didn't see him at first. He felt sick when he saw the way the dark-haired guy looked at Malachi. That should have been him. The guy leaned forward, and from where he stood it seemed like the two were kissing. Cole clenched his teeth. *Fuck!* The guy moved off and Malachi, now alone, turned slightly. Cole, his heart in his throat, held Malachi's gaze. And as much as he wanted to rush to him, his iron-weighted legs wouldn't move. That was a sign. After everything that had happened, why should he be the one to make the first move? *Fuck, have a little self-respect. If he's interested, he'll come to me.*

He flinched at the touch of a hand on his arm and turned to see Dean looking at him. *Jesus, he's still here?* He fixed his attention back on the spot where Malachi stood but it was empty. *Christ!* He was on edge — partly because of Dean, but mostly because seeing Malachi revived the restlessness and agitation that enveloped him. And being on edge became a call to arms to the demons desperate to seize control of his mind. He could have stayed home, perfecting his role as a recluse — barricaded first in his Liberty Village loft, and now in his Annex home — watching Charlie Chaplin films or reading Tom Clancy novels. It was how he coped in the days immediately after Paul's death, how he tried to hang on to his mind.

There it was again, the pressure on his arm, and Cole drew in a deep breath. He turned to Dean, but didn't know what to say. Even though the evening with Dean held no promise, it did help him to escape the psychotic unfurling that was set to destroy him.

"Who was that?" Dean asked, curt.

Cole shrugged. "No one important." He waited for Dean to test him, push him for a better response.

"I'll be right back," was all Dean said. He pushed past Cole, grabbing playfully at Cole's belt buckle as if he was going to undo it. He winked and made his way towards the washroom.

Cole watched with relief as Dean shoved his way through the mob that wasn't always eager to step aside for him. Everything about Dean made him cringe — his clinginess, his need to always touch him, the sense of feeling possessed. When Dean was out of sight, Cole made a beeline for the stairwell near the entrance, which was winding, narrow and dimly lit. There was a steady stream of people moving in both directions. He held onto the railing to keep his balance as he sometimes twisted his body, pressing up against the wall, to avoid the hard thump of someone's shoulder as they barrelled past. He found himself stuck halfway up as the people in front of him stopped moving. Taking in the snippets of conversations of those near the front of the line, he realized they were managing the number of bodies on the rooftop patio at any one time.

When he emerged outside he did a quick inventory of the area. The bar was immediately to his left. The white patio tables and chairs took up a lot of space since everyone seemed to be standing. The small area to the right, marked off as a dance floor, was empty. He glanced behind him and, thankfully, Dean was nowhere in sight. He edged his way through the multitude, graciously accepting the sheepish smiles and slight nods of head offered to him as he headed for the bar. None of the faces were recognizable and that didn't surprise him. Most of his friends were coupled, and not gay. And the few gay friends he did have were bookish and liked to hold candlelight suppers *à la Hyacinth Bucket*.

With a beer in hand, he weaved his way through the crowd, gawking at the guys who all looked like supermodels. It slowed him down, taking a moment to study each handsome face, as he attempted to reach the front area of the patio that looked onto Church Street. The music, the roaming clouds of cigarette smoke encircling him and the sudden outbursts of laughter pushed him near to a state of delirium. Certainly the beer, together with the wine from dinner, was contributing to the effect — light-headed, an anxious breathlessness, feeling as though he was being watched. There were noticeable beads of sweat on his brow that he regularly wiped away with his hand.

As Cole neared the front of the patio, he froze. He spotted Malachi among the guys leaning against the railing and observing the goings-on on the street below. It was as though Malachi was being deliberately put in his path, like some sort of test. He closed his eyes and inhaled, the unpleasant whiff of cigar smoke filling his nostrils. He needed a moment to find his bearings and calm himself down. Then Cole opened his eyes and felt his throat constrict as he studied the one man able to possess him.

Walk away. Turn around and walk away. Yet he couldn't walk away. The night he'd spent with Malachi haunted him. Not because of the sex, but because of the intimacy with which they talked. It created a bond. Cole was certain of that. That made it so he needed to understand why Malachi had stood him up and never bothered to call. Better his heart was open to forgiveness and reconciliation. He was also still angry and hurt, wishing he could erase the imprint Malachi had left on his life. There his heart was open to vengeance, or so he thought. His grip tightened on his beer, and the fingers of his other hand curled into a fist, his nails pressing deep into his palm. With his head titled slightly upwards, it looked like he was praying for the courage to face down his Goliath.

He went over to Malachi and, leaning sideways against the railing, contemplated him. There was no immediate acknowledgement of his presence. He didn't feel nervous anymore, just a little unsettled. At times when he knew he had to be strong, or strong-minded, he gave the impression of a weak man, some flowery wallpaper no one ever took notice of. He placed his hand on Malachi's shoulder. "You don't look that surprised to see me," he said when Malachi looked at him.

"Should I be?" Malachi turned away.

"What the fuck's your problem?" Cole let his hand fall from Malachi's shoulder and shoved it into his pants pocket only to pull it out again. He turned his body so that he could, like Malachi, rest his forearms on the paint-chipped railing and watch the people and cars moving about on the street below. The heavy bass-laden music streaming from the speakers around the patio couldn't distil the street noises or the conversations colliding into each other. His last swig of beer seemed to stay lodged in his throat, and no matter how hard he tried he could not force it down, disconnect from it. That would be like disconnecting himself from the things that love was all about. Yet he was fully connected to the idea of love — being completely devoted to one person for the rest of his life — that had implanted itself in him like a confounded cold that he could not shake.

He wanted to be like Malachi — show no emotion or give any indication of being affected. He remembered the look they shared earlier, and how the iciness of Malachi's dark brown eyes was both terrifying and seductive. It only took that brief exchange to call up the tenderness, despite everything, he still had for Malachi. He smiled. If there were any man he wanted to possess him, it was definitely Malachi.

Two guys pushed in beside Cole, who was forced to shift to his right. When his arm brushed against Malachi's and their eyes locked, his smile broadened. But Cole, betrayed by a resurgent adolescent shyness, couldn't hold the gaze.

"There you are…"

The deep voice made Cole look up and to the right. His eyes widened as the tall, Billy Zane lookalike cupped his hands to Malachi's shoulders. Right then he was prepared to surrender in defeat. He heard the two whispering but couldn't make out what was being said. Then the guy turned and eyed him. Cole stood up straight. "Have a good night, Malachi." They looked at each other again with the same intensity as on that night they were wrapped up in each other's arms.

"Cole…"

Cole waited a moment, but all that followed was Malachi hunching his shoulders. "I don't know why I fucking bothered," he said and walked away.

***

What's the matter with you? Malachi thought, trying to track Cole in the crowd, but all the heads blended together. He caught Shane's raised-eyebrow look and rolled his eyes.

"That was Cole?" Shane asked, his voice brimming with an odd mixture of excitement and anxiousness, as if he'd met the man who replaced him in his lover's bed. "What happened?"

"Nothing." Malachi took up his earlier position against the railing.

"I don't understand." Shane spoke with a hint of insincerity. "How can you let him walk away? You could explain —"

"Explain Zach Brennan?" Malachi asked, then sucked his teeth.

"Zach's only part of the problem. It's the same goddamn thing every time someone tries to get close to you. You push them away. You're like a record stuck on repeat." Shane's voice trailed off when Malachi shot him a knowing look. "Why do you keep pretending like you're not interested in Cole? Who are you trying to kid?"

"Shane, don't," Malachi said pointedly.

"In case Cole hasn't told you yet, you're being a prick. Maybe it won't be Cole. Maybe it'll be someone else, but one day you'll wake up and realize what you missed out on."

"Fuck off, Shane."

"Hey ... don't take this out on me." There was a silence. "So, then what happened to your friend Chad?"

"Go away, Shane."

Shane laughed and wrapped his arm around Malachi's neck, like he'd done as they waited to enter Urbane, another gesture of reassurance. "This is just a rough patch. You're going to get through it. You know that, right?" There was no response. "We're downstairs if you want... All right. I can take a hint." He removed his arm and dragged his hand down Malachi's back as he moved off.

Left alone, Malachi placed his free hand to his face and slowly slid it downward. His whole world was spinning out of control and he was exhausted. He backed away from the railing, sat down at a nearby table and finished his beer. He set the empty bottle on the table, gripped his hands to the arms of the sturdy plastic chair and leaned back. He stared up into the dark night sky, the noise around him fading as if he was willingly blocking it out. There weren't any stars in the sky, just an expansive blackness blanketing the earth. That blackness was in him, a heaviness wedged deep in his chest that he couldn't pry free.

Malachi kept trying to think of Cole as a beautiful stranger who had provided a 'quick fix.' But deep down he knew it had, *bon gré mal gré*, been much more than that, and that made him anxious and confused. He had no defence against such feelings. They were a menace that went straight through him — strangling, cutting and ruthless. Zach was dead, and now there was no possible future for them. Had there ever been? And was there a possible future with Cole? Or was Malachi destined to live a solitary life?

The crowd on the patio buzzed with excitement when Gloria Gaynor's "I Will Survive" streamed through the speakers. The energetic partiers charged onto the dance floor, and that was when Malachi saw Cole emerge from the washroom. Their eyes briefly met until Cole turned away. It was a type of shunning, a good ole kick in the teeth that cut through Malachi. *Maybe Shane's right and I'm being a prick. But Cole and I ... it couldn't work. Not now. Not with everything that's happened. I'm not ready. I'm not open to it. Not now. Maybe not ever.*

Malachi stood and approached Cole, who stood in line at the bar. He glued his eyes to Cole's black jeans showcasing the firm cyclist's arse he'd paid great homage to. The bartender set down a Corona in front of Cole. Malachi, cutting in to hand over a twenty-dollar bill, said, "Make it two."

"I can buy my own drink," Cole said without looking at Malachi. He slapped down a ten-dollar bill on the bar and moved off.

Malachi paid for his drink, then searched for Cole, who was lost in the mob exiting the dance floor. Making his way back towards the railing, a tingling sensation raced over his body when his eyes latched onto that dark full mane seated at the table he'd vacated earlier. He pulled out the other chair and said, "May I?"

"What's the point?" Cole asked, swung his head away from Malachi and took a swig of his beer.

The music blaring through the speakers over the rooftop patio held them in a sort of suspended animation. They barely exchanged glances, letting their eyes rove — as if this were the first time they'd met and were embarrassed to show the other that they were, perhaps, the object of their affection. They both felt uncomfortable, wanting to speak but not knowing what to say.

Malachi sat down and pulled his chair closer to the table. "I know this may seem awkward —"

"Seem awkward?" Cole interrupted, his wild eyes trained on Malachi. "I try talking to you and you bite my head off. And you pretend like nothing happened between us."

"We had a one-night stand," Malachi said dryly. "Then we have to deal with its aftermath. I mean, of course it feels good in the moment. It's afterwards, in the morning, when we're trying to see it for more than it really is."

Cole rolled his eyes. "Spoken like a true philistine."

"Look, Cole … I'm sorry if you expected more."

"Sorry doesn't cut it. And an apology from you at this point doesn't mean much. Christ, I don't get guys like you."

"Guys like me?" Malachi gave a little shrug and continued in a calm voice. "Guys like me tell you how it is, straight up. I made it very clear that I wasn't looking for anything beyond —"

"Then why the fuck did you agree to have dinner with me?" Cole shot back.

Malachi dropped his gaze, his heart thumping in his chest. He waited until his breathing normalized and then, without looking at Cole, said, "I think I'm going to call it a night."

"Run away." Cole pursed his lips. "Is that what you do best?"

A loud, crowing laugh soared across the patio. Cole and Malachi, like many of the other patrons, turned their attention to the group of guys near the bar who were doubled over laughing. Malachi pushed back his chair from the table and stood. He looked at Cole but stared past him at the brick wall of the building next door.

Cole chugged the rest of his beer. "Do you ever wonder if there's anyone out there who's happy?" he asked as Malachi started to walk away. "I mean, really happy?"

Malachi stopped and spun around. "No."

Cole, still not looking up, traced his index finger around the top of the bottle. "Sometimes I wonder what they've done to get there. How have they stayed there … *in* that happiness? Did they risk their soul and what did it cost them?"

"I didn't realize that happiness had a cost. But I'm just a philistine, so what do I really know."

"Everything has a cost of some sort," Cole said, slowly lifting his head. "To know what happiness —"

"I'm not interested in debating the metaphysics of happiness with you. I don't care if other people are really happy. That's for them to decide, and to live with." Malachi bit down on his lip. "Look, all I needed was one night where I could have a little fun. And that's what I had. I didn't want the responsibilities, stress and the pain that comes with a relationship."

"I'm glad you got what *you* wanted. Jesus…" Cole sucked his teeth. "And is that what you think relationships are?"

Malachi shrugged. "Sooner or later."

"So, you've studied every relationship in the history of mankind and know how each one has ended? This I've got to hear."

"They end in pain," Malachi said, matter-of-fact. "There's either a breakup or someone dies. Doesn't really matter, it still ends. And frankly, Cole, I'm not about to risk exposing myself, or you for that matter, to that sort of suffering. I'm starting to think … there's nothing wrong with a little free-style love. You know, no strings attached. How's everyone calling it these days? Oh, yeah … fuck n' go."

"That explains everything," Cole said in a loud voice, leaning forward. "There's this huge force field around you that repels everyone and everything. And you're afraid to take it down." He leaned back in his chair.

They looked at each other, with misgiving and desire. They were caught in separate, entangling webs that reeled them back from the edge of the daring vistas that held the promise of love and possibility. They were both in search of something that would give their lives meaning — for Cole that was love, for Malachi it had yet to reveal itself.

Malachi looked down at Cole. "You were wrong, you know."

"Wrong about what?"

"I was never waiting on happiness. You don't 'wait on' happiness. Happiness waits on you."

"I never said —"

"It was implied."

Dean came into view and approached the table. He looked suspiciously at Malachi and coolly at Cole, and then lifted his beer bottle to his mouth. "I wondered where you had disappeared to," he spat at Cole, but his fiery eyes were trained at Malachi.

"I should have…" Cole blinked. "I'm sorry."

"So am I." Dean turned and walked away.

Malachi started to move off.

"Malachi…" Cole rose and moved to block Malachi's path.

"You like to imagine what happiness looks like," Malachi said, shoving his hands in his pockets.

"What does that mean?" Cole asked.

Malachi locked onto Cole's narrow blue eyes. "If *you're* not happy, do something about it." He stepped around Cole and headed for the stairs.

"Isn't that what I'm trying to do?" Cole shouted, ignoring the people who turned and looked oddly at him, as if he had had too much to drink. But he didn't care. "And for that matter … why don't you take your own damn advice!"

***

Malachi, pushing his way through the crowd, almost let himself be baited but kept walking. He ran down the stairwell and towards the exit. Outside, breathing in the warm night air, his tight muscles loosened. He stood on the sidewalk for a time, staring at the bright white light shining on the sign above the entrance that read, 'Urbane,' cut out in large wood letters. He was tempted to venture back inside, but for what? Shane was occupied, and he had as much use for Cory and Eric as they had for him. He decided to return to the hotel.

"Malachi…"

Malachi, walking northward along Church Street, spun around when he heard his name echo through the air. He couldn't help but smile at the black-haired beauty jogging towards him.

"You're not leaving already," Chad said as he closed the gap between them. "It's still early."

Malachi shrugged. "Like I said, this really isn't my scene."

"Then let's go somewhere and have some fun." Chad took another step forward. "No strings, nothing complicated. Just good old-fashioned fun."

Malachi glanced away. He flinched at the feel of Chad's velvety hand on his face, the hair on the back of his neck standing up. He didn't resist when Chad gently turned his head and, looking at each other again, his lips curled into a smile. Then Chad leaned in and kissed him. And Malachi lapped it up, smiling through the kiss as he thought about Taylor's brashness on their second date. Was this night going to end the same way?

"Get a room!" someone shouted amid the whistling as a group of guys navigated around them on the sidewalk.

Malachi pulled away. "Chad —"

Chad placed his index finger to Malachi's lips. "Don't resist. Let's just enjoy the moment." He reached for Malachi's hand and led him into the street, flagging down the approaching taxi.

Malachi didn't resist. He needed something to distract him from the chaos swirling about his mind. And he needed to, one more time, feel loved in an uncomplicated way.

Chad never let go of his hand during the ten-minute ride, the pressure keeping his manhood hard as steel. They didn't say anything, yet whenever their eyes met they broke out in giddy laughter. Malachi tried not to think about what was happening or if it meant anything. He wanted, like Chad had encouraged, to 'just enjoy the moment.'

Once inside the hotel room, Malachi wasn't sure what came over him. He lunged at Chad and, in no time, had him pinned down on the bed. *Let it go,* he thought as he kissed Chad passionately, their tongues tangling. *Let it all go.*

TEN

CHAD, NAKED AND STRETCHED out in the bed, kept his gaze trained at the bathroom door. He was spent and recovering from the sex that had almost made him pass out. What was he thinking? He hadn't gone out with the intention of picking up a stranger, but he'd been drawn to Malachi since that first glance on the sidewalk. It was the coy smile that had hooked him, made him swoon. It was wrong for a myriad of reasons and right for just as many. Given his circumstances, what he'd done was wrong. Deep down, he knew that.

The bathroom door swung open, and Chad quickly moved to pull the bedcovers up to his waist. He smiled when Malachi came into view, his heart leaping into his throat. He hadn't felt this silly in a long time, like when he was a teenager and had a crush on his father's secretary. "What are you doing?" he asked, panic rising in his voice.

"I'm going back to my hotel," Malachi said, scavenging the floor for his clothes.

"Why? You can stay —"

"I don't do that." Malachi pulled on his underwear. "Besides, no strings, remember?"

Chad moved off the bed and crossed to Malachi, who wouldn't hold his gaze. When Malachi went to put on his T-shirt, Chad snatched it away and thrust it to the floor. Then he wrapped his arms around Malachi's waist, picked him up and carried him back to the bed. Chad fell backwards, Malachi falling on top of him. There was a brief scrimmage as they jockeyed for the dominant position. As he usually did in such situations, Chad won out, straddling Malachi's waist and pinning him down.

"I'm not asking to marry you," Chad said, searching for Malachi's hands. "I'd just like you to stay and maybe we could cuddle a bit."

"That's a bad idea," Malachi said, dodging Chad's eyes. "That tends to complicate things. And my life is already complicated enough."

"So is mine." Chad offered a faint smile, then leaned forward and kissed Malachi. His lips parted to let Malachi's tongue slip into his mouth. He straightened his legs and, with their hard cocks rubbing against each other, moaned. He broke the kiss and buried his face in Malachi's neck. *God, I wish this could last forever*. He drew in a deep breath, lifted his head and gazed at Malachi. "I need to tell you something."

Malachi, sucking his teeth, shoved Chad off him. "Don't. Don't ruin this."

"It's not what I want to do," Chad said weakly. "But I want you to know that this isn't something that I do regularly."

"I don't care what you do." Malachi's tone was dismissive. "I mean, we had sex. And there's a reason they call them one-night stands."

"Well…" Chad sat up. "In a perfect world, I'd love to make it a multi-night stand. It's just … I'm not exactly single."

Malachi bolted upright. "I don't think I know what 'I'm-not-exactly-single' means."

"It's complicated."

"I'm sure it is," Malachi said. "It proves, like I told a friend earlier, that relationships don't work. Somebody always ends up getting hurt."

When Malachi went to move off the bed, Chad tackled him, one more time holding him down. "All I wanted to-night..." His voice trailed off as he tried to push down the emotion surging in his throat. "Do you know what it's like to be in a relationship that's suffocating you? You know you have to pull yourself out, but you can't. Or won't. Now it almost feels too late, like I have to just serve out the sentence."

Malachi flinched. "Why? Why would you do that to yourself?"

"Because..." Chad ran his hand through his hair. "Because despite everything, having Trent in my life fills a void. I have someone to look after and pamper. I'm not stupid, and I know Trent loves my money more than me. But I watched all my friends coupling up and I felt like the odd man out."

"You're staying because staying is easier," Malachi said, matter-of-fact.

Chad slid off Malachi and rolled onto his back. "I don't know why I'm staying."

"Then why not end it?"

"There's just something comforting about waking up in the morning with someone beside me."

"Even when you know they don't love you?"

Chad turned his head and locked his eyes on Malachi. "I thought you didn't care."

"Not that you'd care, but a lot has happened in my life lately," Malachi said. "And I've been a bit of a prick to a few people. Well, to one guy in particular. I'm trying not to be one with you."

"Because you like me?" Chad winked.

"I think I do like you, but I don't get involved with married guys."

"I'm not married."

Malachi rolled his eyes. "You know what I mean."

"Please don't go," Chad pleaded when Malachi went to stand. "We don't have to cuddle. We could just talk for a bit."

"I have rules for one-night stands," Malachi said bluntly.

"Mali —"

"And I've already broken a couple with you."

"I'm a firm believer that rules are made to be broken." Chad flashed a generous smile. He reached out and drew Malachi into him. His whole body relaxed as Malachi's arms tightened around him. He felt protected, like he'd finally escaped the pain cruising through his life. "Will you stay?" he said into Malachi's ear.

Malachi pulled out of the embrace. "I shouldn't. You and I ... I don't think we should invite each other into our labyrinths."

"I'm not asking that," Chad said. "This is a breather, a reprieve from the pain."

"The best reprieve would be to remove yourself —"

"I will," Chad broke in. "Right now, I want to enjoy us."

They wanted to look away from each other but couldn't, their eyes gleaming compassion as much as understanding. They both needed relief from the chaos implanted in their lives, but spending the night together was dangerous. Chad knew that. He'd confided in Malachi about his troubled relationship, something he hadn't even done with his friends. That scared him. He wasn't falling for the guy, but it just felt nice to get that off his chest. And it gave him a glimpse of what love could look like. First things first. He had to boot Trent from his life, but he wasn't sure he had the courage for that. Being with someone who wanted to be with you, even if they weren't truly in love, was better than being alone.

Without saying another word, they settled into the bed. Chad rolled into Malachi, resting his head on Malachi's chest. With Malachi's arm wrapped around him, Chad couldn't help but think about Trent, who'd given him nothing in return, nothing of substance. It wasn't the cheap gifts on his birthday or that Trent barely helped out with the expenses that bothered him. All he wanted was to feel loved, and with Trent that came with a price.

Whatever he gave Trent — tickets to see Madonna, a weekend trip to New York City, a Kenneth Cole watch — it was never enough. And Trent came to expect more because he'd set the bar high. And he bought the gifts and took Trent out for nice dinners because it was, on those nights, when they had sex. Sex had to be earned. Some nights Trent didn't come home at all, partying it up with his friends. When Trent did stumble into the house, sometimes in the morning, other times late in the day, Chad smelled the sex on him. There was never a hint of guilt or shame, like it was part of the package deal. *Why* do *I put up with it?* Chad knew why. He truly didn't believe that he deserved better. And he didn't want to look like a fool to his friends. Malachi was right. He let Trent stay with him because it was easier.

Chad fell asleep, a smile on his face, feeling for the first time in years like he was safe in the arms of his personal saviour.

***

The sculpted torso stretched out on the bed had Malachi second-guessing himself. Should he open the door and slip away unnoticed? Or should he undress and climb back into the bed? His eyes sidled over to the desk and the note he'd scribbled on the hotel stationery. *Coward. Maybe that's true, but it's the right thing to do.* There were already too many distractions in his life. He couldn't afford another. He felt an ache in his heart as his gaze fell on the white sheet covering Chad's round ass and then followed down the exposed hairy, muscular legs. Just when he thought he knew what to do, he found himself hesitating. Then Chad shifted slightly in the bed and Malachi, panicked, opened the door. He rushed into the corridor and quietly closed the door behind him. That chapter was, at least, over. Right?

Twenty minutes later, he was back in his own hotel room that showed no signs of Shane having slept there. For some reason, that both surprised and disappointed him. He checked the time. Twenty-three minutes past seven. He had lots of time before meeting up with Shane, Cory and Eric for breakfast at ten. That was the plan before the night of dance and drink had opened the door to new possibilities. He'd quickly closed the door on that possibility, unwilling to see where it could lead. *God, why did I sneak out like that? Yes, I'm a coward. And pathetic.* He showered, changed and made himself a cup of coffee. Comfortably seated at the desk, he wrote until it was time to meet up with the others.

At five minutes to ten, Malachi made his way down to Hearth, the hotel restaurant. Since there was still no sign of Shane, he was confident that he'd end up eating alone. He shuddered at the thought of dining alone with Cory and Eric, and requested a table for one. He beamed with relief when the hostess led him to a quiet corner of the restaurant. A few minutes later, a middle-aged woman appeared at his table with a carafe of coffee, filled his cup and took his order.

He poured some cream into the dark liquid that began to turn caramel brown. It had him thinking about how his life had evolved, the odd components that fused together in ways he'd never imagined. Stirring a spoonful of sugar into his coffee, that was when he understood. Chad, Zach and Cole weren't the real antagonists in his life. He was. They kept him distracted, focused away from himself. He could see that now. That didn't mean that he knew what to do. He'd yet to find a way to shield himself from the flying shrapnel of the life that'd been shattered years ago. He didn't want to think about the past, as if that allowed him to outrun it. But it was always there, in his subconscious, along with the pain that influenced the choices he made. Could he not see how much his past was a part of him and his present? No matter how desperate he was to escape it, his past hovered over him like dark storm clouds waiting to unleash their wrath.

"More coffee?" The middle-aged woman was back and topped up his coffee without waiting for a response. "Your breakfast should be up shortly."

As the server walked away, a chortle laugh rang out through the dining room. Malachi's hand shook and he was unable to pick up his coffee cup. The laugh had transported him back to his second year of university, when he was just beginning to step into the man he hoped to become.

"Tip it forward a little," the deep voice said.

Malachi looked to the right and saw the smirking brunette reaching for the box of wine. He held his glass steady under the sprout as the guy tilted the box. "Maybe this is a sign that I've reached my limit," he said once his glass was full.

The guy laughed and extended his hand. "I'm Taylor."

"Malachi."

"Malachi..."

"Bishop." Malachi's body tingled when Taylor didn't let go immediately. Those smiling greenish-brown eyes had his insides spinning. The tousled brown hair made it look like he belonged on the cover of *Out*. And Malachi was already imagining how it would feel to drag his lips across every inch of those toned muscles.

"I was just thinking I like that name." Taylor winked. "Malachi Bishop ... that sounds familiar."

"You mean you don't know who I am?" Malachi made an 'x' in the air with his index finger. "Strike one."

"Ha-ha." Taylor grabbed a plastic cup from the buffet that housed the makeshift bar. He surveyed the offerings, then made himself a rye and ginger. "How did you end up here tonight?"

"I was invited."

"I meant..." Taylor sipped his drink. "Are you friends with Jay or Glen?"

"Neither. I came with my friend Patrick. He's friends with Glen and Jay." Malachi lifted his cup to his mouth and looked about the room. *Where is Patrick, anyway?* He'd met Patrick

Knowles, a young scholar of English literature, six months ago at an interschool symposium. Maybe it was because he was older and more experienced, but Patrick became a sort of mentor. He did more than help Malachi navigate Ottawa's gay community. They became lovers. Or were they more than that?

"I'm Glen's cousin."

"Strike two," Malachi teased. He didn't know much about Glen, but when Taylor's eyes widened, he felt the heat burn in his cheeks. "You know, I was just kidding."

"I figured it out."

Malachi's gulp of wine went down the wrong way and he coughed. "Figured out what?"

"'The App.' That was your story in *Prism*."

"Yes. But —"

"I think I just hit a homerun." Taylor imitated swinging a bat. "I liked it. You're a good writer."

Malachi opened his mouth to speak, but nothing happened. He couldn't even squeak out a thank-you for the compliment. He was still in shock that a gorgeous, seemingly well-read stranger knew who he was and liked his writing. It was too good to be true, but the timing was horrible. Too late. Holding his gaze to those magnetic eyes with their aristocratic eyebrows, he was hooked. Yet he still couldn't bring himself to say anything and glanced at his watch.

Taylor downed his drink, crumpled the cup and tossed it into the nearby bin. "Enjoy the rest of your evening."

Before Malachi could react, Taylor had slipped away into the crowd. He raised himself up on his toes, searching the faces for those thin pink kissable lips. With most guys he sucked at small talk and never knew what to say. Something about Taylor had him wanting to share his life story. Malachi began to frantically edge his way through the throng, grabbing every guy with brown hair by the arm and spinning them around. Each time he was met with a snarl or a questioning look. Where the hell was Taylor?

In the kitchen, he saw Patrick in the corner chatting with Glen. The last thing he wanted was for Patrick to see him. He had to do something about that, but now wasn't the time. He set his unfinished drink on the counter, then pushed his way into the front hall. Even with the loud music, he heard the thunder of feet on the staircase and stepped to the side as a stream of men filed past him and into the living room. The last guy moved a bit slower, like there wasn't any reason to rush. This time, it took only a split second for Malachi to react. He leaped forward and reached for the bare arm. When their eyes met, he smiled.

"Let's have a drink soon," Malachi said.

Taylor raised an eyebrow. "Soon?"

"Tomorrow."

"Can't." Taylor gently peeled Malachi's hand off his arm. "Already have plans."

"Then Sunday."

"Dinner with my family."

"Then breakfast," Malachi said, working to tamp down his frustration. "The Elgin Street Diner. Sunday morning. Nine o'clock. Final offer." He held his breath, his stomach tightening, as he waited for a response.

"Don't be late," Taylor said nonchalantly and moved off.

Malachi exhaled. His heart pounding and his hands shaking, he staggered onto the front porch and leaned against the railing. He didn't know what was happening, how Taylor had gotten to him in a way no other man had. Was this what it felt like to fall in love? No, that was crazy. They didn't even know each other. But there was something between them. He felt it. Did Taylor feel it, too? Recovered, Malachi skipped down the stairs and started for home. He couldn't wait for Sunday, his lips curling into a smile as he thought — without really knowing why — that his life would never be the same.

And on Sunday morning, Malachi showed up at the diner at quarter to nine. A stocky blond seated him at a booth in the middle of the restaurant. He fidgeted with the menu and repeatedly checked the time while he waited. Of all the scenarios that had played out in his mind in the last thirty-four hours, he'd never imagined being stood up. As the clock ticked closer to nine, he was beginning to panic. He hadn't had that much success with dating. His relationships, if he could even call them that, were short-term — two or three weeks, maybe a month. And he and Patrick … that wasn't a relationship as much as it was a booty call. Whatever it was, Malachi was tired of it. It wasn't that he was looking for love, either, but he wanted something different. He wanted to get to know a guy on a more personal level — his dreams, his hopes, how he saw himself in the world. He was tired of feeling cheap. Did he believe that Taylor would be different from the other guys he dated? Yes, but he wasn't quite sure why he believed it.

At ten minutes past nine, Malachi felt his throat constrict. Was Taylor going to show? They hadn't exchanged numbers, so if something had come up there was no way to get in contact. He'd been too shy to ask a guy out before. And when he did, what happened? He got screwed.

The stocky blond appeared at his table. "Would you like to wait a little longer?"

Malachi, not looking up from the meu, shrugged. "There's no point. I'll have —"

"Malachi…"

He recognized that baritone voice and, lifting his head, felt giddy at seeing Taylor's generous smile.

"Sorry I'm late," Taylor said, sliding into the other side of the booth. He turned to the server. "Could I please get a black coffee?" Then, when they were alone, he added, "I'm really sorry."

"I thought you might have changed your mind," Malachi said.

"Thought about it." Taylor, taking a moment to catch his breath, winked. "Kidding. It's a date. No pressure. But if I hadn't shown … I didn't want to be that guy looking back twenty years from now and wondering if I'd missed out on the best thing to come into my life."

"That sounds like pressure to me," Malachi said, reaching for his coffee.

"Relax. I don't propose on the first date." Taylor grabbed a couple of paper napkins from the metal holder and wiped his forehead. "Again, sorry for being late."

"Stop apologizing."

Taylor took a few more serviettes and ran them across his lips. "I didn't hear my alarm. No, that's not true. I forgot to set it. Last night was weird."

"How so?"

"Oh, you know…" Taylor chuckled. "Alcohol and pot don't really mix that well. Don't look at me like that. Pot isn't my thing. But people do some crazy shit when they're high. Sorry, I'm not normally like this. I'm just nervous."

He's nervous? Everything I ate last night went straight through me. I spent half the night glued to the toilet, and this morning it still hurt to wipe my butthole. "Well, I'm glad you made it."

"Me, too." Taylor leaned back as the server set down his coffee. "Thanks. I really need this." He took a couple of sips, then looked at Malachi. "I'm glad I haven't struck out yet."

"The other night you seemed to think you hit a homerun."

"You're the umpire. You tell me." Taylor grinned.

Malachi quickly discovered that there was something different about Taylor. Taylor made him laugh. After leaving the restaurant, they made their way to the canal and ambled along the pathway towards Parliament Hill. They sat down on a bench and, looking out at the Ottawa River, felt an inner peacefulness. They talked about everything and nothing — their 'crazy' families, the Conservative leadership race, the friends who'd come and gone from their lives, and, to their surprise, Jesus. Every time Taylor looked at him, Malachi felt as though he was being penetrated. Taylor's dreamy greenish-brown eyes delved into his core, and he felt that, finally, someone understood him. It was an odd feeling, one that both excited and terrified. Was it possible that he was wrong, that there was such a thing as a kindred spirit or soul mate? Did love really exist? Did it exist in him?

They weren't distracted by the cyclists or runners speeding by, or the walkers and their energetic conversations. They were held in a trance, swept up in the majesty of something new and wonderful. Taylor searched for Malachi's hand, held it in his briefly, and let go. They looked intently at each other and smiled.

Taylor was the first to break the silence. "I need to go and work on a paper that's due next week."

"I see," Malachi said, disappointed, and dropped his gaze. "What about dinner tomorrow?"

Malachi lifted his head, a broad smile on his face. "I'd love that. You could come over to my place."

Three hours after they'd left the diner, they stood and retraced their footsteps until they reached the staircase that led to Wellington Street. They raced up the stairs like school children, laughing giddily.

At the top, Malachi, panting, reached into his pants pocket, pulled out a folded piece of paper and handed it Taylor. "Call me later and we'll shore things up for tomorrow." He started walking backwards and, grinning, said, "Maybe I'm the one who's hit a homerun." He waved, turned around and walked away.

The hand pushing down gently on Malachi's shoulder startled him. He sighed as Taylor's image faded from his mind. He looked up.

"Can I get you anything else?" The server placed the salmon benedict on the table in front of him.

"This is perfect," he said, picking up his fork and knife. He popped a home fry into his mouth and chewed thoughtfully as he stared blankly into the restaurant. His focus found the family, seated midway across the room, laughing as they studied their menus. The young father, with his mussed up brown hair and wearing a blue T-shirt, reminded him of the young Taylor Blanchard he'd fallen in love with. The guy's chortle laugh and how he looked so much like Taylor made Malachi's throat constrict. It'd been a long time since the past had rattled him so much that it had him seeing Taylor everywhere. The coy smile the husband shot at his wife had Malachi back reliving that first night he'd welcomed Taylor into his home.

"I'm late again," Taylor said, stepping into the apartment. "Sorry, I —"

"It's okay." Malachi closed the door, his anxiousness beginning to ebb. He'd called Taylor's cell phone three times and never got an answer. This time he truly believed that Taylor wasn't going to show.

"I hope that this will make up for my tardiness." Taylor handed over the bottle of Masi Bianco Delle Venezie once he was inside the apartment.

Malachi read the label and then looked at Taylor, who wore a dark sea blue ringer T-shirt and form-fitting blue jeans. And his smile — coy and slightly mischievous — had Malachi swooning. "Let's find out."

Malachi asked Taylor to open the chilled wine while he plated their meals. They sat down at the square bistro table and clinked their wineglasses together in a silent toast. With the first bites of the spaghettini with speck, arugula and cream that he'd prepared, there was no doubt that the wine — with its hints of ripe apples and bananas — went perfectly with the meal.

"What do you think?" Taylor asked, reaching for his wineglass. "About the wine…"

"It's delicious."

"Excellent."

There it was again, that smile that made Malachi dizzy. *Who is this guy?*

Like their breakfast date, conversation came easily to them. And the wine, relaxing their inhibitions, had them revealing their secret desires, hopes and dreams. Malachi wanted to be a writer. Taylor saw himself becoming the country's first openly gay prime minister.

"No second fiddle for you, eh?" Malachi said, chuckling.

"Me?" Taylor threw Malachi a mocking look. "You said you wanted to win the Booker Prize."

"I guess we're both deluded."

They laughed, then talked about how some of their friends ridiculed their 'pipe dreams,' but they were determined to succeed regardless. *And he'll do it*, Malachi thought. *He's actually going to be the prime minister some day.*

After dinner, they sat on Malachi's frayed wool-upholstered blue sofa with a white floral pattern and drank more wine while listening to a compilation CD of classical music. In between sips, they stole sidelong glances of each other and exchanged sheepish smiles. They finished their drinks and set their wineglasses on the wooden coffee table. Malachi went to stand, but Taylor stretched out his arm, holding him down. Then Taylor leaned over and kissed him.

Malachi trembled as their tongues darted and prodded, but eagerly absorbed Taylor's sweet taste. He reached out and drew him close. Feeling Taylor's solid, muscular body pressed against his had his excitement bolting up a notch. No one had ever made him feel this way before, like he was on fire. He wanted Taylor. Badly. They kissed deeply, shifting into a position that knitted their bodies perfectly together. Taylor suddenly pulled away, looking at him with hard eyes and breathing deeply. Malachi's gut tightened. *Slow down. Don't rush and screw this up.* Then Taylor smirked, stood and held out his hand. Malachi, his pulse racing and that ache burning in his veins, was slow to rise. It was the last thing he expected to do, but it was too late. He had to go all the way. He gripped Taylor's warm hand, led him down the hall and took him into his bed.

Neither of them expected what followed. They were inseparable. They met in between classes for coffee just to check-in and see each other, or to help each other prepare for exams. Their late-night phone calls, when their schedules kept them apart, lasted for hours as they recounted their day's events. Either over the phone or in-person, Malachi would sometimes read an excerpt from whatever he was writing and loved Taylor's thoughtful feedback. He tried to be as gentle when listening to Taylor ramble off his list of future campaign slogans. Wherever they were, laughter and smiles abounded, and it was contagious. People studied them, dissected them in the hope of tapping into that energy. When their leases were up at the end of the following summer, they found an apartment together on Gladstone Avenue in Centretown.

A loud crash made Malachi go rigid. He looked about the restaurant and saw a couple of waiters rushing to the aid of one of their colleagues. He dropped his gaze and sighed. He'd barely touched his food, the sight of which had him feeling nauseous.

"Was there something wrong with your food, sir?" the middle-aged woman asked, cautiously approaching the table.

"No, no." He dabbed the white serviette to his lips. "It's fine. I wasn't as hungry as I thought."

She picked up the plate. "Can I get you anything else?"

"Just the bill."

Malachi checked the time. It was almost eleven, and Shane, Cory and Eric had stood him up. *I guess we all got lucky.*

But in the end, maybe luck had nothing to do with it.

ELEVEN

THANKS FOR A WONDERFUL night! C.

Malachi scratched the back of his head as he again read the note on the tiny card sticking out of the full vase of red roses, the centrepiece on the dining room table. Then he winced. The internet made it too easy for fans and stalkers to track him down. And it didn't matter to the tech-savvy ones that his phone number was unlisted. They managed to find him anyway.

He picked up the crystal vase, inhaling the sweet fragrance, and moved it to the sideboard. Then he proceeded to set the table. He was expecting Shane at any moment for their annual tradition — a celebratory dinner to mark the survival of yet another year at the college. It was his turn to host and he'd spent the day preparing some of their favourite dishes. Sauerbraten. Potatoes Anna. Green beans with toasted almonds and asiago cheese. And for dessert, strawberry-rhubarb pie. He set the royal blue napkins next to each place setting and sighed.

He headed into the kitchen and took out the chilled bottle of Wolf Blass chardonnay. He poured himself a glass, feeling a sudden anxiousness that he hoped to wash down with the first gulp. He'd come to think of the end of the school year as a beginning, where he had the chance to restart his life once the summer break was over. But he couldn't … start again. Now more than ever Taylor's legacy poked at him.

Constantly. After Taylor's death, he'd been determined to never feel like that again or risk getting hurt. Yet Zach had left an imprint on his life that couldn't be exorcised. And after Zach died, Malachi walked the college corridors with his head down to dodge the disapproving looks being thrown at him. He still imagined the students, and staff, blamed him. Maybe they were right. He returned the wine bottle to the fridge. *You don't really begin again. Not if you can't pretend like nothing ever happened.*

And life happened, brandishing an overabundance of experiences that lifted Malachi high, held him there, and then sent him tumbling. Zach Brennan, Chad Whiting and Cole Malcolm were the most recent and colourful happenings in the city he'd fled to, and where he'd wanted to begin again. He lifted his wineglass to his mouth, and that first gulp went down the wrong pipe and he coughed several times. It reminded him of Patrick, who had somehow wrongly gotten into his life.

He was nineteen with a future of possibilities before him. He still hadn't decided on a major, swinging back and forth between English and political science. He was learning towards English, mostly because he had a bit of a crush on his British Literature professor. At his teacher's prompting, and hoping to impress, he registered for the Eighteenth-Century Fiction Symposium. An interschool event held at Carleton University, he wasn't about to miss the panel discussion on politics and literature hosted by his professor.

It was a Thursday afternoon, the last week of September, and Malachi lingered at the back of the auditorium. He wanted to speak to his professor and tell him how much he enjoyed the discussion — a moment to shake hands and stare into those probing camel-brown eyes. He went to move forward, not paying attention to where he was going, when he collided with the tall man coming towards him. He watched the books slip out of the guy's hands but couldn't immediately react. His gaze was locked on the almost predatory hazel eyes of the blond in front of him. After a few moments, Malachi bent over to pick up the books that were scattered on the floor.

"I think those are mine," the man said, taking back the books.

"Sorry," Malachi said, adjusting the straps of his backpack. "I was distracted."

"I noticed." He held out his hand. "Patrick."

"Malachi." The handshake was over, and Malachi kept glancing at the front of the room.

"He's straight, you know," Patrick said, shoving the books into his satchel. "You're not the first to crush on Professor Dunn."

"I don't..." Malachi swallowed hard and looked down. He'd been found out and felt like a fool.

"Patrick," a croaky voice called out. "You coming?"

Patrick tapped Malachi on the arm. "A few of us are heading to the Imperial Pub. Care to join us?"

Malachi lifted his head, one more time looking in Professor Dunn's direction, but this time he didn't feel that usual giddiness. He turned to Patrick and said, "Sure."

It was a short walk from the auditorium to the pub, which was located in the University Centre. The seven men and women squeezed into a booth, and before long pitchers of beers were on the table. Malachi, the youngest one there, didn't say much and hardly drank. He wasn't sure why he'd come and wasn't participating in the conversation, either. But he didn't leave. It made him feel like he had a circle of friends and people who cared about him, even though it wasn't true.

Around nine o'clock, people started to clear out. Malachi went to get up when he felt a hand on his arm.

"How about one more round?" Patrick asked.

Malachi didn't know what to think, and with everyone else gone, he wasn't sure he wanted to be alone with Patrick. What he really wanted was to avoid another night of awkward sex. The last few guys he'd been with didn't like to kiss, had no endurance, or were too drunk to get an erection. Real duds in the sack. And even though Patrick was the pretty-boy type he didn't necessarily go for, he heard himself say, "Sure," and that was it.

A few minutes later, Malachi watched as Patrick filled their empty beer steins. Still, he didn't say much and didn't have to. All he asked was, "What's your specialty?" and Patrick told his story.

Patrick was preparing to defend his thesis on the absence of a moral order in Defoe's *Moll Flaunders*. He didn't seem that enthusiastic about it, and made it sound like it was his own life that lacked order. He admitted that this wasn't where he'd thought he'd be. He'd wanted to be a writer instead of writing about other people's work.

"Have you had anything published?" Malachi asked. "I mean, like a short story or poem."

"I don't have time for that shit," Patrick said. "Someone else telling me if my writing is 'worthy' or not."

Malachi took a big gulp of his beer. "I sent out my short story fourteen times before it was finally accepted."

"Fourteen times?" Patrick's voice rippled with disbelief. "Doesn't that prove that it's a lot easier to criticize than create? Some smug literary wannabe, who probably hasn't written a word in his life, sitting behind a desk and deciding if your work is publishable. And all you get in return is an impersonal rejection letter."

"Isn't that how the process works?"

"The first letter," Patrick said, shifting to look squarely at Malachi, "you shrug off as part of the learning process and try again. The second rejection feels more personal, but by the eighth … you're asking yourself what's the fucking point?"

"What was it?"

Patrick polished off his beer. "A novel."

"None of us like rejection. But unless we try —"

"I'm done trying." Patrick refilled his glass. "I'm sorry."

"Let's talk about something else," Malachi said softly. "So, are you…"

"Oh, yes," Patrick said proudly. "Gay and single." Then he got more personal, talking about how he struggled at first with being gay. "I just wanted to live a normal life," he'd said, "whatever that meant. My father, although he never said it, was the type of man who'd have thrown me out of the house for being gay. I didn't want to disappoint him further." His father wanted him to become a lawyer, but instead he'd spent a year studying theology. He never imagined becoming a United Church minister, like his mother, but it was a temporary diversion. He wanted to dispel the 'perversion,' to fit in with the rest of society and go unnoticed. Yet it was a brief love affair with a fellow theology student that dramatically changed his life.

"How so?" Malachi asked.

"For the first time in my life..." Patrick, staring into his half-empty beer stein, raised his head. "I was happy."

Malachi checked the time. "It's getting late..."

"Sure." Patrick scanned the pub for their server and, when he caught her eye, signalled for the bill.

They headed northward along the campus, retracing their earlier path. Malachi listened as Patrick pointed at various buildings along the way and provided obscure historical facts about them. When they reached Colonel By Drive, they looked searchingly at each other, both of them aware that something was different between them. They shook hands and, under the quiet veil of night, Malachi found himself being pulled forward and into Patrick.

The kiss caught them off guard, but they readily accepted it each time their tongues met in between their short gasps for air. Malachi was surprised first by his full state of arousal, then by how the kiss ended abruptly, and again when he found himself crawling naked into Patrick's bed.

Six months later, they were still meeting up for sex. It didn't feel like they were dating, not to Malachi, anyway. They never met up for dinner or drinks. After that first night, they never talked intimately about themselves. They simply showed up at the agreed upon time, stripped naked and got down to business. And afterwards, no cuddling. No words. No looking at each other. But now something had changed.

Malachi had met Taylor. They'd talked for less than ten minutes at the party, yet Taylor made him feel alive in a way that Patrick never did. It was crazy, wasn't it? Not to Malachi. It was real. Now he had to make sure he was starting on a clean slate.

"Thanks for coming," Malachi said.

Patrick wrinkled his nose. "What happened to you last night? You left the party without saying a word."

"I was tired," Malachi said, dodging Patrick's eyes. "Do you want a coffee or something?" They were at the Starbucks in the Rideau Centre.

"No, I'm fine. I could have just gone to your apartment and…" Patrick winked.

"That's what I want to talk about," Malachi said, lowering his voice. "We should … I guess … we need to end things."

"Weren't you having fun?"

Malachi nodded. "I was, sort of. I mean, it's just sex and I … I think I want something more."

"You're twenty with your whole life ahead of you. What's the rush?" Patrick shifted in his chair. "Why not just enjoy it?"

"Because I'm ready for something deeper." Malachi sipped his Americano. "I'm ready to be with someone who knows me or wants to get to know me, who doesn't just think that I'm a good fuck."

"Wow!" Patrick slouched down in his seat. "All right. Let's get to know each other. Let's go on a date."

"Patrick, I…" Malachi's voice cracked. "I didn't mean with you. I've met someone and —"

"You've met someone?" Patrick's eyes went wide. "When did that happen?"

"It's not important."

"Fuck, you met him last night at the party. So, you spent one night with him and you think he's the love of your life?"

"I didn't have sex with him," Malachi said, curt. "I can't explain it. There's just a connection between us, and I need to see where it could lead."

"You don't think we have a connection?" Patrick asked.

"Not like that," Malachi said bluntly. *You wouldn't even read my short story after it was published. Taylor, a complete stranger, knew all about it.*

Patrick pushed back his chair and stood. "You're a real asshole, you know that?" He walked away.

Malachi kept his gaze fixed on Patrick as he moved off down the long corridor, eventually folding into the eager Saturday shoppers. Had he misjudged Patrick's feelings for him? No. There was nothing emotional between them. It had been all about sex, being satisfied, and mostly on Patrick's terms. And Malachi was tired of wasting his time. *I did the right thing. I didn't cheat. I told him. That counts for something, right?*

He rose from the table, his coffee cup in hand, and made his way back to his Stewart Street apartment. He couldn't get Taylor out of his thoughts and didn't know how he'd possibly make it through the rest of the day without losing his mind.

The phone rang, the double ring from the lobby, that jolted Malachi to attention. He answered it and buzzed in Shane. Waiting for the knock on the door, he downed his wine and poured himself another glass.

"Starting the party without me?" Shane asked when he entered the unit.

"Absolutely." Malachi gulped his drink.

They laughed.

Shane went into the dining room and grabbed a wineglass from the sideboard. When he joined Malachi in the kitchen a short time later, he smirked. "So, you and Cole managed to patch things up?"

"No," Malachi said tersely.

"But … the flowers … and the card…"

Malachi chuckled. "They're from Chad."

"Chad?" Shane took the wine bottle from the fridge and poured himself a generous glassful. "You're dating Chad?"

"No, I'm not dating Chad, either."

"Why would Chad send you a dozen roses?"

Malachi shot Shane a knowing look.

"Oh…" Shane accepted the plateful of food held out to him, then followed Malachi into the dining room.

They sat down and ate their first few bites in silence, a silence that, for whatever reason, was both necessary and awkward. Was it proof that Zach had somehow even affected their friendship?

Shane broke the silence with, "Do you want to talk about it?"

"Talk about what?" Malachi shoved a forkful of potatoes into his mouth.

"Zach, Taylor … anything, everything." Shane said, matter-of-fact. "I don't think you see how much Zach's death has affected you. It's churned up all your past pain. I mean … maybe you should see someone. Don't look at me like that. I mean a therapist. You keep pretending like it doesn't matter, like Zach didn't matter and that everything's all right. But it's not all right. You're not all right."

"I'm fine," Malachi spat, reaching for his wine. He sighed annoyance as Shane opined about the benefits of therapy. *What good would it do?* he wondered, staring blankly into his plate. He wasn't ready to move on, to concede defeat. He wanted to hang onto the image he and others had of himself — that he was strong, rational and emotionally stable. A rock. When 'bad' things in life happened, they ricocheted off him without leaving a trace. That was why, wherever he lived, his friends looked up to him. He knew, *knew*, that Zach's death stuck to him and shook him to his very core.

He sat there, with his head down, unable to drown out Shane's deep voice that was beginning to crescendo. He couldn't hold back the tears banking in his eyes. He didn't moan or groan or wail. He simply let the tears roll down his face, finally allowing himself to grieve for Zach, grieve for Taylor, grieve for the perfect life that he'd been robbed of.

***

It wasn't necessarily the right move, bringing his whole sense of judgment into question, but Cole didn't know what else to do. Ever since he'd seen Malachi at Urbane, he couldn't get him out of his head. Were they fated? No, and it would have been silly for him to think so. But he felt something between them, and it was very real to him. It was crazy and he knew it — to be so caught up in a guy who showed nothing but disdain for him. But Cole couldn't forget how they'd lain in bed together and how right it'd felt. He couldn't forget, as he talked about the practical jokes he and Paul played on each other, how Malachi's hand stroked his back. He couldn't forget the intensity of their stare before each kiss. Perhaps it was the move of a desperate man, but he didn't care. Cole touched the screen on the wall, scrolling through the electronic directory until he came to M. Bishop. He tapped the name and heard the dialling sound.

"Hello," was the brutish greeting through the intercom.

"I'm downstairs in the lobby," Cole said.

"Who is this?"

"Malachi, it's Cole."

There was a long silence. When Cole heard the click of the door unlocking, he reached for it, pulled it open and raced inside. *Stay calm*, he counselled himself as he rode the elevator to the twelfth floor. He knew exactly what he wanted to say. He'd rehearsed all day long and fine-tuned it during the drive to Claredon. He'd be bold, say what was in his heart and stop being Malachi's doormat.

The elevator doors slid open and he walked cautiously towards Malachi's unit at the end of the hall. He stood in front of the door, unable to raise his hand. He drew in a deep breath, then knocked twice. A moment later, the door opened wide and he involuntarily flinched when greeted by the familiar-looking, unsmiling brunette.

"You must be Cole." Shane extended his hand. "I'm Shane."

"We kind of met at Urbane last weekend," Cole said as they shook hands.

"Come in," Shane said, stepping to the side. "Malachi will be right out."

Cole entered the condo and stood in the middle of the foyer with his hands shoved in his pockets. His eyes roved, but he saw the way Shane looked at him … with misgiving. *How much does he know? I suppose Malachi told him everything.*

"How was traffic?" Shane asked as he slipped on his shoes.

"Oh, fine." Cole shrugged. "The 401's always busy it seems nowadays."

Malachi came into the foyer, and he and Shane hugged.

"Call me later," Shane said, pulling out of the embrace. At the door, he turned to Cole and said quietly, "Try to be patient with him." Then he was gone.

Cole and Malachi stood there looking at each other, neither of them sure what to do or say next. He cleared his throat. "Is this a bad time?"

"What do you want, Cole?" Malachi asked with no emotion in his voice.

"I'd like us to talk."

"The last thing you said to me was, 'Fuck you.'" Malachi folded his arms. "What could we possibly have to talk about?"

"That wasn't what I said to you," Cole corrected. "I told you to take your own damn advice."

"That sounds like 'Fuck you' to me."

"Well, maybe it wasn't my best moment, but that night you were impossible, a real ... prick!" Cole looked down, breathed deeply, then raised his head. "There are a couple of things I'd like to say, and I think you at least owe me —"

"I owe you?"

"Yes," Cole said. "You owe me the courtesy of hearing me out."

Malachi unfolded his arms and raised his hands in the air, like he was surrendering in defeat. "Fine." He gestured Cole into the living room.

Cole pulled his hands out of his pockets as he kicked off his shoes. He went into the living room and sat down on the sofa. Malachi remained standing just inside the doorway. Cole then clasped his hands together and stared at the dark hardwood floor. Now, face-to-face with Malachi, he didn't know where to begin. "I've been thinking a lot about truth," he said, lifting his head, "and about what you said."

"I said a lot of things."

"You told me that if I wasn't happy to do something about it," Cole said harshly, unable to squash the frustration surging in his voice. "So, I'm … I'm doing something about it."

"They don't give out the Victoria Cross for that." Malachi started to back out of the room.

"Where are you going?" Cole asked, almost shouting. There was no answer. He pursed his lips and bit down on them. *What's the point? Why do I keep doing this to myself? What's wrong with me?*

What was wrong with Cole? He was a man desperately looking for love and to be loved. He easily developed affections for others, eager to look after them, pamper them. He wanted that with Malachi. It was the vision of happiness that came to him, that he wanted to somehow manifest.

He was ready, ready to shake off the heaviness that swept over him every morning when he woke up. Ready to let go of the idea that there was something sinister about his world. The only thing sinister about his life was that he was alone, and that terrified him. His younger brother's tragic death possessed him, left a scar. Paul was his connection to a world that held him on the brink of madness, and now he had none. No one to ground him, steady him, in a way prepare his heart for harvest.

Try to be patient with him. It was hard advice to swallow when he felt that familiar loneliness swarm over his body and make him tremble. Malachi made him believe in a love that could endure. And if he could thoughtfully articulate his feelings, he was convinced that Malachi would also see just how good they could be together. He was tired of losing connections that were important to him. He'd lost his older brother Owen to a pious woman who disagreed with Cole being gay, a disagreement that forced a wedge between the brothers. He and his younger sister, Leslie, had a terrible row shortly after their mother's death. About what? He couldn't recall, but after nine years of not speaking they were completely divorced from each other. And despite everything, they were the only 'family' he had left. That was why Malachi was so important to him. Malachi was a connection that offered hope, peeled away the madness of his world. He was that missing link.

Malachi was back and came towards him. He accepted the drink offered to him and immediately took a sip.

"So, you're doing something about your unhappiness," Malachi said, lowering himself into the leather club chair opposite the sofa. "What's that got to do with me?"

"I came here tonight because…" Cole drew in a deep breath. "I … I like you."

"That's supposed to cure your unhappiness? Some silly declaration of —"

"It's not silly!" Cole interrupted.

"You don't even know me."

"But I want to. That's the fucking point." Cole made a grunting sound. "I want to get to know you better. I want you to talk to me again the way you did that night we were together. I got a glimpse inside of you, and what I saw —"

"Sometimes what you see is false, a half-truth." Malachi sipped his scotch. "It's like looking in a cracked mirror. All you see are fragments, disconnected fragments that don't necessarily form something whole. We think they do, but it's an illusion."

"That's a bit extreme."

"Maybe. Maybe I'm not like you. Maybe I don't believe in love." Malachi yawned. "Do you want another drink?"

"Please."

Malachi left the room, returning moments later with the bottle of Lagavulin. He poured generous amounts of the golden liquid into their glasses before sitting down again.

"You really don't believe in love?" Cole asked cautiously.

"I don't know anymore." Malachi tipped his glass forward and, before taking a sip, added, "I know it never ends well, it never lasts."

"I think you're wrong. It can last. But I don't think you're open to it." Cole downed his drink in two large gulps, then let out a loud belch. "Sorry … I should go." He stood, took a step towards the foyer and then turned around. "I didn't mean to intrude tonight. I just wanted … I thought that by coming here that we'd possibly admit that we have a connection. That didn't happen, so now I'm hoping for some type of closure."

"Closure." Malachi weighed that up, trying not to laugh, and stood. "And do you have it now? Closure, that is."

"Yes," was Cole's snappish response. He abruptly turned away, strode into the foyer and stabbed his feet into his shoes.

"Cole…" Malachi came into the foyer.

"I get it." Cole's tone was harsh. "You're not interested in me. I foolishly made what happened between us into something bigger than it was. That's my fault. So, I'll leave and get out of your life for good." He gripped the doorknob, started to turn it, then stopped and spun around. "You don't believe in love or that it can last. Then what's the point of living? It's like you let yourself be mummified alive, wrapped up in some goddamn cloth that you think can protect you from every hurt. And you likely won't get hurt when you run away from every chance of a relationship. Then you're going to wake up in twenty years, look at the old man staring back at you in the mirror and say, 'Good job, Malachi … that's twenty years without a single day of pain.'"

"Or I'm that guy looking back twenty years from now and wondering if I'd missed out on the best thing to come into my life," Malachi whispered and ran his hand over his face. "You're right," he said urgently when Cole went to open the door. "I'm a prick. I've been mean and disrespectful to you." He began to choke on his words. "And I'm sorry. It's just…" He folded his arms around his chest like he was trying to hug himself. "You have every right to walk out that door, but I hope you'd be better than me and let me explain —"

"Explain what?"

"Why I never showed up for dinner."

Cole's grip tightened on the doorknob. "I don't think it makes much of a difference now."

"Maybe not, but you said you wanted closure. Maybe I need it, too."

Cole let go of the doorknob. "So, what happened?"

"That day…" Malachi's arms fell to his sides. "I lost a student. I mean … he killed himself."

Cole heard the way Malachi's voice cracked and, in that moment, he knew he was lost. He'd have to touch him, hold him, console him. A force immediately took him over, gave him the courage to act in a way he'd always wanted to. Boldly. He went over to Malachi and held him. Holding Malachi, feeling the warmth of his body, he was more certain than ever of his feelings. No matter how silly it sounded or how foolish of him to even imagine, he loved him. But how could he prove it? How could he make Malachi believe him?

They pushed apart. Malachi wiped the tears off his face while Cole took off his shoes. He wasn't going anywhere. They returned to the living room, this time both of them sitting down on the sofa. Cole took the bottle of scotch and refilled their glasses. He made himself comfortable and listened attentively as Malachi began explaining the history of Zach. Occasionally, Cole reached for Malachi's hand and held it, a gesture of reassurance as much as understanding. He knew by the way Malachi's eyes fluttered that the grief was real and present, that he'd yet to expunge Zach from his heart and mind. Zach had succeeded where he hoped to — penetrate Malachi's heart and open the door to love. Could he?

The confession proved that Malachi did in fact believe in love, and now so did Cole. He sensed that Malachi had, by confiding in him, released another burden. That was significant. On that first night they'd met, Malachi had told him of the love of his life, Taylor. Now he heard of the other great love, Zach. There it was. Proof that they'd forged a bond and were perhaps willing to glue together the disconnected fragments of that cracked mirror. First Taylor and then Zach, and Cole couldn't help but wince every time Malachi's eyes glistened when he said their names. *God, I'd love it if he felt that way about me.* He wanted to feel that pure love, the kind of love he craved and had been searching out his whole adult life. He'd never experienced that type of love, but thought it was possible with Malachi — a love not created *ex nihilo* but borne out of a desire exalted in that first moment they'd lain down together. In that holy clinch, Cole had felt such inviolable trust, hoping that the pure light of love would finally displace the dreary, petulant world of one-night stands.

Cole reached for Malachi's forearm, tugging at it tenderly until he had once again secured Malachi's hand in his. "I wish you'd have told me this sooner," he said gently. "About Zach, that is. I would've understood." He pushed himself off the sofa and had a difficult time keeping his balance. "Gotta take a leak."

"End of the hall, last door on the left ... in case you've forgotten."

Cole heard Malachi giggle as he staggered down the hall. The bottle of scotch, which was two-thirds full when he'd first arrived, was almost empty. He had to place one hand to the bathroom wall to keep his balance as he relieved himself. It seemed to take forever, his head beginning to spin and the scotch backing up in his mouth. He fumbled to flush the toilet, then washed his hands quickly and returned to the living room. He stood in the entryway and glanced at his watch before shoving his hands in his pockets. It was almost midnight. "I really should get going."

"You're in no condition to drive," Malachi said as he stood.

Cole took his left hand out of his pocket and ran it through his dark full mane. "I can't stay here." He dropped his gaze, trying to swallow the metallic taste in his mouth. "I want to hold you. I want to feel your body next to mine. It's all I've thought about since that first night … to the point of demons engulfing me." He looked up and, with Malachi now standing less than a foot away from him, his heart raced. He couldn't take Malachi's penetrating glare and lowered his head. A long silence settled in, then Cole felt the weight of arms around his neck and the hot breath in his ear.

"Then hold me…"

***

It was morning. Malachi, seated at his oak desk in his office, was writing in one of his black hardcover notebooks. In the middle of a sentence, his hand froze and he stared abstractly at the lined pages of his notebook. *What have I done?* He knew exactly what he had done. One small act — wrapping his arms around Cole's neck — had changed the *mise en scène* in ways he had not anticipated. He still didn't know what had compelled him to throw his arms around Cole's neck in the first place. He had been in withdrawal ever since Zach's death, a sort of emotional sobriety. All he had to do was avoid Cole and then avoid falling for him. Mission failed.

In lying down again with Cole and then waking up next to him, Malachi could almost feel his past's stranglehold loosening. Maybe his heart could be mended. On his face came the beginnings of a smile and, almost too easily, he put a name to the giddy feeling quietly awakening within him: happiness.

It was here in the present and not some unknown entity belonging to that unforeseeable future to which Zach alluded. Nor was it the 'hell' Zach spoke of and from which he had escaped. And while Malachi still tried to make sense of everything that had happened, he knew the future was still speculative, but not daunting or dire.

He closed his notebook and placed it in the top drawer of his desk. He made his way down the corridor and into the kitchen. He saw Cole standing outside on the balcony wearing only his jeans and drinking a cup of coffee. The bright sun bounced off his olive skin and lit up the blue sky. He stared at Cole's broad bare shoulders and back, and smiled. He moved gingerly about the kitchen, trying not to be detected, quietly opening the cupboard doors. He glanced at Cole, who still had his back to him, and felt relief. He went to the fridge, and pulled out the egg carton and open package of bacon.

Malachi waved when Cole spun around, smiled and mouthed, "Good morning." There was something in the look that he recognized. *Oh, God!* He could feel himself trembling. He'd let himself be hooked. But he wasn't really sure as to who had done the hooking. When he wrapped his arms around Cole's neck, he'd felt it. It was real despite what he wanted to believe. He'd felt the joyful pang of love. *Did he feel it, too?* The sex that followed was tame yet vocal, passionate yet tempered. And that moment when Cole reached up and held his face, he could see how much Cole wanted to say, "I love you," and mean it. He'd closed his eyes to shut him down but it was too late. There it was between them. The scent of endurance of *real* love.

Cole pushed open the balcony door and stepped into the kitchen. They smiled sheepishly at each other. He set his coffee mug down on the counter and hugged Malachi from behind, pressing his lips to Malachi's neck and holding them there. He stepped away as Malachi started to vigorously beat the eggs with the large stainless steel whisk.

"I hope you're hungry," Malachi said as he crowded the bacon strips into the frying pan.

"Famished," Cole said, picking up his coffee mug.

Malachi adjusted the gas flame under the pan, then stole a sidelong glace at Cole. Was he really ready for this?

Absolutely … not.

When Love Falls

(Three and a half years later)

TWELVE

"ARE YOU COMING TO bed?" Cole asked from the door-way to Malachi's office.

"Not yet," Malachi said without looking up, his fingers dancing across his laptop's keyboard. "I want to finish this tonight."

"How long?"

"I don't know."

"Malachi…"

"I need to finish this tonight, Cole." Malachi, levelling his gaze at Cole, spoke harshly. "It'll take as long as it takes."

"Right…" Cole drawled and watched, pained, as Malachi resumed typing. He stood there a moment longer, wondering what had happened to the man he'd fallen in love with. Did he still exist?

Cole spun around and made his way upstairs to the bed-room. He moved around in the darkness, a way of keeping the present at bay. Mostly he didn't want to see his reflection in the mirror, didn't want to see the man he'd become. He un-dressed down to his underwear, leaving his clothes bunched in a ball on the floor of the walk-in closet. Then he went into the en suite bathroom, turned on the light and staggered. *Christ! Who the hell are you?* he wondered of the guy staring back at him in the mirror. He noticed that there was a hint of grey in his short brown hair, and the lines around his eyes were deeper. He brushed his teeth quickly and turned out the light.

He climbed into the king-size bed and drew the covers up to his waist. He lay there, still, with his hands cupped to the back of his head and stared into the blackness. He didn't know what was happening. Worst of all, he didn't know why it was happening. He and Malachi had started out happy after an unconventional debut to their romance. Now, three and a half years later, everything had changed. The proof was in the way Malachi looked at him, like he didn't exist. Silence reigned where laughter once had dominion. At the dinner table, when they ate together, conversation was limited to, "Pass the salt." And lately, most nights Malachi took refuge in his office where he wrote or read while Cole stole away in the den watching his collection of Charlie Chaplin films. *Am I losing him?* Panic burned in his chest. *Maybe I've already lost him.*

He rolled onto his side and his gaze found the red digits of the clock on the nightstand. It was almost midnight. It was the fifth night in a row that they'd gone to bed separately, Malachi staying up late to write. It seemed to be part of the new reality that was easier for them to acquiesce to than challenge. It was also why Cole couldn't shake the feeling that there was something terribly wrong about the world that would destroy him and the life he'd come to depend on.

Cole had always led a simple life, even after meeting Malachi. How long had he searched for something compulsory in his life to claim him? Too long. But when he and Malachi finally gave in to each other, that something compulsory did claim him. It was love, which became his anchor and gave a 'why' to his life.

Now, the thought of losing Malachi made Cole squeamish. If they were 'losing each other,' he knew why. He felt like they hardly saw each other anymore. He tried not to work long hours and to be home on weekends. Malachi, on the days he taught, spent at least three hours commuting between their Kendal Avenue home and Claredon College. Too much. He worried about Malachi travelling the 401, especially in winter. But more importantly, he wanted them to spend more time together, continue to harvest their love. That was why he'd asked Malachi to consider finding a teaching position closer to home. That 'request' created a wedge. Was it also the moment they began to fall apart?

At the sound of the heavy footsteps on the staircase, Cole closed his eyes. Then he listened to Malachi, who moved quietly about the room, and felt that ache from years ago when they'd first met. Back then, everything seemed simpler. Could it be that way again?

After what seemed like an eternity, Cole felt the mattress compress as Malachi slipped into the bed. He waited a moment, then rolled over onto his other side and slid his body up against Malachi's. He didn't want to seem pushy, and held off another few minutes before manoeuvring his head onto Malachi's stomach. He lay there motionless, for the first time in days feeling like their connection was still alive. *Does he know how much I want him?* When there was no resistance, no act of deterrence, he glided his hand inside Malachi's underwear.

"Not tonight," Malachi grunted, shoving Cole's hand away.

"Fuck!" Cole rolled onto his back and briefly hid his face in his hands. "It's been 'not tonight' for the past three weeks. What's going on?"

"I'm tired."

Cole turned on the lamp on the nightstand and sat up in bed. He looked down at Malachi, who lay there with his eyes closed. "You've been tired a lot lately."

"Yes, I have." Malachi's voice brimmed with anger. "It's late. Turn off the light and let's get some sleep."

"Maybe if you weren't commuting…" Cole's voice trailed off when Malachi pushed back the duvet and got out of the bed. "Where are you going?"

"To the guest room," Malachi spat, walking heavy-footed towards the door. "I can't take this tonight. I'm too tired."

"You've been 'too tired' all week," Cole shot back just before the door banged closed. Then the sound of the guest bedroom door thundering shut made him stiffen. Defeat pinned him down the way he remembered André the Giant holding his opponent down for the count. He had until the count of three to throw off his aggressor, stand up to him and make him see his worth. If not, it was game over.

Cole bounced out of bed, stomping out of the room and down the hall to the guest room. He threw open the door, which crashed into the wall, and switched on the ceiling light. "We're going to talk," he said firmly, for the first time in years like a determined man.

"For the love of God —"

"Enough!" Cole shouted. He sat down on the edge of the bed and made a play for Malachi's hand. He seized it on the third attempt and held it tight. "You may not want to talk, but for once we're going to do what I want."

"Cole —"

"Stop!" Cole couldn't tamp down the rage rumbling in his voice. "Something's going on. You're distant, uninterested in me, in us." He blinked rapidly to prevent the tears pooling in his eyes from flowing. It didn't work. "I need to know what's going on. I need to know what's wrong."

There was a long silence.

Malachi jerked his hand free and sat up in the bed. His eyes, locked on Cole, were on fire. "Do you really want to know what's wrong?"

"Yes," Cole said with an air of desperation.

Malachi gave a languid shrug. "We are."

***

Malachi entered the kitchen the next morning shortly after nine. He refilled his coffee and took a few sips, hoping that the caffeine would begin to take effect. He hadn't slept well. Every time he tried all he could see was the colossal hurt in Cole's eyes from his stunning admission. *We are.* The savageness in his voice had, in the moment, surprised him. He'd hoped to remain calm and rational, but he'd been holding everything in for months. No wonder he'd finally snapped. The worst part of all was that he didn't feel remorse or regret. *Maybe I'm a monster,* he thought, turning to leave the kitchen. He froze. Cole, seated at the island bar-counter, had his eyes glued to him. Malachi dropped his head and started moving again.

"Malachi…"

Malachi spun around at the doorway and stared into his coffee, unable to look directly at Cole. "About last night —"

"Did you mean it?" Cole asked, his voice hoarse. "Do you think we're wrong together?"

"Maybe. I don't know. I just…"

Cole pulled down the zipper of his blue cycling jersey, exposing his chest. "I remember when we couldn't get enough of each other."

Malachi's heart sank as he thought, with both nostalgia and sadness, about how he used to meet Cole at the door when he arrived home. They'd kiss, their duelling tongues the tinder for their passion that had them peeling off each other's clothes. When they crawled into bed, they searched for each other, sparking another round of ravenous lovemaking. On rainy weekends, they snuggled together on the sofa, watching action films or romantic comedies. Sometimes they drove down to Niagara-on-the-lake for wine tasting tours. They did things together. Now all of that was over. They barely spoke or touched each other. And when it came to physical intimacy, Cole tried but Malachi kept pushing him away. Why? What had changed?

"I don't know what happened to us. I don't want to think…" Cole sat up straight on the backless stool and ran his hand through his sweaty hair. "Is there someone else?"

Malachi levelled his gaze at Cole. "What?"

Cole's eyes were moist. "Would you tell me if you've met someone else?"

"No, I haven't met someone else," Malachi said, his voice dropping to a whisper. He stepped forward and set his mug down on the counter. "I've never … I'm not cheating on you."

"Something's wrong, Malachi. I mean, look at us. It's not like it was before, in the beginning. Last night made me feel like I repulse you. That hurt. It hurts."

"Cole, I —"

Cole raised a hand. "I love you, but I don't know what I'm supposed to do. Is there something you want me to change? Tell me and I'll do it. I do know that I don't want to lose you, I don't want to lose us."

Malachi shrugged. "I don't know what it is you want me to say."

"I'd like us to spend more time together."

"Fuck, Cole, not that again." Malachi ran his hand over his face. "I'm not leaving the college. I love my work and I love my students."

"You seem to love everything and everyone but me."

"That's not fair."

"You could stay home and write full-time," Cole said. "Isn't that your dream?"

"Stay home so I can have your dinner on the table, do the laundry and clean the house?" Malachi sucked his teeth. "I'm not Edith Bunker."

"Christ, if Taylor had lived long enough to ask you to marry him," Cole said, his voice rising with each word, "you'd have done it for him. You'd have fuckin' become Mary Poppins."

"Things were different then."

"I'm sure they were." Cole cupped his hands to the top of his head, then dragged them down his face and let them fall to his sides. "I'm sorry, but I … I don't understand why you aren't happy to do the same for me."

"Back then I hadn't spent ten goddamn years earning tenure. Now I'm supposed to give that up and my pension?"

"Malachi, I just want —"

"You want me to give up everything I've worked so hard for," Malachi said bitterly. "Why is it that I'm the one who's supposed to make the big changes? You're on the road a lot, too. Travelling comes with what we do."

"I'm gone once a month for three or four days."

"Sometimes you're gone longer than that."

"There's got to be a solution. I'm concerned about you spending all that time on the highway, especially in winter. I worry about you being in an accident."

"There *is* a solution. We can move to Claredon."

"Don't be ridiculous."

"What?" Malachi flicked his eyebrows. "That's not an option?"

"Not a realistic one, no."

"Why not?"

"I pay the mortgage, I earn —"

"You earn more money than me?" Malachi interrupted, his eyes widening. "You think you're the breadwinner, so what you say goes, right? So, I need to make the sacrifice because I live in *your* house? Fuck that!" He shook his head. "Do I not contribute enough? Do you want me to give you more money each month? I can give you more." He was shouting again. "I can pay the fucking mortgage if you want."

"That's not what I meant," Cole said ruefully.

They looked at each other, immured in a long, stony silence.

"Maybe we should take a break," Malachi said and picked up his mug. "Maybe we need some time on our own."

"I don't want to 'take a break,'" Cole said. "I want us to talk. I want us to figure this out."

"You seem to already have it figured out."

"That's not fair."

"I have work to do." Malachi left the kitchen.

"You always have work to do," Cole shouted into the air.

Malachi didn't want to take the bait, but that comment cut through him. He returned to the kitchen and stared down the man he now saw as a stranger. "What's that supposed to mean?"

"Have you even noticed what's happened to us?" Cole, speaking harshly, stood. "We don't eat dinner together anymore. We may sit at the same table, but that's all. And sex ... I can't even remember the last time we had sex. It's like we're two roommates who can't stand each other and who do everything to avoid each other. I try ... I try to get close to you but you keep pushing me away." He spoke with emphasis. "You're always too busy with your writing and teaching and ... it's like you try to squeeze me in in between classes if it's convenient. Do you know what it's been like for me whenever we go out to dinner or a movie, or to the god-damn grocery store? There's always someone clamouring for your autograph. It's been a gong show ever since Zach's book came out and that bloody dedication. Don't get me wrong..." He drew in a deep breath. "You worked hard to make sure the royalties from Zach's book went to mental health charities.

That's admirable. And I'm truly happy for your success, but I feel like I'm second-rate. I've attended faithfully to your needs, your career, while sacrificing my will to yours."

"How? How the hell have you 'attended faithfully' to my needs?"

"I've never missed a book launch," Cole said. "Every time you had a function to attend, I was there. Even if it meant rescheduling a client meeting, missing out on my own career development opportunities, or skipping a cycling race."

"I never asked you to do that," Malachi countered.

"You don't have to ask. It's what you do when you love someone. You support and encourage them."

"I get it." Malachi snapped his fingers. "You want me to get a job closer to home as payback. You think I owe you."

"You owe *us*," was Cole's unexpected and brutal response. He rolled his pursed lips, then let out a nervous laugh. "You're right. I do think you owe me because I've become your silly plastic shadow. That should be worth something."

"I ... owe..." Malachi placed his coffee mug on the counter. "You think I'd have done all that for Taylor. And you know what? Maybe I would have. But one thing's for sure ... Taylor would never have asked me to, he'd have never demanded that I do this or do that. And he sure as hell wouldn't tell me I owe him."

"Well, I'm not bloody Taylor!"

"Don't I know it!" Malachi said, unable to censor himself. He felt his rage smouldering underneath the surface. He wasn't the one who'd chased this relationship or who'd refused to take No for an answer. Yet now, somehow, he was the one being told he fucking 'owes' the relationship. *Walk away. Just walk away.*

Malachi made his way into the front hall, grabbed his keys and wallet off the occasional table, and then stabbed his feet into his shoes. He rushed out of the house, slamming the door closed so hard the window pane cracked.

***

"Nothing's changed," Cole mumbled, staring at the bed he and Malachi shared.

Two days after their big blowout, they carried on just like before. That despite the promises made when they finally spoke to each other again.

"Look, Cole," Malachi had said when he returned home after storming out of the house. "I'm trying to get my next book out. College finals are less than a month away and I'm … just a bit stressed. But I don't need to work in Toronto to fit in more time for us."

"I don't want you to fit me in," Cole said askance.

Malachi drew in a deep breath. "That's not what I meant. Just be patient. I'll try to make more time for us, okay?"

"Sure," Cole said somewhat dismissively. "And I'll stop acting like a New Jersey housewife."

"That'd be fantastic," Malachi said.

They laughed like they hadn't done in months, and that made Cole feel hopeful that maybe their love would blossom. Afterwards, they fell into a loose embrace, but it didn't lead to anything. Not a kiss. Not makeup sex. Nothing. Once they'd pushed apart they were back in their own corners — living in the same house yet separated from each other. Cole had wanted to say something, but he was too afraid of another argument and being reminded how the glorious Taylor was so much better than him.

"Not a goddamn, fuckin' thing has changed." Cole picked up his heavy grey suitcase and made his way downstairs. In the foyer, he dropped his suitcase to the floor and checked the time. Nine minutes to noon. *Where is he?* he wondered, panic beginning to rise. Four weeks ago, he'd signed up for a customer relationship management conference in Banff. His flight to Calgary left in three hours, and Malachi had promised to drive him to the airport. But now he didn't want to go, not with everything that was happening between him and Malachi. *Maybe he's right and a break will do us good.* He decided to call a cab. As he pulled out his cell phone from his back jeans pocket, the front door swung open.

"Oh, fuck!" Malachi shook his head. "Your flight. I forgot."

"I'll take a cab," Cole said, trying to hold Malachi's gaze.

"No." Malachi, who hadn't fully closed the door, opened it wide. "I said I'd drive you. Let's go."

They left the house, silence their only friend.

"I'll be back Thursday," Cole said, frequently glancing at his watch. Vehicles weren't moving on the QEW and that had him worried. He didn't want to miss his flight. Or did he?

"Remember that's my late day at the college."

"I know," Cole said with disappointment, studying Malachi. "This reminds me of when we first started dating." He let out a nervous laugh when Malachi turned his head slightly to look out the driver's side window. *God, he knows exactly how to cut through me.* He held his gaze to his lap, a thin smile on his lips, as he thought about the early days of their relationship. His secretary kept his schedule clear after three o'clock on Friday afternoons so he could head to Claredon and hopefully beat the traffic. In the beginning, he did all the travelling and would have done anything to shore up their connection. He knew that long-distance relationships had their challenges, but it wasn't as if the Atlantic Ocean separated them. On a good day, they were only a ninety-minute drive away from each other. Yet sometimes it was a look, or how Malachi would refer to their relationship as 'weekend love,' that had Cole wondering if they'd survive.

It wasn't until the seventh month of their courtship, when Malachi started coming to Toronto, that Cole felt they stood a real chance. It proved to him that the loving wasn't one-sided, that someone — Malachi — actually loved him. That had him living on a high. And he loved those weekends with Malachi in Toronto, guiding him around like a foreigner in the city for the first time. They visited the CN Tower and had dinner at 360, taking in the magnificent view as they revolved around the city skyline. He showed him the shops along the harbourfront, inspecting some of the artist studios. They attended theatrical performances at the Royal Alexandra and Princess of Wales theatres. He threw lavish dinner parties to introduce Malachi to his friends, show him off like a long sought-after trophy. Their weekends in Claredon were quiet, and he loved them all the more for it. They woke up early Saturday mornings, when Cole could have slept in until ten, and went to the Claredon Market. They bought fresh fruits and vegetables, and exotic meats like elk and venison, for the dinners they cooked together. In the afternoons, they went for long walks along the Kawartha trails and talked about their future plans as if they knew the other would be somehow implicated. At night, they surrendered themselves to each other, and in those crushing embraces everything about them — and the world — felt magical and right.

The car lurched forward and Cole along with it. They were moving again. He stole a sidelong glance of Malachi and resisted the urge to touch him. He wanted to believe that there was still something good in their love that could sustain them, see them through. Yet it felt too eerily familiar, the way Malachi so easily cut him off. One thing he knew was that he wouldn't fight for them if Malachi wasn't just as committed to the cause. *You can't force someone to love you.* Cole turned away and stared out the window, watching the city roll by. Overwhelmed with a sense of loss, he wondered if he could ever find himself in this city again? Could he still call this home?

The car came to a stop in front of Terminal One at Toronto Pearson International Airport, on the departures level. They both got out of the car and, once Cole had retrieved his suitcase from the trunk, stared searchingly at each other.

"I'll call you later tonight," Cole said, setting his suitcase down on the edge of the curb, "to let you know I made it safely."

"Sure," Malachi said, looking past Cole.

Cole cupped his hands to Malachi's face and leaned forward until their foreheads touched. He stared intently into Malachi's eyes that held him in a trance. "I love you," he said with emphasis. "Please believe that. And I believe we can get through this. I want to get through this." He kissed Malachi on the lips, but he was doing all the work. He pulled back, reached for Malachi's hands and applied pressure. He hoped the message was understood and let go.

"Safe travels," Malachi said.

"That's it? All you can say is 'safe travels?'" Cole bit down on his lip. "I'm pretty sure I deserve more than that." He waited for Malachi to say something — the 'I love you' that would make them okay — but, one more time, silence reigned. "Maybe you're right," he said, his voice elevated, "that we need a break. Perhaps a permanent one because I'm not going through that shit again. I won't let you put me through the wringer the way you did when we first met. Christ, I may love you, but goddammit Malachi … I deserve fucking better than this."

Cole grabbed the handle of his suitcase and started for the terminal. He'd always imagined himself as being the one to fight, fight for them. But somehow everything they had had gone to seed. And if Malachi wasn't interested in salvaging them, neither was he. He was done.

THIRTEEN

"I DON'T KNOW HOW you do it," Shane said when Malachi stepped out onto the veranda.

"Do what?" Malachi asked, handing him a Corona.

"Live in this city." Shane tapped his beer bottle against Malachi's wineglass and took a gulp. "It's so busy and the traffic…" He'd left Claredon at three, and it still took him almost three hours to get to Malachi's home in the Annex. "I think I'd shoot myself if I had to drive in that every day."

They laughed.

"You get used to it." Malachi, dodging Shane's eyes, sat down in the empty Muskoka chair.

"Sure." Shane shook his head. "Where's Cole, anyway?"

"In Banff at some conference."

Shane heard the hint of annoyance in his best friend's voice and sat up straight. "Is everything okay?"

"Not really." Malachi lifted his wineglass to his mouth and took a couple of sips. He locked his gaze on Shane. "Cole thinks we don't spend enough time together. So, he wants me to leave the college and get a job in Toronto."

"Is that true?" Shane asked, matter-of-fact.

Malachi shrugged. "Maybe."

Shane recognized the change in tone, from dismissive to petulant. His friend was in transition. "What's really going on, Malachi?"

Malachi shot out of the chair and stood by the veranda railing. "It doesn't feel right anymore. It feels like we're moving in different directions."

"You're about to go on sabbatical for a year," Shane said. "Maybe this is the perfect time for the two of you to get to know each other again."

"Or maybe it's the perfect time for us to separate."

Shane's body went rigid. "Are you serious?" *He's never had to look for love. Love always finds him. I don't think he really understands what it means to be alone.* "Don't you want to try and work it out?"

"You don't understand." Malachi drained his drink.

"Because I haven't been in a long-term relationship lately?"

"Have you ever been in a long-term relationship?"

"That's just mean." Shane took a large swig of his beer. *Dammit, he's right. No one's ever wanted me like that.*

"I'm sorry." Malachi took up his earlier position in the Muskoka chair. "I just don't know what to do, what I really want."

"Has he done something to change the way you feel?" When there was no response, Shane drove his foot into Malachi's. "Has Cole cheated on you?"

"No. Or at least I don't think so. I don't think he would."

"Then love him, Malachi. Love him like your life depends on it." Shane spoke with the conviction of an evangelical preacher trying to convert the unsaved. "You're right. I haven't had a long-term relationship. Maybe one day it'll happen for me. And when it does, I'd love to have what you and Cole have. He'd do anything for you. I mean, my

God ... have you forgotten what he did when you first started dating? He drove to Claredon *every* weekend to see you for the first six months. And everyone sees the way he looks at you ... with desire. His face just lights up every time you come into a room. We're all envious."

"Things change."

"Do they? Or is it just your perception that's changed."

"I don't know."

"Stop comparing your relationship with Cole to the past."

"That's not what I'm doing!" Malachi barked.

"It's exactly what you're doing." Shane's tone sharpened. "In your mind, no one will ever be better than Taylor. You're hanging on so tightly to your first love that it's blinding you."

"Can we talk about something else?" Malachi sat back in his chair.

"Sure," Shane said. "Where are we going tonight?"

"I invited you over for dinner," Malachi said askance. "I'm not going out dancing so you can score. Besides, do you remember what happened the last time we went out together?"

"That was before you and Cole got serious," Shane said. "And you said you cut off contact with Chad."

"I did."

"So, there's no reason we can't go out for a drink, right?" Shane polished off his beer, then let out a loud belch.

"Classy," Malachi said, reaching for his wine.

"Bite me." Shane slid to the edge of his chair. "Maybe getting out of the house will help. I'm suggesting going for a drink or two, not a night on the town. Besides, you're in a relationship and hooking up with —"

"Actually, I'm not," Malachi cut in.

Shane raised an eyebrow. "You're not ... what?"

"In a relationship. At least I don't think I am." Malachi gave a nervous laugh. "I proposed that Cole and I take a break, and that pissed him off. He thinks we should make it permanent."

"What are you leaving out?"

"At the airport..." Malachi's knee bounced up and down. "He told me he loved me, and I couldn't say it back."

"Jesus, Malachi."

"I told you things have changed."

"One thing hasn't changed," Shane said as he stood, "and that's how much of an asshole you can be sometimes. Oh, don't look at me like that. You know it's true." He placed his hand on Malachi's shoulder and offered an encouraging smile. "Come on. We're definitely not staying here."

Malachi, slow to rise, followed Shane back inside. "I'm going to regret this," he said, closing the veranda doors.

"Really?" Shane's voice was filled with indignation. "You're worried about regretting going out for a drink? Don't you think you might 'regret' losing Cole and what that would mean?" He watched Malachi, who wouldn't look at him, move into the foyer. Shaking his head, he joined Malachi at the door.

"Where do you want to go?" Malachi asked, opening the front door.

"You're hopeless," Shane grunted, passing over the threshold. "Absolutely hopeless."

***

Malachi roamed the house, trying to let it possess him, feel himself in each room. But he felt nothing. *Nothing*. That didn't surprise him. It wasn't his house. It was Cole's. It had always been Cole's. From the beginning. And he'd never tried to feel at home. The proof was in his decision to put most of his belongings into storage after he'd agreed to move in with Cole. Malachi brought his piano and the furniture from his office to set up his new workspace, but nothing more than that. Cole, who didn't share his taste in abstract art, had encouraged him to bring a few paintings from his collection into the home. There, too, Malachi resisted even though he thought the rooms — painted beige, brown or blue — were bland, and had no character or warmth. Yet he refused to bring in anything that represented him. Was it any wonder this house had never become his home?

Did any of that matter? Home was supposed to be with Cole, the affirmation of their love and commitment to each other. Yet it felt stilted, stale. He couldn't pinpoint exactly why. He'd tried, one more time, to explain it to Shane when they were out last night at Urbane, but he couldn't. It was a gut feeling, something that had him doubting Cole, doubting them. Why? He went into his office and sat down at his desk. He pulled open the bottom drawer and took out the small photo album he kept there. He set it on his desk and flipped through it.

He studied the picture of the smiling brunette with his arm wrapped around him and knew Shane was right. He still couldn't stop comparing everything to the past even though it was unfair. He just couldn't help himself. He abruptly closed the album and spun around in his chair, staring blankly out the window. The morning fog that had settled over the city, obscuring his distant view of the CN Tower, was beginning to lift. It made him feel cut off from the world, like everything was blurry and spinning out of control. It resuscitated that feeling, from so long ago, when his life came unhinged.

He'd felt that feeling before, too. It was ten years ago, almost to the day. He stood in the foyer of the house on Regent Street, the silence bearing down on him again. He felt his heart tightening, his breathing rapid and shallow. He ran into the living room and thrust himself onto the sofa. He curled up in the foetal position and stayed like that until he'd calmed down. But it never lasted. The calm … it was so easily shattered.

Beads of sweat formed on Malachi's brow as his eyes, moving across the room, landed on each of the unopened boxes. He couldn't bring himself to do it — open them and the world of hurt awaiting to be unleashed. Over the course of the three weeks he'd been in the house, he'd tried to unseal the cartons covered with Taylor's spidery handwriting. But every time he went to unpeel the tape, he stopped. He couldn't, just couldn't, bear any reminder of the man he'd loved and who'd been viciously taken from him.

Malachi launched himself off the sofa and, undoing his tie, careened his way upstairs to the bedroom. He went into the walk-in closet, turned on the light, and froze. Seeing Taylor's suits hanging there made him choke every time. His friends had encouraged him to give Taylor's clothes away before the move, but he couldn't. He had to hang onto everything that belonged to Taylor. The clothes, still impregnated with Taylor's scent, made Malachi's heart race. He fingered the sleeves of the suit jackets and, for some reason, slid his hand into the pocket of the black pinstriped suit. That was Taylor's favourite, and the one he'd planned to wear to a literacy fundraiser scheduled to take place the day after he was killed. Malachi stiffened at the touch of something smooth. He pulled out a folded piece of paper and felt himself smirking. Taylor always kept his daily to-do list folded and in a pocket. After tentatively unfolding the paper, Malachi staggered, feeling faint, as he read the list:

1. Confirm dinner reservations at Bekta
2. Pick up ring at lunch
3. Ask Malachi to marry me

Ask Malachi to marry me! Tears flooded Malachi's eyes. He knew then that the nightmare would never end. It had, in fact, just begun.

A car horn, somewhere off in the distance, thrust Malachi out of his daydream and left him breathless. For a moment, he'd forgotten where he was. Then, glimpsing the photo of Cole on the bookshelf, he knew exactly where he was. He was in the middle of that nightmare that wouldn't end. He listened. The silence eerie and comforting. He felt nauseous. Maybe it was time to let go, to let Cole go. Didn't Cole deserve better?

He grabbed a piece of paper from the printer, picked up a pen, and poured out his thoughts onto the page. Afterwards, he gathered up the manuscript pages on his desk and shoved them into his satchel, which he then carried into the kitchen along with the piece of paper. Then he ran upstairs to the bedroom and, as fast as he could without thinking, shoved clothes into a suitcase.

Forty minutes later, Malachi stood in line at the Via Rail ticket counter at Union Station. He'd already decided on his destination, and it didn't surprise him. He was going to the one person who — for whatever reason, and despite what he'd told Shane — he hadn't completely let go of.

COLE TURNED THE KEY in the lock and pushed the door open wide. He stepped into the quiet house, setting his suitcase and briefcase down on the floor by the foot of the staircase. He looked back towards the driveway, Malachi's car still parked there, before closing the door. "I'm home," he called out, but it bounced off the moody walls. He kicked off his shoes and went first to check Malachi's office. Empty. Worse than that, it looked undisturbed, like it hadn't been used in days. *Where is he?* he wondered, engulfed by a sickening angst. He looked in each room as he made his way towards the kitchen, an acidic taste building in his mouth when he saw the paper on the counter. He picked it up and read the missive.

> Cole,
>
> After what happened at the airport, I couldn't stay here, couldn't face you again. Maybe you meant it, maybe you didn't, but I think taking a break — even if it's permanent — makes sense. To me, anyway. I'm sorry I couldn't say "I love you" back. I think that says more about me. Something is wrong with me, something is broken inside. That makes you right again. You deserve better.
>
> I don't know what happens next. I can't

think that far ahead. At the moment, all I know
is that I need to be on my own and think.

M

He marched into the dining room, grabbed the bottle of
Sky vodka from the sideboard and returned to the kitchen. He
filled a glass to the brim and gulped half of it. He winced, his
chest burning and his heart thumping. "Fuck!" He swiped at
the glass, knocking it off the counter. It crashed to the floor,
breaking into pieces. He didn't care. His fingers curled into
fists, which he raised in the air and tapped against his head
three times. *I didn't mean it. I didn't mean to push him away.
I just hoped that he would have fought for us. I'm the fool,
always the fool.*

He stepped around the broken glass and vodka pooled on
the floor as he made his way into the living room. He turned
on the CD player, Diane Reeves's powerful voice filling the
room. He found the remote control on the coffee table and
turned down the volume. He fell onto the sofa and, as he
closed his eyes, tears streaked down his face. Reeves was one
of Malachi's favourite jazz singers, but tonight she was also
one of Cole's. She held him and Malachi together, no matter
how loosely, amidst the rumblings of thunder occurring outside and inside his head. How long had he and Malachi been
on a collision course? He'd seen it coming and had tried to
do something about it. Nothing he did was ever good enough.
Did that mean he was ready to give up?

He opened his eyes just as lightning lit up the sky and the
lights flickered. *Call him. Find out what's going on. Don't
let him dictate how things will unfold. Have your say, too.*

Be a man. He flew off the sofa and patted himself down. His cell phone wasn't in his pocket. He went into the foyer and searched through his briefcase. It wasn't there, either. "I'm not in the mood for this!" he shouted. The doorbell sounded. He hesitated a moment, rubbed his eyes and then checked the time. He strode to the door and opened it. He staggered when Jeremy Turner came into view.

"Christ, you look like hell," Jeremy said, then held out the black phone. "I think this is yours."

"Thanks," Cole said in a barely audible voice as he palmed the phone. "Would you like to come in for a moment?"

"Sure," Jeremy said with surprise and stepped into the house.

Cole closed the door and drew in a deep breath. Jeremy had also attended the conference in Banff and they were on the same flight back to Toronto. They still worked together and fed off each other's dry wit, which occasionally allowed a residual sexual tension to surface. It was there now. He felt it. He wanted it. He needed it.

He led Jeremy into the living room and they sat down on the sofa. They didn't say anything, just sat there letting their eyes rove the room and smiling coyly when their gazes met. It was what they did long ago, during their affair, as a prelude to sex.

"I should offer you a drink," Cole said and stood.

"No, I'm good, thanks," Jeremy said. "Maybe it's a bad idea for me to stay." He rose and locked his eyes on Cole.

"Maybe you're right." *Why did I invite him in? Be stronger.* When Jeremy went to leave, Cole grabbed him by the arm. "Please stay for a drink." He disappeared briefly into the kitchen and returned with two Heineken, handing off one to Jeremy. "I guess it's lucky we landed when we did. Otherwise, we might have been up there circling for hours because of the weather."

They moved back into the living room, taking up their earlier positions on the sofa and not looking at each other.

"Are you all right?" Jeremy asked, levelling his gaze at Cole.

"Not really," Cole groaned. "I've fucked everything up."

Jeremy lifted his beer to his mouth and took a swig. "Are you talking about Malachi?"

Cole fell backwards into the sofa. "Christ! I don't know why I love him. I just do. But lately…" He turned to Jeremy. "I can't get Malachi to talk to me about anything. Not his writing, not what he's feeling, not the goddamn weather. It never used to be like this. I mean, he used to tell me everything."

"So, what's changed?" Jeremy asked, glancing away.

Cole shrugged. "I don't know. Getting a 'Hello' in the morning is like pulling fucking teeth." He blinked rapidly, trying to force back the oncoming tears. "It's like he doesn't want to have anything to do with me. God knows he certainly won't touch me."

"Let me ask you this…" Jeremy shifted his body slightly, his eyes roaming Cole's torso. "Why do you love him? More importantly, why do *you* stay?"

Cole dropped his head and didn't say anything. What could he say?

"Don't you think you deserve better, Cole?" Jeremy kicked Cole's leg when there was, again, no response. "You do deserve to be happy, and to be with someone who wants to make you happy."

"We were just…" Cole's voice broke off as a feeling of sadness overwhelmed. "In the beginning, once we got together, it was just so easy." He looked up. "He says there's no one else, but —"

"You don't believe him?" Jeremy placed his hand on Cole's thigh, two inches from his crotch, and squeezed.

"He won't have sex with me," Cole said, his gaze landing on Jeremy's hand. Finally, someone had touched him, made him feel wanted. He raised his head. "What am I supposed to believe?"

"You're supposed to believe what I say is true," Malachi said from the living room entryway, his fire-blazing eyes glued to Cole. "And you could try talking to me instead of your ex-lover."

Jeremy quickly pulled his hand away.

"I've tried talking to you!" Cole shouted as he bounced off the sofa. "God, I've tried."

"No, you tried giving orders, like I'm one of your minions."

"Fuck, all you know these days is how to be mean."

Jeremy stood. "I should go." He set the beer can on the coffee table and slipped out of the house.

Cole and Malachi stood there staring quizzically at each other for a time. Then Malachi rolled his eyes, turned and walked away.

"Malachi…" Cole ran after Malachi, running to catch up to him in the kitchen. "I'll be the bigger man here and say I'm sorry. Let's talk —"

"Talk about what?" Malachi took a bottle of water from the fridge. He kept his back to Cole as he unscrewed the cap. "At the airport ... didn't we break up?"

"I was angry," Cole said ruefully.

"Angry or not..." Malachi spun around. "You were right, like I said in my note. You deserve better."

"I want you."

"Why? You're right that all I've been to you is mean and cruel. Why would you still want me?"

There was a silence.

Cole sighed. "If you think I'm right, then why did you come back here?"

"Honestly, I don't know." Malachi gulped his water. "Are you sleeping with Jeremy?"

Cole's eyes widened. "Where the fuck did that come from?"

"Why else would he be here?"

"He drove me home from the airport and I left my cell phone in his car. No, Malachi, don't look at me like that. I haven't slept with Jeremy, despite what hasn't been going on in our bedroom."

"No, you just give him puppy dog eyes and bitch about me while he feels you up. Fuck, I ... I can't do this." Malachi went to leave the kitchen.

"I'm not the bad guy here!" Cole yelled as he chased after Malachi. "Jesus!" He stopped in his tracks, looked down and saw the blood pooling under his foot from the broken piece of glass he stepped on. Then came the thud of the front door slamming shut.

Let him go, just fucking let him go.

***

Malachi navigated his grey Range Rover through the darkness covering the 401. He was headed west, finally on his way to the one person with whom he knew he could be himself.

Earlier he had balked. As he waited in line to board the train at Union Station, he knew he'd been unfair — to Cole, to *them*. Cole had done everything to salvage them, and he'd turned a blind eye. He wasn't ready to admit that there wasn't anything wrong with them. He was the problem. And when Cole had finally given him a way out, he took it. Part of him wanted to articulate what it was that had him pulling away from Cole and the life they'd built. It was deeper than them not talking or not having sex, deeper than the imprint Zach had left on his life. When he was honest with himself, it came down to this: he wasn't happy with his life and didn't know what to do. Maybe it still had something to do with Taylor. Or his work at the college. Something wasn't right with him, and he had to work that out. Fair or not, Cole became his scapegoat and he didn't care. Actually, he had to care a little. That was why the part of him that wanted to get on that train couldn't. So instead, he roamed around downtown, dragging his suitcase behind him, and tried to think. He ended up at Hair of the Dog in the Village, ordering whiskey after whiskey to help make sense of it all.

If he and Cole were to survive, something had to change. Maybe Cole was right, and they needed to spend more time together — get to know each other again. That was the first thing to tackle. Maybe he could suggest that they buy a home together. Not Cole's house, not Malachi's, but *their* house. And he couldn't expect them to move to Claredon. That was just as silly and selfish as Cole asking him to leave the college. Perhaps they could move somewhere in between, some place new that they could choose together. Was that the answer?

But to walk in on Cole talking about him with Jeremy felt like the ultimate betrayal. He began to feel angry again. How dare he tell someone else about their sex life. That was their business and nobody else's. And maybe what bothered him most wasn't that Cole had talked to someone about their relationship as much as who it was. "His ex-lover!" Malachi screamed. "He fucking brought his goddamn ex into our mess." The burger and fries he'd had for dinner were backing up in his throat as he tried to tamp down his anger. He had to think about something different, something happy in his life. He turned up the volume on the radio, not in the mood for Bette Midler singing "The Wind Beneath My Wings," and changed the channel. He stopped on the station playing a Leonard Cohn song, and that allowed him to quiet his mind. He pressed down on the accelerator, the car gathering speed as he raced away from his past and to an uncertain future.

Two and a half hours after he'd stormed out on Cole, Malachi swerved onto Baycliffe Place and drove slowly as he tried to see the numbers on the houses. He pulled into the driveway with the black Audi A7 and parked beside it. He turned off the engine and sat there for a time. *What am I doing here? If I go in there, everything is lost.* But in that moment, he didn't care. He needed to be around someone he trusted, someone who understood him and his struggle. He saw the head peek through the crack in the curtains. Now he had no choice. He got out of the car, grabbed his suitcase and satchel from the rear cargo space, and made for the house. As he mounted the porch steps, the outside light came on and the front door swung open.

"Malachi?" Chad stepped out onto the porch in his sock feet.

"I didn't know where else to go," Malachi said. His eyes filled with tears and, at seeing Chad's reassuring smile, let them flow.

"Come in," Chad said, reaching for the handle of Malachi's suitcase. He moved aside to let Malachi enter first, then followed behind with the suitcase. He closed the door and locked it. Hesitating, and not really knowing why, but eventually went to Malachi and held him.

As Chad's strong arms held him, Malachi cried — for the love that once was, for the love that floundered, for the love that could never be. He held on tightly, his face nuzzled in Chad's neck, until he felt calm. He pulled away and dried his face with his hands. He stared at Chad, wanting to speak but unable to call forth his words. He shoved his hands in his pockets and pinched his lips. The silence didn't bother him, seemed almost perfect. "I'm sorry," was all he managed to say.

"Don't apologize." Chad grabbed the strap of Malachi's satchel, slid it off his arm, and set the bag on the floor next to the suitcase. "How about something to drink?"

"Oh, I think I've done enough of that lately." Malachi gave a nervous laugh.

"Come on." Chad tapped him on the arm. "I'll make you some tea."

Malachi followed Chad into the kitchen and stood in front of the island counter, watching as Chad filled the kettle and set it on the stove. It gave him a chance to study Chad in a way he hadn't done four years ago, assess his beauty. Chad's narrow brown eyes sparkled with as much of a hint of mystery as mischievousness. Something about his movements, graceful yet rough, made him think of a baseball player at bat. He wasn't sure why that was when he didn't even like baseball. Or maybe … something in the way Chad stood — his sturdy frame — reminded him of Taylor. Chad's black hair was cut short, which made his face seem fuller. Even through the loose-fitting brown and white checkered shirt he wore, Malachi could tell he still worked out regularly. *We were such an odd match back then. I don't know what he ever saw in me.* His eyes travelled down to Chad's jeans that hugged his round butt and awakened a longing that had never really been dormant. It'd always been alive through the years. "God, I'm such an idiot."

Chad spun around. "What?"

Malachi moaned. "Nothing."

The kettle whistled. Chad poured the hot water into a white porcelain teapot, which he then shifted to the table in the dining area. He invited Malachi to sit, which he did. They looked intently at each other from across the table, both of them knowing just how much they still mattered to each other. In the aftermath of their one-night stand, they knew they had to hang onto each other, shore up their bond. They exchanged, at rapid intervals, long e-mails that detailed the struggles they faced and the difficult choices they had to make. They encouraged and supported each other like two lovers separated, each trapped in some foreign land and unable to escape. With a view to a platonic friendship and even from behind a computer screen, they felt themselves becoming close. Too close. He disclosed his liaison with Chad as he began his romance with Cole, who wasn't initially bothered by it until he understood that Malachi wrote to Chad almost daily. That was odd for two people who were supposedly just friends. Three weeks into dating Cole, Malachi sent his last e-mail to Chad stating they had to let each other go. Their worlds were too chaotic to let them blossom. Chad must have agreed because he never responded. But then a year later, a friendship request on Facebook — initiated by Chad — brought them back to each other. So began a clandestine friendship by social media, and it was as if they'd never been apart. He had his confidant back, and that was exactly what he needed. Should he have told Cole? Maybe. But he could be friends with whomever he wanted. Cole had no right to pick and choose his friends. That wasn't what he'd signed up for.

"Do you want to talk about it?" Chad asked as he filled Malachi's mug with the fireweed and mint tea.

"I wouldn't know where to begin." Malachi looped his finger through the mug handle. "Everything's just upside-down at the moment."

Chad blew on his tea and took a sip. "What do you mean?"

"I don't know." Malachi sighed. He did know, but did he have the courage to actually hear himself say it? "Lately, I've been questioning everything. Me and Cole. My writing. Remember Zach? He wrote a book, one freakin' book, and it sold twice as many copies as my last two combined. He was my student, and I'm proud of him and his memory —"

"But?" Chad interrupted.

Malachi rolled his shoulders. "Maybe, I'm … a little jealous. I've been at this game for over a decade and I'm still not as good as him. He found his voice in a few months. Me … maybe I haven't found mine yet. Not my true voice, anyway. Maybe I'm a fraud." He wrapped his hands loosely around the warm mug. "Then there's my work at the college."

"Malachi, stop!" Chad sat up straight. "You have it all. You're a bestselling author and I think you've found your voice. I mean, come on, you're a genius. Do you read the reviews on Amazon? I love your protagonists, especially Caleb in your last book. Actually, I love to hate him because he's a goddamn jackass. Yet you still manage to make us root for him. That's what I enjoy, what everyone likes about your writing. And don't you love teaching?"

After a long silence, Malachi offered a faint smile. "I do. I get excited helping my students, young and old alike, hone their writing skills. It's especially great when one of them gets a story or poem published. I just…" He sat back, then dragged his hands down his face and let them rest on his lap. "What does it all mean?"

"Bloody hell, Malachi," Chad said bluntly, "don't bullshit *me*. You love to write. It's what you're compelled to do. So, what's this really all about?"

The tears were banking again in Malachi's eyes and he felt his chest tightening. He levelled his gaze at Chad and didn't blink. "I think…" He looked down. "I think I've fallen out of love with Cole. I don't know how it happened or when. I don't even know why. I just know that when I look at him, I don't feel that spark anymore. I don't think he gets me. I don't think he understands."

"Understands what?"

"Who I am. Who I've become."

"Have you tried explaining it to him?"

"Christ, you sound like Shane."

"You're the one in crisis," Chad said, matter-of-fact. "How's Cole supposed to know what's going on in your head if you don't talk to him?"

Malachi lifted his head and locked his eyes on Chad. "He told me he loved me and I couldn't say it back. What's the matter with me?"

"Malachi…"

"I pushed him away, cut him off." Malachi's voice cracked with each word. "Now … it's … all … over."

"Are you sure you've fallen out of love with Cole?" Chad asked. "To me, you don't sound so sure."

"I don't know." Malachi finally took a sip of his tea. "Maybe I do still love him, and maybe on some level I'd like it to work out between us. I just don't know how. And if that's the case, maybe I shouldn't be here, either. I can hardly be mad at Cole for talking about me with his ex if I'm here spilling the beans to you." He pushed back his chair and stood.

"Mali…" Chad reached out and grabbed Malachi by the arm. "Stay. Please, stay."

Malachi slowly lowered himself back down into his chair. He stared blankly into his tea and worked hard to keep the tears from flowing. This was exactly where he had to be. He knew that. It was why he fled to Chad. Over the years, he'd written to Chad the way he'd talked to Cole in the beginning. With blind trust. From the safety of his computer, he didn't have to filter his thoughts, letting them spill onto the page. They were raw and real. Sometimes, especially lately, he felt he had to censor himself with Cole. He wasn't sure why that was or whose fault it was. Well, actually, it was his fault because he'd slipped away from himself. Now, face-to-face with Chad, he wanted their intimacy to reign over him, give him new life.

Chad sidled his eyes to the microwave clock. Twenty minutes past eleven. "I have to work in the morning. Stay up as long as you like, but I'll show you to the guest bedroom."

"I'm sorry if this is an inconvenience," Malachi said and stood.

"I'm glad you're here." Chad offered another reassuring smile. "I'm glad you came to me."

They made their way upstairs to the room at the end of the hall. Chad entered first, turning on the light and setting Malachi's suitcase and satchel down near the foot of the bed. He studied Malachi who, looking somewhat disoriented, stood in front of the nightstand. "Stay as long as you like," he said, walking towards the door.

"Thanks," Malachi said. "Maybe a day or two. Just until I can figure out what to do."

"There's no need to rush." Chad reached for Malachi's hand, applied a little pressure, then left the room.

Malachi drew in a deep breath and blew it out slowly through his nose. He closed the door and leaned up against it, his eyes roving the cosy room with light-blue walls and one window that provided a view of the neighbour's house. A blue, white and green quilt covered the queen-size bed that took up much of the space. He took a step forward and touched his hand to the oak-stained bureau that looked like an antique, but he couldn't say for certain that it was. Did it have a history? Where had it been before being brought into this room and had it been wounded? He couldn't find any scratches.

He sat down on the bed with his hands clasped together on his lap, his head bowed and he cried. He cried for his long dead mother whom he had still not managed to forgive, for his father who had not said a word to him even as he lay dying, and for Cole and the home that was in ruins. Damnit, he cried for Zach because he feared he was living in the same *hell*, and for himself for being weak. He cried, still, for Taylor and the love he couldn't let go of.

Malachi fell back onto the bed and curled up in the foetal position, his face covered in tears, his lower lip quivering. He wanted to pray, but the words fell silent. All he could do was hope that this pain would pass, and that he would find a way back to himself, and to the life he imagined.

FIFTEEN

STRETCHED OUT ON ONE of the wooden loungers, the backs of his tanned hairy legs warm against the blue cushion with a flowery design, Cole let out a boisterous laugh as he flipped the page. Two days ago, he'd picked up Malachi's latest book, *Never Really Alone*, and hadn't been able to put it down. It was good, real good, and the first one he'd actually read. He'd only ever skimmed the others, spending most of his time reading books on business, entrepreneurship and leadership that he thought would help advance his career. But Malachi had a way with words and a unique, almost cynical, perspective on the world to which he could, oddly enough, relate. Cole turned the page and the next one was blank, and the next one after that. The story was over, but he wanted it to go on. He wanted to stay in Malachi's world. Then his body went rigid. For the first time in almost four years, he understood Malachi — everything he'd done, said, or tried to say but couldn't. "Fuck!" he growled. "I really did screw this up. I gave him every reason to fall out of love with me."

Cole closed his eyes. He turned his focus to his breathing, a way to steady his mind, feel a certain calm. He gave up two minutes later. Nothing could calm his mind. Well, one thing could, and that was for Malachi to walk through the door and them sitting down and, *une fois pour toutes,* talking. But he was beginning to believe that that was never going to happen.

It was the end of July, late in the afternoon, and the sun had already crossed the backyard and left it shaded. More than three weeks had passed since Malachi had walked out on him. And during that time he hadn't heard from Malachi, didn't know if he ever would. *God, you're such an ass.* It was how he chastised himself every day, as if that would change the past and allow him to reinvent himself. It changed nothing. He knew that, and that had his stomach doing regular somersaults.

He stood, picked up the empty glass balanced on the lounger's arm and went into the house. In the kitchen, he retrieved the jug of lemonade from the fridge and stared a moment at the glass. He knew what he was about to do wasn't a good idea, but that didn't stop him. He needed some type of reprieve from this world and the pain that continually pricked at him. He grabbed the ice cube tray from the freezer and dumped as many as he could into the glass. The vodka bottle had become a permanent fixture on the kitchen counter. He picked it up, filled his glass two-thirds full and topped it up with the lemonade. He took a gulp and didn't wince. How many had he had already? He'd lost count.

It didn't matter because he'd taken time off work to 'grieve.' He'd barely slept since Malachi had left. He couldn't. He wasn't eating either, and had lost a few pounds. He stopped shaving, the brown and grey beard becoming wild like he belonged in some badass motorcycle gang. Some days he didn't even shower or brush his teeth. Like today. It didn't matter. At the moment, nothing did.

He was about to return to the veranda when the dingdong of the doorbell rang out through the air. He took another large gulp of his drink before heading into the foyer. He opened the front door and rolled his eyes when Shane came into view.

"Is Malachi here?" Shane asked, barging into the house.

"No, he's not," Cole said askance.

"Where is he?"

"You tell me." Cole held onto the door handle. "I don't know where he is."

"How do you not know where he is?"

"Because he left." Cole let go of the door and ran his hand through his longish hair. "I thought he might have run to you."

"He didn't," Shane shot back, his eyes glued to Cole. "How long has he been gone?"

"Three weeks." Cole staggered to the staircase and sat down. "He doesn't answer my calls, e-mails or text messages. His sister called last week and I just told her he was away. If he's not with her, where could he be?" He saw the colour drain out of Shane's face and he stiffened. "You know where he is…"

"No, not really." Shane shrugged. "I have an idea."

"Tell me." Cole shot up off the stairs. "Damn it, I have a right to know!"

"Calm down," Shane said, moving to the door. "Let me see if I can find out for sure. Maybe I'm wrong."

Cole moved to intercept Shane, grabbing him by the arm, before he could slip out of the house. "Promise you'll tell me, whatever you find out."

"I won't promise that." Shane jerked his arm free. "Malachi's my friend. My loyalty is to him, not you. The rest is up to him." He rushed out of the house.

Cole slammed the door closed, his heart racing and his fingers balled into fists. *He's gone. Let him go. If he doesn't want to try to fix us, fine. Just let him go.* He went into the bathroom at the end of the hall, ran water in the sink and when it was hot splashed it on his face. He grabbed the blue hand towel to dry his face and then, seeing his reflection in the mirror, sighed. At forty, he thought he looked old. The beard didn't help, his face sallow and poised upon the terrible fear that the unwelcome end of he and Malachi had in fact arrived.

He tossed the towel on the counter, then made his way to the living room. He stood in front of the piano, running his hand back and forth across the polished ebony lid edge. He contemplated the picture of them, taken shortly after they'd met. *I think we were happy then.* He pulled out the piano bench and sat down. He didn't play, but he'd sneak into the living room and listen as Malachi practiced. The way Malachi moved — the music speaking through him — stirred his arousal, became an unexpected aphrodisiac. Growing up, there used to be music in the house all the time. His mother played the piano, and like he did with Malachi, he'd sit on the sofa and applaud. He often wondered why his mother became a lawyer when it seemed like music was her true passion. Something about it all seemed incredibly tragic to him. He felt his lips curling into a smile. He loved coming home to find Malachi at the piano, to once again have music in the house, to feel at home in the world.

"God, Cole, what the fuck have you done?" He cupped his hands to the back of his head, which lifted up his white T-shirt and exposed his hairy stomach. He let his arms fall to his sides and let out another grievous sigh. The ringing of the phone brought him out of his dream-like state. He bolted from the piano, answering the phone on the third ring. He slammed it down when the telemarketer started in on some spiel. Tears escaped his eyes and rolled down his face. His life was unravelling and he didn't know what to do. His parents were dead. He still had no contact with his siblings. There was, at least in the beginning, no play-acting with Malachi. That was what he liked. He could be himself, and not an illusion of what others wanted him to be. This was the concept of home, long missing from his life but which came to him when they'd met, that he hoped would sustain him through this unexpected, unforeseen mess.

***

Chad stared at Malachi through the window above the kitchen sink. His body tingled as he thought about that night, standing on the sidewalk and kissing Malachi for the first time. He'd felt buttery inside and his palms were clammy because he was so nervous. That buttery feeling was back, although he wasn't yearning for Malachi, not in that way. Back then, Malachi had shown up at a time in his life when he knew he was vulnerable. Now they were together and he was vulnerable in a new way. Maybe by being in each other's presence they could release themselves from the burdens weighing them down. Or perhaps Chad would have to find a saving force elsewhere.

He picked up the two wineglasses and returned to the back veranda. He handed the glass of the Wolf Blass chardonnay to Malachi, keeping the Cave Springs merlot for himself, and sat down at the patio table. "Did you get any writing done today?"

"A little," Malachi said after tasting his wine. "I spent most of my time just staring at the screen. Can't seem to focus much."

"Maybe you need to talk to Cole," Chad said. "If it's over —"

"Call me a coward, but I'm not ready for that." Malachi looked at Chad and smiled. "Thank you for opening up your house to me, but I feel like I've overstayed my welcome."

"You haven't," Chad reassured him. "You can stay for as long as you like."

Malachi sighed. "For a while after we first met, I wondered what might have happened if we'd met, say, a month earlier. And if you'd been single."

"I like to think that things turned out for the better." Chad winked. "I mean, I wouldn't trade our friendship for the world."

"Translation…" Malachi let out a nervous laugh. "Not interested."

"That's not what I said."

"God, my life is such a wrecking ball." Malachi shook his head. "I can't love the one I'm with and I can't…" He rubbed his eye. "I'm leaving tomorrow."

Chad sat up straight. "To go where?"

"To my sister's," Malachi said. "I haven't seen her or my nephew in a while. If you don't mind, I'd like to leave my car here and pick it up on the way back. My flight leaves in the morning."

"Sure." Chad paused. "Malachi —"

"I have to go, Chad. I've always…" Malachi set down his wineglass, rose and moved to the other side of the table. He lowered himself into the chair next to Chad and held his hand. "Fuck, I've screwed up and I don't know how to fix it. But if I stay here, I'll probably make things worse." When Chad's pressure matched his own, he leaned forward.

Chad pulled his hand away and placed it to the centre of Malachi's chest, holding him at bay. "Malachi…"

"Oh, Jesus!" Malachi shot out of the chair. "I'm sorry." He made a beeline for the house.

"Malachi, wait!" Chad bolted after Malachi, catching up to him before he could enter the house. He cupped his hand to Malachi's shoulder and spun him around. "It's not that I'm not interested, but you have to admit that the timing's not great. You don't even know what you want from Cole. You have to figure that out first and…" He hesitated, biting down on his lip. "I don't want to be your rebound guy or, worse, another piece of ass in your collection."

"That's not…" Malachi's voice trailed off. He took in a deep breath and sighed. "I should go tonight."

"No." Chad now had both hands on Malachi's shoulders. "Stay. And let me be your friend."

Malachi looked down.

After a long silence, they returned to the table to finish their wine. They didn't say anything, and that was both comforting and necessary. Chad's focus was on the fence that needed to be painted. He was glad that Malachi, in his moment of crisis, had come to him. He'd be, as he'd promised, his friend. It was the best thing he could do. For both of them. He looked at Malachi, who was staring off at some unfixed point in the other direction, and kicked his foot. "What would you like to do for dinner?"

"Let's go out." Malachi looked at Chad. "My treat."

Chad collected their empty wineglasses as he stood. "How about Pierre's Bistro? I haven't been there myself, but several of my colleagues rave about it."

"Sounds good." Malachi eased himself out of the chair and started for the house.

Chad walked slowly behind Malachi, that ache from years ago on the rise and gnawing at his heart. *Be his friend*, he counselled himself. *Be his friend!*

SIXTEEN

MALACHI TOSSED HIS PEN onto the manuscript pages spread out over the mahogany dining room table and pushed back his chair. He stared to his left, his gaze held to the rain-drops splattering on the window. Everything beyond a blur, like his life. *What went wrong?* he wondered, rolling his head back. He brought himself forward and hid his face in his hands. *It wasn't supposed to be like this.* He uncovered his face, picked up his pen and tried to focus on the pages before him, the galleys of his latest novel. His publisher checked in with him daily to make sure the corrected proofs would be delivered on time. The release date had already been delayed once, but Malachi didn't really care.

"I love days like this," Sarah said as she came into the dining room. She carried a plate with a roast beef sandwich in one hand and a glass of orange juice in the other.

He looked up, saw the raised-eyebrow look his sister threw at him and shuffled his papers to one side of the table, which he'd claimed as his writing space upon his arrival. "Sorry about the mess." His sister liked to keep a neat, orderly house while he thrived on organized chaos. A dictionary, thesaurus and grammar book cluttered the table along with his writing, just like the way he'd kept his desk back in Toronto.

"Do you even know where anything is?" Sarah asked when there was finally a place for her to set down the plate and glass.

"Absolutely!"

Sarah disappeared long enough to collect the other sandwich and drink from the kitchen. "I could never work in this ... mess."

Malachi took a bite of his sandwich and studied his sister, who was tall and slim like him. She had their mother's fair complexion, and most people thought she was biracial. She wasn't. Seated across from her, he remembered that the table had belonged to their parents. Their childhood home had been the gathering place for the family at Christmas and Thanksgiving, the feasts his mother prepared eaten at this very table. Aunts, uncles, cousins ... somehow everyone managed to sit around the table. That was a much happier time in his life, before his mother's illness and her death that had left a mark. At least the cancer took her quickly, but it left behind old wounds and misunderstandings. Was that why, when he left for university, it felt natural for him to stay away?

She looks so much like dad, he thought, taking in his sister's large, wild brown eyes and the strong, sturdy nose they shared. He chuckled. He knew their mother wouldn't have approved of the fire engine red lipstick covering the full lips of her round mouth.

"What?" she asked with a hint of annoyance.

"Nothing," he said, half grinning. "But really, sis, you don't have to cater to me."

"You wouldn't eat otherwise." She touched her hair a couple of times, smoothing it down gently. She'd returned about an hour ago from the beauty salon where she had her tight black curls relaxed and cut short. "Look at you now. You're as thin as a toothpick."

"You sound like mom," Malachi said with his mouth full. "Funny."

Malachi knew by her petulant tone that she wasn't amused. He watched her chew thoughtfully, their eyes locked, and was grateful for the silence. When he showed up unannounced on her doorstep, she welcomed him into her home as if it were the natural thing to do. No questions asked. *Is she trying to make up for the past?* he'd wondered then, and was asking himself the same question now. It wasn't necessarily in what she said or didn't say, but it was in the look — deep and probing — that had him thinking that she believed she'd failed him. Or worse yet, that she'd deserted him when he needed her the most. She hadn't.

Unlike their parents, she didn't care about him being gay. He sensed at times that she wanted to ask questions that, to some, may have seemed ridiculous. But she always held off because he was, to use the French term, *sensible* growing up. Then, when their mother was first diagnosed, they both hoped for some attempt, no matter how meager, at reconciliation between him and his parents. But Malachi and his mother were cut from the same cloth. They felt things strongly and could not be moved from their positions.

"Shall we continue this little dance?" Sarah asked before tossing the last piece of her sandwich into her mouth. When Malachi didn't say anything, she drummed her long fingernails against the tabletop. "All right, so I'll go first. You know, it's nice to have you here, and you know you can stay as long as you want. Maybe it'll give us a chance to get to know each other better. I mean, I know we don't have the closest of relationships, but Malachi ... I had to read in the *Chronicle Herald* that you were nominated for the Man Booker Prize. Didn't that warrant a phone call?" She raised a hand when Malachi opened his mouth. "No excuses. I'm your sister. We're blood. We should be celebrating each other's successes and encouraging one another through difficult times. That's what family does."

She's always been there for me, even when I didn't deserve it. She always made time for him — when she had her hands full with a teething baby, while she earned her degree, and as she tried to save a marriage she wasn't sure needed saving. "It's just..." He hesitated as her stare bore into him. This wasn't the time to hold things back. She'd opened her home to him and deserved the truth. "Cole and I are in trouble. It's been a rough year and I needed a breather. I walked out on him. Maybe for the right reason, maybe not. I don't know anymore. But I didn't know what else to do. I needed time to think."

"Do you love him?" Sarah asked bluntly.

Malachi shrugged. "I don't know. I don't know what I feel."

"You've been together a long time —"

"Does that mean I'm supposed to stay?"

"It means you owe him the truth."

"But I don't know the truth," Malachi snapped. "I don't know why I want out. I don't know why one day I love him and the next I don't. Or why I'm a freakin' prick."

Sarah was no stranger to dysfunctional relationships. She'd been through two husbands, and surely she understood the feelings of loss and confusion consuming her brother? Love was supposed to endure ... for a lifetime. That was the hope. But when the love ebbed, its premature ending could upend everything in its path. And, instantly, home fell apart.

"Malachi..." Sarah contemplated him, his surly face, his eyes skirting to avoid her gaze. "We all make mistakes. I know it's not always easy to forgive, but imagine a world without forgiveness and what it would look like." She reached across the table and placed her warm hand on top of his. "I don't know what Cole's done or not done, and nor do I need to know. Or maybe it's about what you've done or haven't done. Forgive him or don't, forgive yourself or don't ... that's up to you. But if you could imagine yourself in that world without forgiveness..."

Malachi jerked his hand away, grabbed his pen, and slid his papers back in front of him. He glimpsed Sarah's hand reaching for his empty plate and raised his head to see her disappearing into the kitchen. *We all make mistakes*, reverberated in his mind. That was just it. Cole hadn't made a mistake. Malachi had. Because he was in crisis, he'd treated Cole ruthlessly, wouldn't even have sex with him. Could he really fault Cole for wanting them to spend more time together? Was his life falling apart all because of Cole pressuring him to find a job closer to home? Was that the real strain on their relationship? He ran his hand over his face. Sometimes he felt like Cole didn't trust him, especially on the wintery nights when the roads were icy and he crashed at Shane's. When he arrived home the following day, Cole looked accusatorily at him and rebuffed any attempts at affection. What happened to that love that appeared as a symbol of romantic poetry and had swept them off their feet? *He's right.* He felt sick. *We share a bed, sometimes eat together, but live like roommates who know they won't renew the lease together.*

Was their love salvageable? If only he knew what he wanted, if only he could — for once in his life — be honest with himself and with Cole. Maybe the crisis was all in his head. Maybe he'd finally lost it, lost his mind.

He resumed reading the manuscript where he'd left off before Sarah had brought him lunch, a temporary escape into a world where he *could* forget the heartache of his own life.

***

The eerie silence in the house had Cole on edge. He had to find a way out of this labyrinth before it destroyed him completely. He had only one play left, and he knew it was risky, but didn't feel like he had any other choice.

In the bedroom, he tugged at the zipper of his navy-blue suitcase. His head felt heavy, not out of drunkenness but because the sleepless nights had caught up to him. He was beyond worn down. He felt dead inside. He grabbed his wallet off the mahogany chest of drawers and shoved it into his back pocket. As he went to pick up his watch, it slipped through his fingers and crashed to the floor. He bent over and picked it up, his hands shaking so much that he couldn't do up the clasp. He sat down on the bed and breathed deeply as his entire body trembled. *Don't panic*, he repeated to himself as it took him two more attempts to affix the watch to his wrist. Then he stood, yanked the suitcase off the bed and made his way downstairs.

He set the bag on the ceramic tile floor near the front door and headed to the kitchen to grab his keys off the hook next to the back door. He then roamed the lower level of the house to make sure all the lights were off, also ensuring the windows were closed and locked. He came into the living room, slipped his hands into his pockets and stood in the middle of the room. *How the fuck did I end up here?* he wondered, enveloped in loss. He was alone, again, in a world in which he felt conflicted. *I'd give anything to hold him again.* He felt safest when Malachi held him. He thought about the times they cuddled on the sofa and the joy that filled him, like he knew anything was possible. Sometimes they'd listen to music, exchanging coy smiles and gliding their hands over each other's bodies — the preamble to a passionate lovemaking session. Other times they talked energetically about their dreams, like when they first met and everything was new, held the promise of love.

He sighed as he pulled his hands out of his pockets. He wasn't sure if they could find their way back to each other or if it was too late. But he thought he had to try one last time. The house, without Malachi, was empty and nothing but a shell of his former life. This was supposed to be home, their home together, and then it dawned on him. Malachi had never tried to create his own imprint, made no attempt to change the décor or the furniture placements. Malachi had never, in that way, committed to *them*. How, then, could Cole expect it to really be home?

"Fuck, you're stupid!" Cole dragged his keys out of his pocket as he made his way into the foyer. He was about to pick up his suitcase when the doorbell sounded. His grip tightened on his keys, which dug into his skin. The doorbell rang a second time. He stepped forward, opened the door and his eyes went wide. "What are you doing here?"

"I thought you might want to talk," Jeremy Turner said, his gaze immediately falling on the suitcase behind Cole.

"Well, I don't." Cole picked up his valise and stepped onto the front porch, pulling the door closed behind him. He jammed a shiny, square-headed key in the door and locked it. Avoiding eye contact with Jeremy, he rushed towards his silver Hyundai Sonata, opened the trunk and tossed in his suitcase. He closed the trunk with a bang and moved around to the driver's side door.

"I know you're not all right," Jeremy said, grabbing Cole by the arm. "I know you, remember?"

"No, you don't know me, not like that." Cole twisted his arm out of Jeremy's grasp.

"If that's the lie you want to keep telling yourself, fine," Jeremy said.

"Fuck off!"

"Hey, I'm not your punching bag." Jeremy sucked his teeth. "I know you've been searching for love your whole life. You thought you found *the one* with Malachi, yet it's all fallen apart. And you're desperate to hang onto it, to him, and for what? I heard the way he spoke to you, I saw how he looked at you —"

"He was upset," Cole cut in. "I shouldn't have aired our dirty laundry to you."

"You needed someone to talk to, someone who'd listen." Jeremy took a step forward. "What's wrong with that?"

"Look, Jeremy…" Cole opened the car door. "I'm not interested in having this conversation. I'm late and have to go."

"Did he leave? Is that why you haven't been to work? Do you think he'll come back to you?" Jeremy shook his head. "So, now what? You're going to chase after him? For fuck's sake, Cole, why would you fight for him?"

"You couldn't possibly understand —"

"I understand that *he* walked out on you." Jeremy was almost shouting. "Are you that desperate? Do you think there's no one else out there who'll love you?"

"It's not that simple."

"But it is," Jeremy spat. "You seem to be the only one fighting for your relationship. When has Malachi ever fought for you? You were the one who drove every weekend to see him. And now it seems like you're contemplating giving up your job for him ... and for what? Where the hell is he?"

"I can't just walk —"

"Walk away, Cole. Walk out on him. It's exactly what you need to do because ... Christ Almighty, you deserve better than this, better than him. He constantly turns down sex. He won't talk to you. His happiness always comes first. Has he ever put you first? Ever? Can you even name one time?"

"Malachi moved in with me," Cole said, "a long way from his work."

"He moved out of his shitty one-bedroom condo into this grand house. Big sacrifice."

Cole's lips parted, but no other words came out. At the tears banking in his eyes, he dropped his head.

"Don't you see, Cole..." Jeremy touched his hand to Cole's arm. "You deserve someone who does these things, someone who'll love you no holds barred."

"I have to finish this," was Cole's tempered reply as he looked up. "Maybe you're right. But I've got to do this my way." He took a moment to draw in several deep breaths. "I guess the secret's out that I'm leaving the firm."

"If you were doing it to save your relationship with Malachi, it's not too late to change your mind."

"No." Cole bowed his head as if he was about to pray. "I won't change my mind. It's final. I'm leaving at the end of the month." He lifted his gaze to Jeremy, pursed his lips and rolled them. "I'll be in next week to debrief the team on the projects I've been leading. But as far as I know, Tom has already reassigned most of my files to the other associates. I'm going to have to bring you up to speed on everything else, but I don't want it to be difficult, Jeremy. I'm leaving because I need a new start, and that means having you out of my life. Permanently."

"I see."

"I hope you *do* see," Cole said bluntly. "Even if it really is over between Malachi and me, I won't run to you. I mean, there was never going to be an us. I've never thought of you like that."

"You never gave us a chance," Jeremy said bitterly. "You were never open to it."

"Maybe you were right about something else, too."

"What's that?"

"I've always been looking for love. Maybe I need to learn to be happy on my own." Cole got into the car and flipped the engine. He fastened his seatbelt and backed out of the driveway. As the car rolled down the street, he kept checking the rear-view mirror until Jeremy finally disappeared out of sight.

He pressed down on the accelerator and raced towards the airport. He'd made a decision, one that would bring down the curtain on what should only have been a one-act play — a decision he hoped he could live with.

SEVENTEEN

MALACHI STOOD AT THE edge of the gravel path and watched the ducks scurrying to feast on the pieces of bread being tossed at them by a silver-haired man. It was the same guy he had seen every day since he started taking his afternoon constitutionals through the Public Gardens. He watched the man reach into a plastic bag and wait for the ducks to quack before throwing the breadcrumbs high into the air, laughing as the ducks chased after them. Other onlookers in the park speculated about the man's mental stability, but his child-like smile seemed to reveal a great sense of joy. Why did feeding the ducks have to make him crazy?

The morning fog had lifted, but the sky was overcast, the air warm and humid. Malachi had left the house shortly after Sarah, who ran her own communications firm from her home. She'd gone to the gym for one of the fitness classes she attended daily. He clasped his hands behind his back and followed the gravel path towards the gate at the corner of Summer and Sackville streets. Outside the park, he stood at the intersection waiting to cross the road and found himself surrounded by couples — young and young-at-heart — holding hands and exchanging kisses. He breathed deeply, his eyes blinking rapidly behind his sunglasses as he tried to check his tears.

It took him about fifteen minutes to walk back to Sarah's Clifton Street home. It was twenty-seven minutes past one, and his sister's voice echoed from her office at the far end of the main floor. He went into the kitchen, grabbed a bottle of water from the fridge and then returned to his papers in the dining room. The pace of his progress frustrated him. Cole, Chad and Taylor were too much in his head, breaking his concentration. From the time he sat down at the table at eight to noon, when he went for his walk, he'd reviewed only six pages of the proofs.

It didn't help, either, that he was tired. His sleep had been restless, continuously interrupted by the slightest noise — the creaks of the old house, the howling wind, the early morning rain pelting against the window. And when he climbed into bed, he lay in the darkness thinking about his conversation with Sarah. They'd stayed up late, sharing a bottle of wine and talking like they'd never done before … like friends. Maybe the alcohol broke down barriers, opened them up to a new way of being with each other. Whatever it was, they both felt the shift. They'd come to an understanding about their past and present. So, he decided to tell Sarah about Chad, about the incongruence in his life, but talk about their childhood and parents dominated.

"Mama was furious when you came back from that party smelling of alcohol and barely able to walk in a straight line," Sarah said, smirking. "You were fourteen, I think."

"She only found out because I tripped over the shoes that you always left in the middle of the hall," Malachi said, curt.

"And the next day we both got one of her famous lessons that always ended with, 'Train up a child in the way he should go —'"

"'And when he is old, he shall not depart from it.' God…" Malachi shook his head. "It's the one verse of scripture I can't get out of my head."

"She worried constantly about you," Sarah said, trying to sound convincing. "She didn't want you to become another statistic, running the streets with some gang and ending up in jail."

"Instead I ended up gay and unholy. I think she would have preferred me in a gang."

Sarah cut her eyes. "Don't be silly."

There was a silence.

"And what about you?" Malachi went on the offence. "Mama probably prayed you wouldn't end up a teenage mother on welfare."

"I didn't end up on welfare," Sarah shot back. "And he made an honest woman out of me."

Malachi shrugged. "What does all that mean now?"

"It doesn't mean a thing." She sounded relieved. "Joshua's a fine young man, and I'm proud of him. Mind you, he's stubborn like his stepfather." She looked at Malachi and, in a hushed voice, added, "I think he might be gay, too."

Malachi choked on his mouthful of wine. "What?"

"He's twenty-one and hasn't brought a girl home yet, or even mentioned —"

"Doesn't mean anything," Malachi said, irritated. "Maybe he's a late bloomer, or maybe he's too busy with school."

"Maybe you could talk to him."

"Sarah, really…"

"I don't care if he's gay. But if he is, I want him to know that he can be open about it with me."

"Then talk to him," Malachi said flippantly as he contemplated Sarah, who immediately glanced away. All of a sudden she was unrecognizable to him, as if the possibility of having a gay son had made this normally self-confident, determined woman unsure of her own moral core. "I won't promise anything. If there's an opportunity before I leave —"

"You're leaving already?" Sarah said, alarmed. "When?"

"Monday or Tuesday."

Malachi had climbed into bed around two o'clock, and as he lay awake, there was a different sort of heaviness in his heart. During the five hours that he and Sarah sat out on the back veranda talking, he never mentioned Cole. Not once. Was that a sign that Cole no longer mattered to him, not like he used to? Had everything between them unravelled to the point where they were completely unsalvageable? It didn't seem so unimaginable that he and Cole — and the life they had built together — were a dream, fictitious, make-believe. And now the dream was over. *If it's just a dream, does that make me unreal?* he'd wondered as the heaviness hit his eyes. But he was real, more real than the staid notion of home that tried to claim him.

The clickety clack of Sarah's high heel shoes against the hardwood floor brought him back to the present. He winced. He told his sister he was leaving, and that was true. She just didn't know that he wasn't going straight home.

"Don't you ever take a break?" Sarah said as she came into the dining room.

"Don't you?"

It was Saturday, but it didn't seem that either of them liked to take a day off.

"If you're not going to take that with you when you go out," Sarah said, pointing at the phone on the table, "you could at least put it on vibrate. It's been ringing nonstop."

"Oh, sorry." Malachi reached for the phone and, when he was about to pick it up, it started ringing.

"Are you going to answer it?"

Malachi kept his gaze glued to the 'Unknown Caller' on the screen. "It's a wrong number."

"How many times can someone dial the wrong number?" Sarah asked when the ringing stopped. She pulled out a chair and sat down. "I swear it's the tenth time it's rung since I've been home."

Malachi slid the phone towards him and turned off the ringer. "Thanks for letting me stay here. I don't think I said that yet. I've booked my flight for Monday morning."

"Are you sure you don't want to stay a little longer?" She pointed at his papers spread out over the table. "Despite your 'organized chaos,' it's been nice having you here. It's been great catching up with my little brother."

Malachi took a swig of his water. "I realized something talking to you last night. I've never gotten over losing Taylor. In my own fucked-up way, I expected Cole to be like Taylor. But I've never let myself love Cole the way I did Taylor."

Sarah raised an eyebrow. "You got that from our talk?"

"Well..." Malachi grinned. "There were a few times when I wasn't paying attention to what you were saying."

"Thanks a lot!" Sarah swatted playfully at her brother from across the table. "So, what does that mean?"

"It means —" Malachi's phone began vibrating. "'Unknown Caller' again."

"That's it!" Sarah snatched the phone off the table and tapped 'Accept.' "Hello." She listened. "Yes, he is. One moment."

Malachi reluctantly took the phone from Sarah. "Hello," he said dryly, and immediately sat up in the chair. "Yes, yes, of course. I'm on my way." He hung up and stood.

"What's going on?" Sarah asked and slowly lifted herself out of the chair.

"There's been an accident," Malachi barely got out, levelling his gaze at Sarah. "It's Cole. He's in the hospital."

"Is he okay?" Sarah asked.

"I don't know." Malachi froze. He didn't know what to do, didn't understand the panic burning in his chest. Wait. Yes, he did understand it. It was happening again. And he wouldn't survive it this time. He wouldn't survive losing the man he loved. Not again.

"I'll drive you to the airport," Sarah said quietly.

"He's…" Malachi's throat constricted. "He's here. Cole's at the QE II."

"How did he know you were here?"

"I don't know." Malachi's tuna salad lunch roiled in his belly. "Did you call and tell him?"

"I did no such thing." Sarah pushed the chair into the table. "All right, let's get you to the hospital then."

Malachi didn't move. Struggling to breathe, he remembered standing in front of Taylor's closed casket at the funeral home. He'd wanted to see him, touch him one more time, but there had been too much damage to his body. His insides knotted tighter every time he tried to imagine what Taylor looked like under the lid. He closed his eyes, but immediately opened them wide. It wasn't Taylor he saw. It was Cole. "What if … what if I lose him?"

Sarah went around the table and pulled Malachi into her. "Cole's going to be fine. You've got to believe that." She pushed away, then guided Malachi to the front hall.

The front door swung open as they were stepping into their shoes.

"Hey, Mom," the tall, slim man said. "Uncle Malachi, I've got —"

"Later, Joshua," Sarah said gently. "Right now we need to get to the hospital."

"Why?" Joshua slipped his knapsack off his back and set it down on the staircase. "What's wrong?"

"I'll explain on the way," she said, ushering the two men out of the house.

Malachi walked to the car in a daze. He'd finally realized how much of a cad he'd been to the man who treated him like a god. Just when he was ready to make amends, he couldn't help but wonder if it was too late?

***

Malachi hopped out of the car before it had come to a complete stop. He ran towards the emergency entrance, dodging people along the way, and cut in front of the woman standing at the admittance counter. "Can you tell me where Cole Malcolm is?" he asked urgently.

"Sir, please take a number," the nurse said with restraint.

"Cole Malcolm," Malachi repeated, his tone fiery like a hostage taker who was prepared to risk it all if his will was tested. "Where is he?"

A man wearing a black V-neck scrub top and matching pants appeared behind the counter. "You're inquiring about Cole Malcolm?" he asked.

"Yes," Malachi grunted.

"Come with me, please," the guy said.

Malachi, his heart thumping in his chest, followed the man down the corridor and into a small room. He didn't like this, not at all, especially after the door closed. He could feel himself trembling.

"I'm Dan." He motioned Malachi to sit. "I'm a nurse and I was there when Mr. Malcolm was brought in. He's going to be fine. I'll try to get the doctor to come speak to you when she can."

Malachi, relieved, remained standing. "Can I see him?"

"Mr. Malcolm's already on his way to the operating room."

"Operating room?" Malachi's voice spiked in panic. "You said he was going to be fine."

"The accident caused a fracture in the middle of Mr. Malcolm's thighbone," Dan said, his eyes locked on Malachi. "It's what's called the femur. That requires surgery, and the doctor will explain all of that when you see her."

Malachi ran his hand over his mouth. "How long do you think it'll be before I can see him?"

"The surgery could take a few hours, then Mr. Malcolm will spend time in recovery." Dan checked the time. "It could be a while. In the meantime, there's a cafeteria on the second floor if you wanted to grab a coffee or something to eat." He opened the door.

"Dan..." Malachi took a step forward. "I'm sorry if I was a bit, well, rude earlier."

"Compared to the drama I see here regularly, that was rather mild. But I appreciate the apology." Dan left the room.

Malachi waited a moment before returning to the emergency waiting room, where he found Sarah and Joshua seated together. He updated them on Cole's condition, the little bit he knew, and then they made their way to the cafeteria. He couldn't sit still and kept fidgeting with the napkin under his coffee cup, tearing it into pieces. When Sarah went to touch his hand, Malachi bolted from his seat and paced the area between the two rows of tables.

"Oh, Malachi, sit down," Sarah pleaded. "Cole's going to be fine. The nurse said —"

"What if something goes wrong with the surgery?" Malachi shot back. "People go in for 'routine' procedures all the time and come out dead."

"That's not going to happen with Cole," Sarah said, trying not to laugh at her brother's dramatics. "Just be patient and positive."

Malachi glanced at his watch. It was almost five o'clock. "It's taking forever."

"It's only been three hours." Sarah shook her head. "Do you want the surgeon to rush and do a hatchet job on Cole's leg? That'd be nice. Let's have Cole hobbling around on a cane for the rest of his life because *you* wanted the doctor to hurry up."

Malachi sucked his teeth. "I'm going to see if there's anyone who can give me an update." He charged out of the cafeteria, determined to right the past and reset his life.

***

Cole felt the pressure on his hand and slowly opened his eyes. It took a moment for the room to come into focus, and his eyes quickly fell on Malachi. He thought it was a dream until he went to move and the pain burned in his leg. He opened his mouth to speak but didn't say anything, deciding to take a moment to gather his thoughts. Malachi's grip on his hand tightened and Cole looked away. He couldn't bear it. He closed his eyes and let the silence linger. His heart raced. He didn't know why he was so nervous, why, all off a sudden, he might be losing his nerve.

"I'm so glad you're all right," Malachi said in a whisper.

Cole felt Malachi's lips on his hand and opened his eyes again. Their gazes locked, he recognized the intensity in Malachi's eyes. It was the same as on that night they'd first met. Then, like now, it cut through him. That look had made him swoon, feel like his insides were on fire. Now he felt … nothing. Cole gently pulled his hand away and, taking his time, pushed himself up in the bed.

"Can I get you anything?" Malachi asked.

Cole shook his head. "I'm … fine." His voice was hoarse and unsteady. He lifted his head up a little, and that's when he noticed the others standing near the door. "Sarah?"

"It's nice to see you, Cole," Sarah said, approaching the bed. "Despite the circumstances, of course. We're so happy that you're all right."

"And is that Joshua?" Cole coughed. "He's all grown up."

"He thinks he's all grown up," Sarah said, flashing a bright smile at Joshua. "But he's still my baby."

"It's nice to meet you," Joshua said, remaining by the door.

"Likewise," Cole said, his voice sounding normal again. The one time he and Malachi had visited Sarah together, Joshua had been away on a school trip.

Sarah stepped closer to the bed and loosely hugged Cole, like he was a delicate china doll. "We'll let you two have some privacy," she said as she pulled away. She winked at Malachi, then moved towards Joshua and led him out of the room.

There was that silence again — awkward, necessary and debilitating. They couldn't outrun it or peel it away. Cole dodged Malachi's play for his hand. This was wrong. It was all wrong. Why had it taken so long for him to see it?

"Cole…" Malachi moved off the chair and sat on the edge of the bed. "How did you even know I was here?"

"I didn't," Cole said. "Sarah had called and I told her you were away. Then Shane showed up at the house looking for you and then I knew…"

Malachi sat up straight. "Knew what?"

"That I'd really lost you," Cole said. He saw that Malachi was going to speak and raised his hand in the air. "At the very least, tell me his name."

"Cole —"

"His name."

"It isn't what you think." Malachi dropped his gaze and said in a whisper, "I was with Chad."

"Chad?" Cole's assured voice broke with disbelief. "You told me that was over."

"It was." Malachi lifted his head. "I did cut him out of my life, but then we found each other on Facebook and started chatting again. But that's all. We corresponded with each

238 • MARCUS LOPÉS

other. I never met up with him, not until you and I had that blowout at the house." He sighed. "I just needed ... a friend."

"I was supposed to be your friend," Cole said coolly, then started coughing. "Fuck, I've been such a fool."

"I'm the fool," Malachi said, making a successful play for Cole's hand. "I've been trapped in the past and too stupid to see how much you love me, how much you've always loved me." He smiled. "I want to come home, Cole. I want us —"

"No." Cole yanked his hand free and tried to push down the tears coming into his eyes. "I read your last book, Malachi, and I realized that I'm not Caleb. Right? He's everything you said Taylor was. Free-spirited, ambitious, and out to change the world. You don't think I'm any of that."

"That's not true."

"God, I loved you. Maybe I still do, but I ... I can't do this anymore. I deserve to be happy, and I want to be with someone who wants to be with me."

"I don't think you truly realize what you've got until you're on the verge of losing it." Malachi, his voice cracking, seized Cole's hand again. "Let's not give up on us. You were right about everything. I haven't been there for you, for us, but I want to be. I'll change. I'll do whatever it takes, even leave the college, because I love you, Cole Malcolm."

"I don't believe you, Malachi," Cole said flatly. "I can't expect you to change because, really, it's never been your fault. It's mine."

"Cole —"

"I badgered you into a relationship you were never excited about, never really wanted. I couldn't take No for an answer, so I pursued you for weeks and weeks. Maybe I wore you down and you caved in without really being interested in me. But I didn't care. In my mind, I'd won the love lottery and believed we'd live happily ever after. Stupid, I know, but I expected you to change, to see me as your Prince Charming and be all over me. And I think, in the beginning, we were happy, that we both put in the effort to make sure that that happiness endured." Cole raised his free hand. "Let me finish. I don't think the Malachi I fell in love with was the real you. The real Malachi … he's the one I've seen the last few months. The Malachi who loves writing, loves his job, loves his freedom. You don't need *me*, Malachi. You might have even convinced yourself that you love me and want to be with me, but that's the illusion. This accident … it doesn't change that."

"I do love you, Cole."

Cole squeezed Malachi's hand, then pulled his away. "No, you don't, Malachi. And that's all right. You say you'll change. And maybe, for a time, you will change and make time for me, for us. But it won't last. Taylor's death broke something inside of you, and you just need to be free and on your own. No strings. No attachments. No pain. No one … not me, not Zach, not Chad could ever be good enough because you're still in love with a ghost. That's what's so easy for you. A ghost doesn't fuck up, doesn't ask you to give up your job for the sake of the relationship, doesn't walk out on you when things get tough. A ghost comes to you only when you want it to, lets you live in your imagination and your memories." Biting his lip, his head bopped up and down. "You say you want to be with me, but if you stay you'll never be free, you'll never be who you really are. And you, Malachi Bishop … you need to be free."

"That's not fair."

"Fair?" Cole wiped at the tears streaking down his face. "I've had to compete with Taylor our whole relationship. Do you call that fair?"

Malachi sat still, his eyes glazed over and his mouth open. He had no response, nothing to counter with.

After a long silence, Cole, his tears starting to dry, said, "Just go, Malachi." He closed his eyes and waited. Then it happened. He felt the pressure on the mattress reduce and heard the soft shuffling of feet across the floor. When he opened his eyes, Malachi was gone.

Cole swallowed hard and his eyes were moist again. He'd finally acted boldly, stood up for himself and his worth. He began to sob uncontrollably, his fingers curling into fists. If he'd done the right thing, why did he feel so miserable? When he stopped crying, he felt an unexpected calm. The world — his world — had come into focus. Now he knew what to do.

Once released from the hospital, Cole would return to Toronto. He'd pack up the life that no longer existed and begin again. Maybe it wasn't too late to chase after his dreams, just the way Malachi had done. Ruthlessly. If he wanted to leave a mark on the world, it was time to act. Why not run for mayor? Maybe he wouldn't win, but he could at least say he'd tried. It was worth a shot, right?

All he knew was that happiness wasn't bending over backwards and trying to convince someone to love him. Happiness wasn't sacrificing everything he was to make a relationship work. Happiness wasn't crawling into bed next to his lover and still feeling alone. Happiness was, he finally understood, being true to himself. And if love came, it came. Until then, he would live the life he imagined — on his own terms.

Cole Malcolm would be happy.

EIGHTEEN

THE NEXT MORNING, MALACHI slinked into the kitchen around ten o'clock. He'd gone straight to bed when they'd returned from the hospital. He didn't sleep. How could he? He'd lost everything. And he could now see his own complicity in his undoing. Yawning, Malachi searched through the cupboards for the Alberta Premium whiskey he'd bought just after he'd arrived. He needed something stronger than coffee. He needed something that would let him black out, forget the life he'd let slip away.

"Where the fuck is it?" Malachi mumbled, slamming the cupboard doors shut. Sarah had hidden it. That he was sure of. She'd told him he drank too much and that it wouldn't solve anything. He didn't care, especially now. "You've got to fucking be kidding me," he snarled when he found the whiskey stashed under the sink behind the Liquid-Plumr bottle. He took out a glass tumbler from the cupboard, filled it almost to the brim and went to take a sip.

"Oh, no you don't," Sarah said, rushing across the room. She snatched the glass away, poured the contents down the sink and then trained her gaze at Malachi. "What's wrong with you?"

"Don't start, Sarah!" Malachi barked, then turned to walk away.

"No, no." Sarah moved to intercept him. "You don't get to talk to me like that, not in my house." She raised her hands to his chest and shoved him when he tried to step past her. "Apart from 'Let's go,' you haven't said a word since we left the hospital." She reached for his hand. "What happened?"

"What happened?" Malachi jerked his hand away. He backed up to the counter in front of the sink and leaned against it as he folded his arms. "Cole dumped me. I went to him and he dumped me."

"Malachi, I'm —"

"Don't, Sarah … don't say you're sorry." Malachi took in a deep breath. "I'm sorry. I don't mean to snap. God, Sarah, I fucked everything up."

"Go sit down in the living room," Sarah said gently. "I'll make a fresh pot of coffee, then we'll talk." She walked past Malachi, placing her hand briefly to the side of his face, then headed for the coffeemaker.

Malachi left the kitchen and made for the living room. He found himself studying the photos hanging on the walls or framed and on display on bookcases. It was the first thing he'd done when he arrived. The collection, showcasing three generations of family and clippings of his writing success, projected an image of a perfect family. *Perfect!* He cringed. It was a charade. Nothing in his life before Taylor was perfect. Then Taylor had been plucked away. And the thing that came closest to being perfect since Taylor's death — his and Cole's love — had been ripped apart by his own callousness. Now what was he to do?

He sat down on the sofa, immured in silence. Sarah's words still prodded him. *Imagine a world without forgive-*

ness. He'd been prepared to give those words life, but Cole had shut him down before he could even try. Maybe that was what had shocked him the most. He thought Cole was a romantic who believed in 'for better and for worse.' But their life together went from worse to horrific, and Cole wanted — and got — out. Could Malachi blame him?

Sarah appeared in the living room carrying two mugs. "I hope there's enough cream and sugar," she said, handing off one of the drinks to Malachi.

"It looks fine," Malachi said.

Sarah made herself comfortable on the sofa next to Malachi. "What happened?"

"I told you what happened," Malachi said through gritted teeth. "Cole dumped me."

"Just a moment." Sarah set her mug down on the coffee table, closed her eyes and bowed her head. "Dear Lord, please give me the strength this morning not to hit my snarky brother upside the head. I pray that You'll give me the patience necessary to deal with him today. This I pray in Your holy name, amen." She opened her eyes and reached for her coffee.

"When did you find Jesus?" Malachi asked.

"The moment my little brother started acting like a … jackass." Sarah sipped her coffee. "Relationships don't just end. Things happen, things that change you and how you see the world. More importantly, how you see yourself in the world. And I know losing Taylor hurt, and it changed you. But Malachi … that was ten years ago. You have to let go. Completely." She shook her head when Malachi didn't say anything. "Did you lose interest in Cole?"

"No, it wasn't Cole I lost interest in," Malachi said soberly.

"I don't understand."

"I lost interest in me." Malachi sighed. "Everything was going well, too well, and I ... I kept waiting for it to come crashing down. The way it did when Taylor died. Don't ask me why I kept envisioning the worst. God, ever since Cole and I got together I've been terrified of losing him. I ended up too inside my head and convinced myself that I had to make a change. Any change. But I ended up not knowing what to do, stewing about it and then —"

"You withdrew," Sarah chimed in. "And you cut Cole out."

"Pretty much." Malachi finally tasted his lukewarm coffee. "I couldn't, or wouldn't, see that though. But Cole did. I should have seen it. I mean, why else would Cole have kept harping on me to leave the college? He wanted me closer to home so we could spend time together, but I was —"

"Stubborn?" Sarah chuckled. "Say it ain't so."

"It's not funny, Sarah." Malachi shifted his focus to a spot on the wall above Sarah's head. "I couldn't leave the college. In the beginning, I wasn't sure teaching was for me. Now I love it more than I ever thought I would." That was true. And he loved his students who, each year, seemed to him brighter and more talented than the students who came before them.

"Malachi..." Sarah waited until he held her gaze before continuing. "Do you love Cole? If you do, then maybe you fight —"

Malachi waved her off. "It doesn't matter. If you had seen the way..." He tried, but he couldn't swallow down the sickening feeling rising in his throat. "It was in his eyes. I saw it. He doesn't want anything to do with me. I can't blame him, either." He rose and stood in front of the window, staring blankly at the house across the street.

"But imagine —"

"No, Sarah. No more talk of forgiveness." Malachi spun around, holding his coffee mug in both hands. His look softened as he started to speak. "You're right. I have to let go completely of Taylor before I'll ever be able to open my heart to love. Cole's right, too. He deserves to be happy. And let's face it … I'll never make him happy, at least not in the way he merits. Oh, Sarah, don't cry. I hate it when people get emotional." He moved to the sofa, placing his mug on the coffee table as he sat down, and held his sister's hand. "I'm going to be all right. I need to take a little time to get to know myself again."

Sarah rubbed her eye. "I was just remembering your visit with Cole and how he looked at you. You both seemed so happy." She applied pressure to Malachi's hand. "I want you to be happy."

"Maybe one day." Malachi released Sarah's hand and stood. "I think I'll go for a walk."

"Malachi, if you want to stay longer, you know you can, right?"

"You know…" Malachi felt a hint of a smile on his face. "My sabbatical starts in a couple of weeks, and for the past two, three years I've had this idea about writing in the Mediterranean. Now there's nothing holding me back. Maybe what I really need is a change of scenery. Imagine me renting a villa in the south of France, writing and having coffee with a view of the Mediterranean Sea. You and Joshua could come visit." *Jesus! Cole didn't just break it off so I could be free. He did it so he could be free.*

"Sounds like you're planning on running away," Sarah said and polished off her coffee.

"Maybe. But you have to admit that the Mediterranean is a great place to run off to." He winked. "I'll be back in a bit." He strutted into the foyer and stabbed his feet in his shoes. He opened the front door and turned back towards the living room. "Sarah?"

"Yes?"

"Thanks." Malachi shot out of the house, the bright morning sun coming into his eyes. For the first time in months, he felt at peace with himself. And the idea of going to France — when he heard himself say it out loud — didn't seem silly or farfetched. Maybe alone, in a foreign land, would be the best way for him to get to know himself again.

Maybe 'running away' was the only way for Malachi to escape Zach Brennan's *hell* that still poked at him.

NINETEEN

"I CAN TELL YOU how it ends," Malachi said as he stepped onto the covered front porch. He smiled at Joshua, stretched out on the Victorian-style brown wicker chaise longue. He sat down in the matching chair and worked to make himself comfortable.

"It's homework," Joshua said, chuckling. He closed the book, set it on the table between them and looked at his uncle. "Slim pickings for courses in the summer session, and the Canadian literature course fulfills the humanities requirement. It's a lot of work, but I'm trying to finish my degree in three years instead of four."

"Why the rush?"

"I'm aiming for law or medicine." Joshua repositioned himself on the chaise longue. "It's a long road. I'm hoping to shorten it a bit."

"Don't burn yourself out." Malachi pointed at the book on the table. "And sometimes it's not about the destination, it's about the journey."

"Right." Joshua sounded irritated. He picked up the book and held his finger to the author's name. "It's kind of creepy that my uncle wrote those steamy scenes."

"Steamy?" Malachi laughed. "It's not erotica."

"I'm not so sure." Joshua winked and returned the book to the table. "But it's okay. It's your third book, right? The one that was nominated for the Booker Prize?"

Malachi smiled. "My second, actually."

"My professor asked us to think about morality as we read it." Joshua scratched his head. "I'm halfway through, but I don't get what she means."

"Neither do I," Malachi said coyly.

"Ha-ha." Joshua cut his eyes. "Why didn't you study philosophy?"

"I couldn't make up my mind. I thought about it. I also thought about studying political science. But I had a passion for words and writing that won out I guess."

"Like you knew what you had to do."

Malachi nodded. "In a manner of speaking, yes."

"Did you really think you could succeed? As a writer?"

"No. All I knew was that I had to try." Malachi crossed one leg over the other. "I had a dream and I decided I'd work hard to make it come true. It wasn't easy, especially when I was first starting out. I had a huge collection of rejection letters from publishers and there were times when I felt like giving up. But when it's something you really want, somehow you find the strength and courage to keep pushing on." He uncrossed his legs, leaned back in his chair and stared into the dull grey sky. The air was warm with a gentle breeze. He felt relaxed, at ease, and aware that something had shifted again. Was it him and Joshua? Until now, their relationship mimicked the one with Sarah: presents and cards exchanged on birthdays and at Christmas without knowing each other. Was this an attempt at them moving beyond the polite polemics that they were used to into a more authentic dialogue? Malachi turned his head slightly to the right and studied his nephew who, with his high brow and dark round face, favoured Barry Preston more than Sarah. "You're aiming for law or med school. But what do you want to do with your life?"

"What do you mean?" Joshua asked.

Malachi sat up and moved his chair so he faced Joshua. "If you become a lawyer or a doctor, what would you hope to achieve?"

"Some day I hope to get married and raise a family. I want to be able to provide for them."

"All right," Malachi said, smirking, "but let's dig a little deeper. Being a lawyer or doctor looks glamorous, and people often go into those fields without really knowing what they're all about. Or worse, they don't know why they're there. Then halfway in, they drop out because they realize it's not for them."

"I want to help people," Joshua said quietly.

"All right. You want to help people." Malachi flicked his eyebrows. "Nurses and teachers help people. Social workers help people. Why are you focused on becoming a lawyer or a doctor?"

Joshua opened his mouth but didn't say anything. He tried a second time, and still nothing came out. He succeeded on the third attempt. "For the last year and a half, I've been volunteering at the children's hospital. I spend a lot of time with kids in the cancer ward. I'd like to be able to help them fight the disease, maybe even cure it. They seem like the most courageous people I know." He paused. "Or maybe it's just a silly dream."

Malachi nodded his agreement. "But do you really think that it's a silly dream?"

"What if I don't succeed?"

"What if you do? You have to try. A lot of people don't try, and they end up leading ordinary lives. When you chase after your dreams, something in you comes alive. I know. It changes you. And no matter how silly you think your dreams are ... we wouldn't have iPhones or electric cars if people didn't chase after 'silly' dreams." He caught Joshua's dismissive shrug and kicked the leg of the chaise longue. "You're too young to be cynical. And your mother and I certainly don't want you ending up like your..."

Malachi bit his lip. He didn't like Barry Preston and still held a certain distrust of him although he hadn't seen his infamous ex-brother-in-law in years. Barry wasn't a dreamer or a man with ambition. He roamed from one job to the next, but at least he worked. He never provided child support after he'd walked out on Sarah, who managed quite ably without him. Joshua didn't need that kind of example in his life.

"I'm not going to end up like my father, if that's what you think," Joshua said brutishly. "I know nobody likes him, and I barely see him. He's never showed any interest in me."

That was true. Malachi knew of the 'forced' father-son visits Sarah had insisted upon during the divorce, but when Joshua turned sixteen he cut Barry out of his life.

"What aren't you saying?" Malachi asked.

"I don't know what —"

"Stop right there," Malachi broke in. He stood and moved to the railing, leaning against it. "I'm your uncle, not your mother." He chuckled. "You're quite good. I'm sure you sold your mother on that whole 'fight the disease, maybe even cure it' crap. I almost bought it. Almost. I think you have about as much interest in law and medicine as you do your father." He folded his arms. "What gives?"

Joshua dropped his head. "It's stupid."

"How do you know it's stupid?"

"Everyone tells me it's crazy," Joshua said with an air of defeat.

Joshua went silent, and Malachi again kicked the chaise longue. "I'm not everyone. And when it comes to doing crazy things, I think I have that title locked up in this family."

They laughed.

"I'd like to be an actor," Joshua said. "I was part of the drama club in high school, and my teacher thought I was good. He said I had potential."

"You're a good actor," Malachi said. "With that med school sob story, you should consider writing your own material."

"I wanted to study theatre straight out of high school," Joshua continued with disappointment. "I auditioned and got accepted but…"

"Your mom talked you out of it."

"She said I should get a 'real' degree and keep acting as a hobby."

"Because acting won't —"

"Pay the bills or put food on the table," Joshua chimed in.

Malachi shook his head. "She means well. Your mom told me the same thing when I said I was going to write full-time."

"So, she was right?"

"No, she wasn't." Malachi unfolded his arms and stood up straight. "I chose to teach. I wrote full-time for a couple of months and quickly became a hermit. I discovered I needed something more. Back then … it was shortly after Taylor died and teaching got me out of the house. It took time, but I learned to find a balance between writing and teaching so that I have time to write, to do what I really love." He took up his earlier position in the chair. "I don't think it's all or nothing. What's stopping you from applying again to the theatre program? And there's community theatre if you feel compelled to finish your biology degree to please your mother."

"I don't know." Joshua scratched his elbow. "There just doesn't seem to be enough time."

"You have to make time for what you love," Malachi said emphatically, a metallic taste rising in his mouth. Then his stomach flipped. "I think one of the most courageous things we can do is take that risk that let's us live the life we've imagined. It might work out, it might not."

"You make it sound so easy."

"It's not easy at all. There will always be times when you think that you'll never succeed and you might as well give up. There's always going to be someone doing better than you. So, why not try? We all make choices that decide who we are and who we become." Malachi pointed at the book on the table. "Can you imagine yourself in Sean's position?"

"No. He's a fictional character."

"Right…" Malachi drawled. If he had listened to everyone who had told him he'd never succeed as a writer and that he'd be throwing his life away, he'd have ended up a career civil servant and miserable. Perhaps even suicidal. "Then try imagining yourself in my position. I made time for writing, poured my heart and soul into it. Then Cole came into my life, and for a while we were happy. Then something happened and I ... I didn't make time for the man who loved me and who I said I loved. I shut him out for all the wrong reasons. Now's he gone."

Joshua hunched his shoulders. "I don't follow."

"Whether it's acting, or a boyfriend or girlfriend, we make time for the things and people we love. We find balance." Malachi clasped his hands together. "That's what allows us to live the life we want."

"So, you're a little like Sean in the book," Joshua said, smiling. "Conceited and selfish."

Malachi flicked his eyebrows. "I *am* him. I did whatever I wanted, put myself first. Always."

"Do your friends treat you like a demigod, too?"

"Hardly." Malachi rolled his shoulders. "Sometimes, when you're chasing after a dream, you do have to be a little selfish. But don't be like me and stop carrying about others. Don't lose your humanity."

There was a silence.

"Can I ask you something?" Joshua asked.

"Sure."

"In the book, Sean walked out on his partner. Did you do the same thing?"

Malachi swallowed hard. "No. At least not when I wrote that. Later..."

"Do you regret it?"

"Every day." Malachi shifted in his chair. His eyes met Joshua's and he glanced away.

"That was quite the detour," Joshua said.

"What do you mean?" Malachi tried not to smile.

"I mean," Joshua said in a steely voice, "that mom asked you to talk to me, right?"

Malachi nodded. "Yes."

"She thinks I'm gay."

"Are you?"

"No!" Joshua barked. He dropped his gaze and took a deep breath. "I'm in a little trouble though."

"What kind…" Malachi coughed. "What kind of trouble?"

"I got a girl pregnant. The one fucking time we didn't use a condom."

"That's all it takes." Malachi, leaning forward in his chair, heard the faint gasp and looked in the direction of the door. He saw the silhouette back away. How long had Sarah been listening? He returned his gaze to Joshua. "Are you sure it's yours?"

"No." Joshua looked up. "She says I'm the father, but we have an open relationship."

"Christ Almighty!" Malachi sat back in his chair. "Sorry. I'm not going to lecture you. It's just … times sure have changed since I was your age." He saw the usefulness of 'open relationships' but couldn't imagine himself in one. Could it have saved him and Cole? No, because he didn't see the appeal. He liked the adventure of getting to know someone, how to pleasure them. Like discovering that licking the inside of Cole's ear made him moan, a deep moan from the pit of his stomach. How exactly would that work with a third? Or maybe he was just too much of a prude for group sex. He fixed his gaze on Joshua. "Tell your mother. And when the baby's born, take a paternity test."

"It may never come to that," Joshua said with a hint of relief. "She wants to have an abortion, and wants me to pay for it!"

The front door flew open and Sarah emerged onto the porch. "Absolutely not," she said, pushing aside the book and sitting down on the table.

"Mom…" Joshua, his eyes moist, swung his body around on the chaise longue and planted his feet firmly on the porch floor.

"If she wants to get rid of the baby, fine," Sarah said, reaching for her son's hand, "but she does that on her own, especially if you can't say for certain that you're the father. Now … if she keeps it, your uncle's right. You'll take a paternity test, and if you're the father you'll live up to your responsibilities. And I'll be there to help."

"I never meant to disappoint you," Joshua said weakly.

"No, no." Sarah squeezed his hand. "You haven't disappointed me. Sweetheart, I love you. And just like we've done all these years, we'll get through this … together."

Malachi, watching Sarah and Joshua share a long embrace, felt a great wave of sadness. His time with his sister had brought them closer together, but he still felt disconnected from the place where he'd grown up. Perhaps nothing had changed since the time of Zach, or since Cole entered his life. He felt absolutely alone in the world. Was that because he couldn't let go of the love that haunted him? Would he ever find a way to set himself free? He rose again and made for the house.

"Where are you going?" Sarah said, pushing away from Joshua.

"To pack." Malachi opened the door and disappeared.

"Malachi…" Sarah called out after him.

Malachi ignored the call and bounced up the stairs to the guest bedroom. He retrieved his suitcase from the closet and tossed it on the bed. He unzippered it, then started to fold the clothes piled near the pillows and strategically organized them in the suitcase. There was a knock on the door. He didn't turn around.

"Malachi…" Sarah came into the room and sat down on the trunk at the foot of the bed. "What are you doing?"

Malachi spun around. "I don't know what you mean."

"I think you do." She crossed her legs. "Don't make the same mistake I did. Don't be so stubborn that you can't forgive. And don't roll your eyes at me."

"I'd be naïve to think that Cole would ever take me back," Malachi said, mimicking his sister's testy tone. "Especially after I…"

"After you what?"

Malachi sat down on the bed, crushing a pillow, and fiddled with a pair of socks. "Before I came here, I went to London."

"England?"

"No." Malachi laughed. "London, Ontario." His eyes were moist and he could feel a heavy grey weight pressing down on his chest. "I met someone before Cole and I got serious. It was a one-night stand, but we kept in touch for a while." He told Sarah about Chad and their recent reunion.

"Did you and Chad —"

"Nothing happened," Malachi said, feeling both relieved and disappointed. "There was a moment when … I thought he … I went to kiss him and he stepped back. It was stupid."

"You're being hard on yourself," Sarah said, reaching out her hand and placing it on Malachi's knee.

"I don't know how everything got this far. I mean, I do." He briefly hid his face in his hands. "God, you can't change the past no matter how much you want to."

"Then focus on the present," Sarah encouraged. "And be good to yourself."

"I will." Malachi slid off the bed and continued packing.

"When's your flight?" Sarah asked as she stood.

"Tomorrow morning. Around eleven. I'll take a cab."

"Don't be silly. I'll drive you." Sarah crossed to the door and turned back towards Malachi. "Where will you go?"

"I left my car at Chad's place. I'll pick it up and then head back to Toronto. Maybe I can pack up my things before Cole gets home. I don't think I can face him."

"And after that?"

Malachi shrugged. "I can probably crash with Chad until I figure out —"

"Do you think that's wise?" Sarah checked the time. "We'll leave here in an hour. You haven't forgotten your promise to take Joshua to East Side Mario's for dinner, have you?" She lingered a moment, unable to catch Malachi's eye, then left the room.

Alone, Malachi fell back down on the bed and tears exploded in his eyes. He couldn't outrun the past, he couldn't live in the present, and the future made him queasy. Could he ever be happy again?

He didn't think so, not in the way he imagined.

TWENTY

THE SUITCASE SLIPPED FROM Malachi's fingers and crashed to the floor. He felt a certain sadness for this house, which he had loved as a child. He thought with nostalgia of how he used to run up and down the steps until his mother scolded him to stop. He could almost hear the laughter that rumbled during the holiday gatherings, and smell the aroma of his mother's homemade bread that woke him from his sleep. It'd had been a sanctuary. Until everything changed. He didn't know how his sister could have moved back in. Maybe she was nostalgic about keeping it in the family. Had she been able to strip away the past? Could he do the same with his present?

He walked into the living room and was suddenly thrown back in time to an earlier version of himself: a young boy wounded and terrified. He had a vision of his mother, seated on the sofa, looking at him as if he didn't exist. He drew in a deep breath. That was the past, and there was nothing he could do about it. He had to worry about his present and how he could salvage what was left of his life.

He returned to the foyer, picked up the phone and dialled. A croaky voice answered on the other end and he gave his sister's Clifton Street address. "How long? Thanks." He hung up and stepped into his shoes.

"Oh," Sarah said when she came into the foyer and glanced at her watch. "I didn't realize it was that time. Let me grab my keys."

"I called a cab," Malachi said, slinging the strap of his satchel over his shoulder.

"I said I'd drive you."

"I know but, really, you've done enough." He picked up his suitcase, opened the door and went into the porch. He reached for the door handle of the screen door and turned around to look at Sarah, who had followed him. "Thanks, sis."

She rushed to him, threw her arms around his neck and held him for a moment. "I'm here for you, no matter what you decide." She pulled away and offered an encouraging smile.

"I know. And let me know how things work out with Joshua, and if I need to buy that T-shirt that reads, 'World's Greatest Grandma.'" He winked. "But seriously, if there's anything I can do, let me know."

"I will. Malachi, can I offer one more piece of advice?" She waited until he nodded, then continued. "I know you might be tempted to stay with Chad, but don't. If this is the moment when you start again, then that is the thing that you must do. Go to Toronto, pack up your things and clear the slate. It's best in the long run, for you and Cole."

Malachi didn't say anything, just held his sister's gaze. At the honking of a car horn, he swooped in and kissed her on the cheek. He rushed outside to the taxi parked at the curb and handed off his bags to the driver, who tossed them in the trunk. Moments later, the blue Camry rolled down the street.

He rested his head against the backseat and closed his eyes. He wanted to believe that this was the moment he could begin again. He was battle-worn and tired of fighting with a past that had the power to hold him and his life hostage. He had to break free if he stood any chance at real happiness again. Did he have the courage to do what was necessary?

More importantly, did he have the will?

***

Malachi paid the cab driver and stood at the bottom of the driveway, shifting his gaze between his Range Rover and the Audi A7. Ten hours after leaving his sister's home, he was back in London and losing the battle of wills. Sarah was right. He should go straight to Toronto and begin the process of moving on with his life. But he couldn't. If he couldn't face Cole, he couldn't think of even stepping back into that house. He was broken. All the decisions he'd made in the last six months to a year had unmade him. Going back to that house would drive him over the edge further, shattering his mind for good. Yet there was nowhere else for him to go. Not now. He picked up his suitcase and then, his heart thumping in his chest, reached into the bottom of his satchel and pulled out his car keys.

"Hey…"

Malachi froze. He lifted his head and thought he would collapse as Chad, wearing a form-fitting black swim brief and open-toed sandals, came towards him.

"What's going on?" Chad asked with a slight edge as he hugged Malachi. After they pushed apart, he pointed at the Range Rover. "Were you just going to sneak off?"

"I didn't…" Malachi's voice cracked, his eyes moving down Chad's bare chest. But the swim briefs, putting Chad's manhood on display, kept drawing his attention. And his black hair, cropped and even shorter, made him look like a rock star. "I didn't want to be an inconvenience again."

"Do you have to rush off?" Chad clasped his hands together and then stretched his arms above his head. He leaned to the right, held that position for the count of ten before switching to the left and holding it again. Then he let his hands drop to his sides. "I was just going to cool off in the pool, but how about a drink instead?"

Malachi swallowed hard. "I'd … I'd like that."

Chad reached for Malachi's suitcase, pulled up the handle and dragged it behind him as he made for the house. "Don't suppose you bought a swimsuit while you were in Halifax?"

"No. I was never much of a swimmer."

"I'll lend you a pair of mine."

"With your skinny ass?" Malachi chuckled. "Like they'd fit."

Inside, the air-conditioner blasted cool air and Malachi was happy for the relief from the humidity outside. A typical windy and rainy day when he left Halifax, he was wearing jeans, a grey shirt and a blue blazer. He took off the jacket and, following Chad into the kitchen, hung it on the back of one of the stools at the counter. His eyes immediately found Chad's backside, the briefs clinging to his round bum cheeks, and that long-simmering ache on the rise. When Chad turned around, he looked down. He'd been caught checking him out and he knew it.

"You're too cute," Chad said, handing Malachi a Corona. He took a swig of his own and smiled. "Why don't you go change into something cooler and meet me out back."

"Sure."

They stared at each other for a moment, then Chad headed out to the backyard.

Malachi set his beer on the counter without tasting it. He returned to the foyer, where Chad had left his suitcase, and carried it upstairs to the guest bedroom that had previously been his refuge. As he changed into a pair of knee-length grey shorts and a white T-shirt, there was something familiar about the room that eased his anxiousness. It had been the one place where he'd been able to escape, the chaos swirling about him held back at the door. He was about to leave the room when the oak-stained bureau caught his attention again. Something about its history — and finally seeing its wounds and blemishes — wouldn't let him go. Like Taylor. The memory of their life together, and the suddenness of how it had all fallen apart, stuck to him. He couldn't peel it away, and if he could be honest with himself, he didn't want to. What did that mean?

He headed downstairs and to the backyard, picking up his beer along the way. He sat down on the edge of the pool and eased his legs into the water. He studied Chad, who was swimming laps in the rectangular inground pool, powering through the water like a pro.

Chad, resting at the far end of the pool, held onto the ledge with one hand. When he saw Malachi at the opposite end, he swam towards him and, as he came closer, slammed his arms hard in the water.

"Hey!" Malachi protested playfully, although the soaked part of his shorts felt good against his skin.

"I said I'd lend you one of my swimsuits." Chad lifted himself out of the pool and sat next to Malachi. "God, aren't you hot?"

"It's not so bad." But, really, with his forehead already covered in sweat, it was unbearable.

Chad kicked his feet in the water a couple of times, again getting Malachi wet. Then he leaned over enough to briefly rub his shoulder against Malachi's. "How was Halifax?"

"It started off all right," Malachi said, turning to look at Chad. "My sister and I managed to talk. I tried not to involve her much in what's going on. But then..." Holding back his tears, he told Chad about the accident and the scene at the hospital with Cole.

"Oh, man ... I'm sorry, Malachi." Chad pushed back his wet hair from his face. "I never meant for our friendship to get in the way of your relationship with Cole."

"It wasn't our friendship per se." Malachi bit down on his lip. "It was one thing. Me still being so fucking caught up in the past and not treating Cole the way he deserved."

"And you don't think there's a chance the two of you can reconcile?"

"I don't think Cole wants to," Malachi said, matter-of-fact. "And maybe now ... neither do I."

"The way you used to write about Cole in your e-mails ... I thought you'd be together forever."

"So did I." Malachi tried to smile. "What about you?"

"What about me?" Chad said with an unexpected edge.

"You've been single a long time. I know Trent was an ass-hole, but haven't you thought about trying again?"

"I am." Chad looked away briefly. "I'm trying to keep it casual with Derek and not rush this time. He's a nice guy. You might meet him if you stay around long enough. He's supposed to drop by after work. His shift doesn't end until eight."

"Maybe another time," Malachi said, disappointment rattling his voice. "I really should get back to Toronto, pack up my things before Cole gets home." He set his half-empty beer bottle on the walkway, rose and rushed to the house. In the guest bedroom, he quickly collected his belongings and hurried back downstairs. He choked back his tears when he saw Chad standing in the foyer. It was silly of him to imagine any type of romantic relationship with Chad when he'd just broken up with Cole. But to learn Chad was dating... God, he'd been such a fool. And, really, did he believe that Chad would ever be interested in him like that again? When he had the chance, he chose Cole. No one ever wanted to be the runner-up. And Malachi knew that after what Chad had gone through with Trent, he wouldn't repeat the pattern.

"What's going on?" Chad asked and took a step towards Malachi.

"I should never have come here," Malachi said. "It was a mistake."

"A mistake?"

"I think the best thing for me right now is to be on my own." Malachi stabbed his feet into his shoes. "This way we can both get on with our lives."

"I don't really know what's happening here." Chad sounded frustrated. "But that sounds like goodbye."

"That's because it is ... goodbye."

"But why?" Chad grabbed Malachi by the arm. "What did I do?"

268 . MARCUS LOPÉS

"You didn't do anything but be yourself. It's me. It's all me." Malachi sighed. "I keep reading things into what you do and what you say, and I've managed to imagine a relationship between us that of course doesn't exist, except in my mind." He gently twisted out of Chad's grasp. "Right now, I need to get away from all this chaos."

"Don't include me in that chaos," Chad said. "All I've done is be your friend."

"Unfortunately, next to Cole, you're very much in the chaos. And like I said, it's my fault, not yours." Malachi opened the door and left the house. He headed for his vehicle and tossed his bags on the backseat. He went to open the driver's side door and his gaze locked on Chad, who stood at the edge of the walk. Malachi wanted to say something, anything, but he didn't know what. He smiled, got into the Range Rover and flipped the engine. There was a knock on the window as he fastened his seatbelt.

"I'm sorry, Malachi," Chad said as the window disappeared into the doorframe. "I didn't know you felt... Fuck, our timing has never been right."

"Maybe that's the universe telling us something," Malachi said cheekily.

"Don't. Don't be like that." Chad reached through the window and cupped his hand to Malachi's shoulder. "I'm your friend. I'll always be your friend. And if you ever need anything, I'm here. You know that, right?"

Malachi, his foot on the brake, shifted the SUV into reverse. "You're a good man, Chad. For the record, you couldn't have known how I felt because I never had the courage to say anything. Well, I tried when I went to kiss you, but it was a stupid thing to do. You did the right thing by ... I'm so screwed up that maybe what I feel or think I feel isn't even real. Again, it's just all part of the chaos." He paused, their eyes glued to each other, the stare deep and probing. "You deserve to be happy, and I hope you are with Derek."

"Don't disappear on me, Malachi," Chad pleaded.

Malachi eased his foot off the brake, Chad's hand slipping off his shoulder as the SUV rolled backwards. Shifting into drive, he caught Chad waving to him from the bottom of the driveway. Malachi didn't react. He pressed down on the accelerator and gunned it towards the highway.

Yes, he was running away. From his present and his past. From one love that had been left to asphyxiate itself, and another that would never bloom. From the madness infesting his life.

As the trees passed by in a blur as he sped down the highway, there was no more uncertainty. He had to leave. He'd go away and be on his own. And wherever he ended up, he hoped that he'd run into a better version of himself.

TWENTY-ONE

MALACHI WAS BACK IN the place that he knew would never be home again. He couldn't blame Cole or Chad or the memory of Taylor. He had screwed it up. He saw that now — accepted it — as the last few months of his life began playing themselves out in his mind. The puzzle pieces had moved into their proper places, and he ended up being discarded. Again, he knew he couldn't blame anyone but himself. Seated at his desk, he stared up at the white ceiling, tears gathering in his eyes. He'd gotten so caught up in the idea of a perfect love that he wouldn't let himself see that it had been, always, right in front of him. By the time he'd realized it, it was too late. Home, and the love he'd held so dear, had slipped away.

There had been yet another shift. He'd felt it as he backed out of Chad's driveway. Perhaps, for the first time in his life, he was prepared to let his heart lead him. He wanted to be led to a place he could think of as home. Every time he tried to conjure up that idea — when he could almost *see* the place — he saw himself arriving at some other place, foreign and uncomfortable, where he didn't belong. He'd always felt alone in that place, unable to speak the language.

Malachi, blinking rapidly, felt exhausted. It had been almost a week since his return, and he'd packed up his office, clothes and the few knickknacks he'd collected over the years. He was ready — as much as he could be — to leave.

He was waiting on the movers, who were scheduled now for the weekend. Could he stay in this house that long? That grey weight was back and pressing down on his chest. Sometimes he felt like the house had tried to claim him, like the house where he'd spent his youth, without fully latching onto him. He was an implant, artificial and defunct. Again, whose fault was that?

He moved from his desk and roamed from room to room, meditating on the events that had played out in them, and at the same time trying to feel himself *in* the room. It was his daily ritual, an attempt to be a part of each room's history, yet he was always absent from it. He entered the living room and gasped, surprised by the sense of loss and the tears rolling down his face. He'd always loved this room the most. When he played the piano, Cole always quietly settled into the sofa. He liked that Cole enjoyed listening to him play, but it also made him nervous, unsure of his talent. His hands became clammy, causing him to falter over the keys, as if he were an amateur. Struggling through a section, Cole would sit down on the bench next to him, and he'd find his rhythm again. When he stopped playing, Cole would kiss him on the cheek and then search for his mouth. It was never long before they were upstairs in the bedroom, Cole pushing him onto the bed and climbing on top of him. "God, what have I done?"

Malachi heard the key in the lock and spun around just as the front door swung open.

"If you could just set that there…"

Malachi's body went rigid as he recognized the voice. It was Cole.

"Oh, thank you, thank you," the other voice said with a slight accent. "I wish you a speedy recovery, sir. Have a nice day."

The door closed, and Malachi watched as Cole, who had yet to see him, hobbled along on crutches. Cole leaned one of the crutches against the wall and then tried to pick up his satchel. He couldn't do it, looking awkward and almost losing his balance. Malachi approached him cautiously and said, "Let me help."

Their eyes met, and Malachi immediately recoiled. There it was again in Cole's eyes — the sadness, the distrust and, worst of all, the disappointment.

"I can manage," Cole said, reaching for his crutch. He secured it under his armpit and moved off down the hall.

Malachi didn't move. Not at first. This was not the ending he'd imagined, even if he didn't think he could face Cole again. He knew, at some point, they'd see each other. It was inevitable. They'd need some type of closure. Maybe it was naïve of him to believe that they could be friends, or at the very least remain friendly towards each other. Something in him — the love he still harboured for Cole — made him want to try.

At the loud crash, Malachi ran down the hall and into the kitchen. He stopped just inside the doorway, his gaze locked on Cole. He made his way around the island counter to Cole, who stood by the stove.

"I haven't exactly got the hang of using these bloody crutches," Cole grunted.

Malachi looked down at the floor and saw the glass broken in pieces. He lifted his gaze and said, "I'll clean it up."

Cole didn't say a word. After a moment, he shuffled to the end of the counter and sat down on a stool.

Malachi cleaned up the mess, then went to get the vacuum, making sure all the small shards of glass were off the floor. After he'd put the vacuum away, he returned to the kitchen and took out two glasses. "What would you like?"

Cole, twirling a pill bottle on the counter, sighed. "Just a glass of water to take these damn meds."

Malachi retrieved the bottle of lemon-flavoured sparkling water and filled the glasses. He carried one over to Cole and set it down in front of him. He moved to pick up the other and stayed there, leaning up against the counter. "I didn't think you'd be back this soon."

"They kicked me out of the hospital four days after the surgery. Needed the bed." Cole downed a couple of pills. "Our healthcare system at work."

Malachi's eyes widened. "You went to a hotel?"

"I'd planned to." Cole dodged Malachi's eye. "Your sister wouldn't hear of it."

"My sister?"

"Sarah came to the hospital after you left. Just as I was being discharged." Cole gulped his water. "She insisted that I stay with her."

"You were at Sarah's?" Malachi twisted his face into knots. "I spoke to her yesterday and she never mentioned —"

"I asked her not to. I mean, really, there was no need to stir the pot further."

There was a silence.

"Look, Cole..." Malachi's voice trailed off as he worked to calm himself down. Why was he so upset? "I don't care that you were at Sarah's. I'm glad you're all right. That's all that matters." He downed his drink and set the glass on the counter. "I have everything packed. It was impossible to find a moving company that could come almost on demand. I did find one that'll be here first thing Saturday morning. I thought I'd stay here until then ... in the guest bedroom. But if you'd prefer that I leave, I will."

"I think we can survive under the same roof for a couple of days."

"I can help out a bit," Malachi volunteered. "I've already made a few dinners and put them in the freezer. And I'll make up the pull-out in the den. There's no way you should be climbing the stairs if you're alone in the house."

"You don't have to —"

"I want to, Cole."

Cole winced as a bolt of pain shot through his leg. "It won't change the fact that —"

"I don't expect it to," Malachi interrupted. "I know I screwed everything up and that there's no coming back from that. And maybe we can't exactly be friends right away, but I'd hope that we could at least be kind to each other. I'm asking a lot, I know. And Christ knows I don't deserve any kindness from you after how I've treated you. I guess I hope you'll be a bigger man than I've been."

Cole didn't say anything. The silence lingered, and when Malachi couldn't take it any longer, he started to walk away.

"Malachi..." Cole adjusted himself on the stool. "I may need some help until I can arrange for some assistance. While you're here..." He coughed, reached for his drink and drained it. "If you really want to help, my car's still parked at the airport. I can't drive and —"

"Do you remember where you parked?"

"I took a picture of the letter on the parking lot pole. It's on my phone, which is in my satchel by the door."

Malachi left the kitchen long enough to collect the charcoal satchel from the front hall. As Cole rifled through the bag, Malachi's heart swelled. Suddenly, he felt like he *was* home, and how could he even think of leaving here forever? He heard the faint ding of his phone. Cole had sent him the photo. Malachi checked the time. "I'll go pick it up now." He started to leave, then turned around to face Cole. "Can I get you anything before I go?"

"Well, you'll need these." Cole held out his car keys.

Malachi gave a nervous laugh, then stepped forward to accept the keys. When their fingers touched, a tingling sensation raced over his body. It was torture. Absolute torture. He was thinking about that morning almost four years ago when Cole stood before him — those hairy bronze cyclist's legs and the intent look of unremitting desire, hopeful friendship. He had tried so hard to resist him then, hold him at bay, but had fallen under his spell. And now, just like then, he wanted Cole in a way he hadn't felt in months. The ache was deep, primal and real.

"Are you okay?" Cole asked.

"I'm ... I'm fine." Malachi's throat constricted. "I'll get back as soon as I can." He held Cole's gaze for a moment, then left the kitchen.

Ten minutes later, Malachi was in a taxi bound for the airport. He thought about Cole seated at the counter and how bad he'd wanted to kiss him. He would have looked foolish, and it wouldn't have changed anything. Maybe he wanted Cole now because he couldn't have him. *Christ, Bishop, you're hopeless.* His life had been turned on its head and him along with it. And it sucked.

He closed his eyes and couldn't help but think of all the possibilities that could unfold over the next few days. Would he and Cole talk? Would they come to an understanding? Was there a chance, no matter how remote, that they could rekindle their love? When it came down to it, that was what he really wanted. He wanted to defy the odds, find a way to bring Cole back to him.

Maybe that sounded desperate. Or maybe he was too afraid of, one more time, ending up alone.

Or was it all one terrible long dream, and when he woke up everything would be just as it was — he and Cole heady in love, living the perfect life?

The taxi lurched to a stop and Malachi opened his eyes. He saw the departures sign and cringed.

Yes, the dream was over. The nightmare was in full swing.

***

Cole woke up in a cold sweat and bolted upright, his heart racing. He drew in several deep breaths, his eyes focusing on the small digits of the cable box clock. Twenty-two minutes to eight. He fell backwards, not moving until the heaviness had settled and he felt awake. It took three attempts to lift himself up off the pull-out, trying to balance the crutches and unable to bend the leg in a cast. He shuffled to the bathroom across the hall and felt a bit woozy as he relieved himself. Maybe that was the Percocet. The medication helped the pain, but

taking it made him feel like he was always in a daze. He needed to keep a clear head, especially with Malachi in the house.

He washed his face and massaged his trim beard. It was
time again to dye out the grey. He dried his face and hands,
then slowly made his way to the kitchen. Something was different. He didn't smell coffee. Malachi was never one to sleep
in, and when Cole usually came downstairs there was always
a half pot of coffee there for him. This morning the coffee pot
was empty. Was yesterday a dream? Had he imagined coming
home to Malachi?

"Morning."

Cole cranked his head to the left and locked his gaze on
Malachi, who went straight to the coffeemaker and pressed
'Brew.' He studied Malachi, who took out mugs from the
cupboard and carried them across the room to the small table.
He didn't know what to make of it, them together now after
two months apart. It was both comforting and odd. Would
it change anything? Cole sat down at the table and waited.
Malachi didn't really look at him, and that hurt even though
he thought it shouldn't. The coffeemaker beeped, and Cole
held his gaze to the floor. He heard the splash of coffee into
the mug, and then the table moved. He raised his head to see
Malachi seated across from him.

"How's the leg?" Malachi asked after slurping his coffee.

"Oh…" Cole slid his hand back and forth over the cast.
"It's all right. The Percocet helps."

"You're going to be all right on your own?" Malachi asked.

"I'll manage." Cole's tone changed from somewhat warm
to cool. "I mean, I managed for almost two months on my
own."

"Cole, I —"

"You could have called, Malachi," Cole growled, unable to beat back his anger. "You left a freakin' note and then nothing. For two months I heard nothing. Not a bloody word. Maybe we could have avoided this if you'd called. All you had to say was, 'I'm fine. I just need some time to sort things out.' But you didn't do that."

"No, I didn't."

"And that hurt."

"I wish I could —"

"What? Change the past?" Cole shook his head. "So that it'd be Taylor sitting across from you now instead of me?"

Malachi's mouth dropped open. "That's ... just ... cruel."

"Maybe." Cole picked up his coffee mug. "I just don't think you ever loved me."

"I did love you, Cole. I know I shut you out, but at the hospital —"

"At the hospital it was too late for 'I'm sorry.'" Cole sipped his drink. "It was too late for us."

They let their eyes rove the room. The silence gave them both a chance to calm down. Mentioning Taylor wasn't premeditated, but Cole was tired of being caught in his shadow. How long had he felt like the jilted lover?

"What's next for you?" Cole asked.

Malachi shrugged. "My sabbatical. I've decided to go away for a bit, clear my head."

"Alone?" Cole placed his hand to his forehead. It had come out too quickly, before he could censor himself.

"Yes, alone."

"For some reason, I thought you'd run straight to Chad." Cole shifted slightly on the chair. "I'm sorry. That was a cheap shot."

Malachi stood. "Maybe I shouldn't stay here. I can come back just to meet the movers on Saturday."

Cole trained his gaze at Malachi, who moved to the kitchen sink and poured out his coffee. This was it. The end. *Maybe it's for the best if he goes now. Maybe it'll make it easier.* "Malachi…" Cole, moving with difficulty but as fast as he could, scrambled from the table when Malachi left without saying a word. He heard Malachi's heavy footsteps on the staircase, but Malachi was gone by the time he made it to the foyer. Cole grabbed onto the railing and let his crutches fall to the floor. Then he started hopping up the stairs, resting twice, until he reached the top. He wasn't done yet. He still had to make it to the guest bedroom. But he made it — out of breath and beads of sweat on his forehead.

"Are you insane?" Malachi rushed to Cole, who stood in the doorway and looked as if he was about to collapse. He wrapped his arm around Cole's waist and helped him to the bed. "I don't want to argue with you, Cole. I don't want to upset you either, especially in your home."

"It could have been your home, too … if you would have let it." Cole's breathing was heavy. He grabbed Malachi by the arm, preventing him from moving away. "You're right. After everything we've been through and what I hope we've meant to each other, we can at least be friendly to each other. So, please stay … until Saturday."

Malachi sat down next to Cole and, in an unexpected move, reached for Cole's hand.

Cole didn't, as he thought he would, pull away. Instead, he matched Malachi's pressure. He waited a few minutes, as the silence implanted itself, then pulled his hand away. "Send me a postcard?"

Malachi chuckled as he moved off the bed. "Sure."

"I don't think this is how either of us thought we'd end up." Cole's focus was on Malachi's grey slacks and how they showcased his firm ass. He felt silly, like he did on that first night they'd met.

"I guess not." Malachi spun around. "I truly am sorry, Cole ... about everything."

Cole nodded. "So am I." He offered a faint smile. "My crutches..."

"I said it before that I shouldn't have left like that. If I had stayed, maybe everything before the accident would have been different." Malachi shook his head and started for the door. "I really don't know *how* you survived two months without me."

Cole, alone in the guest bedroom, couldn't shake the feeling that he'd never really recover from this. He knew they couldn't go on as they were, and he did believe that he deserved to be happy. Yet letting go of Malachi was harder than he thought. He wasn't sure how he'd manage. But he had to try. He had to prove to himself, more than anyone else, that he could be happy on his own.

"I really don't know how this is going to work," Malachi said, bursting into the room.

Cole scrunched his eyebrows. "How what will work?"

"You getting down the stairs with these." Malachi held up the crutches. "It might be easier for you to slide..."

"Pfft!" Cole snatched the crutches from Malachi and stood. As he headed for the door, he caught a glimpse of the photo on the dresser. His eyes became moist. He had taken the off-centred photo himself, he and Malachi standing in front of the moving van the day Malachi moved in. He was four years younger, and giddy with joy as he felt his life finally coming together. His position of Vice-President – Financial Institutions with Borden Management Consultants brought him greater recognition in his field. His knowledge and skills were in demand, and he was constantly fielding invites to speak at various conferences. But most important of all, he'd won Malachi's heart and they were living together, building a home. He had everything he wanted.

Now he couldn't shake the emptiness in his heart.

TWENTY-TWO

MALACHI WAS SLOWLY GETTING his life back on track. He'd gone to the south of France, where he rented a one-bedroom apartment in Villefranche-sur-mer. He woke up early every morning and sat at the table on the large terrace, writing under the rising sun. The spectacular bay view distracted him, and hours would slip by with him just staring blankly off in the distance. So, he'd pack up his writing and head to Café Belle Vie on Promenade des Marinières, where he'd become a regular. There he'd write until noon, then order a tuna pizza or croque madam for lunch. Afterwards, he'd play tourist and get lost exploring the narrow cobblestone streets. He was living his dream, and he was happy … for a time. While he roamed the streets in Cannes, visited the Matisse Museum or strolled along the Promenade des Anglais, he found himself scanning the faces of the people who passed by. All the time, he kept searching for Cole. It was torture. He couldn't take the loneliness anymore. The locals were kind to him, but he needed to be near people who supported him no matter what. That was the moment he realized he needed to return. Three months after touching down in France, Malachi was back where he thought he'd always belonged. Claredon.

Well, not exactly Claredon. He'd bought a house in Bridgenorth, just north of Claredon. The lakefront property offered the tranquility he needed to focus, to establish some sort of balance. And although the view wasn't quite the same as the one from the apartment in Villefranche-sur-mer, it still felt like he was living the dream. The mornings were much colder, but he'd put on a jacket and wrote on the covered porch. Sometimes late in the morning or before sunset, he'd go down to the wharf and sit there with his eyes closed. The crash of the water against the shoreline. Birds chirping. The slightest whistle of the wind in the trees. These were the sounds he heard that quieted his mind as he drew in long, deep breaths. These were the moments when he felt calm and, for the first time in months, free.

Things were different now, mid-January, and the time of writing on the porch had long passed. Most days, Malachi wrote in his office, which also offered a view of the lake. This morning he'd settled in at the dining room table, his papers sprawling. He hadn't written more than a hundred words and couldn't seem to focus. That wasn't that unusual. The ground kept shifting underneath him, and he found it harder and harder to concentrate. Even as he tried to structure his day — writing in the morning, reading in the early afternoon before putting in another writing session, and reality TV in the evening — he was easily distracted. He couldn't ground himself, not in the way that he wanted.

The doorbell sounded. Malachi's head swung upwards and he stared into the kitchen. His eyes strained to see the time on the microwave. It looked liked it was seven minutes past noon. He didn't move. It was Saturday, and he had no plans to see anyone or do anything. He wasn't in the mood to deal with his new neighbour, Jack, who was always running out of something — milk, eggs, sugar — and stopping by for a loan.

Malachi thought living in the country would be peaceful, yet it was turning out to be anything but. When the doorbell rang a second time, Malachi jumped up from the table and walked heavy-footed to the front door.

"Oh, it's you," Malachi said after opening the door.

"Thanks for the warm welcome," Shane said as he entered the house, closing the door behind him.

"What are you doing here?"

Shane pulled off his tuque and kicked off his shoes. "I'm checking in on you." He peeled off his jacket and slung it over the banister. "You haven't returned my calls or e-mails. I'm concerned."

Malachi waved him off. "No need to be concerned. I just needed some time alone." He turned away and made for the kitchen.

"You've had lots of time alone ... to brood," Shane said, following behind Malachi. "First in France, now in Bridgenorth. And, Christ ... I still don't know why you moved out here."

Malachi raised an eyebrow, then smirked.

"I'd love a coffee." Shane pulled out a stool and sat down at the island bar-counter.

"I'll make a fresh pot." Malachi dumped out the coffee and grinds from earlier in the morning, then ground some beans. Moving about the kitchen, he could feel Shane's eyes on him. Like he and his movements were being dissected. Shane hadn't just come to check on him. Malachi knew better. It was time for the great interrogation. The coffeemaker started to gurgle and growl, and Malachi levelled his gaze at Shane. "So..."

"How's the book coming?" Shane asked.

"Fine," Malachi said with an edge. "Don't dick around, Shane. Why are you here?"

"That's why I'm here," Shane growled. "The goddamn attitude you keep throwing at me, like I'm the enemy. I'm your best friend, or I was. But ever since things went south with Cole, you've cut me off. I'm not the enemy, by the way. I've been your staunchest ally, or I tried to be. And what I see now worries me. I mean, holing yourself up in the bush —"

"The bush?" Malachi howled.

"In the middle of east bum fuck, if you prefer." Shane's voice was elevated. "You said you came back from France because you felt too cut off from the people who mattered. Yet you're still cutting yourself off ... from the people who matter and the world."

The coffeemaker made a final bust of steam as the gurgling died off. Malachi poured two cups and gave one to Shane, whose grey eyes penetrated to his core. That made Malachi's body go rigid. "I'm not cutting you off."

"Yes, you are," Shane corrected.

"Well, I don't mean to." That was a lie. Almost as soon as he'd moved to Bridgenorth, he retreated into himself. True, Shane mattered to him. He just wasn't sure Shane understood him or where he'd ended up. He didn't want Shane to see how much the break-up with Cole had devastated him. Malachi realized too late that leaving France wasn't the answer. He should have stayed away. He should have tried to build a new life for himself like he had planned.

"Malachi?"

Malachi set his coffee on the counter without taking a sip, then folded his arms. "I'm just trying to get my life back on track, and it's taking longer than I thought it would to…" His voice broke off, his eyes becoming moist.

"Taking longer to what?"

Malachi blinked magnificently. "Get over Cole."

"Malachi —"

"I'm being an idiot, I know." Malachi rubbed his eyes. "I can't stop thinking about him. I don't know what's wrong with me, Shane. I mean, why am I never happy? When I was with Cole, I wanted to run away. When I realized I wanted to be with Cole, he didn't want me. So, I ran away to France, but all I thought about was coming back here. Here again, I'm miserable and want to go back to France, or to Cole, or to a fucking hole in the ground. Or maybe it's just that … the only thing I do well is running away from myself."

Shane stood, went over to Malachi and hugged him. "It'll get better," he said as they pushed apart.

"Fuck, I hope so."

"Focus on your writing," Shane said, matter-of-fact. "It's always been your passion. Give yourself over to it again. Let it rule you, let it have dominion."

Malachi stared blankly into the caramel liquid. "You're right. I have to find a way to get back to myself, and maybe it's through my writing. I have to, as you said, give myself over to it."

"Without cutting off the rest of us," Shane said and winked.

Malachi left the kitchen briefly, and when he returned he tossed the day's copy of the *Claredon Times* onto the counter.

Shane picked up the newspaper and read the headline aloud. "Former Borden Management Consultant Announces Mayoral Bid." He lowered the paper. "So?"

"Keep reading," Malachi said.

Shane returned his focus to the article and, after a moment, he looked up, his eyes wide. "Cole's running for mayor? Of Toronto?"

"I didn't even know he had political ambitions. How did I not know that?" There was a silence. "Christ, why did he stay with me so long? I'm such a fucking cad." He took another swig of his coffee.

"You're being too hard on yourself."

"No, I'm not. Cole was right. I stopped making time for us. I didn't deserve his love." Malachi's attention returned to the newspaper headline. Cole was free and chasing his dream. *Good for you, Cole. Good for you.* He felt his lips curl into a smile and fixed his gaze on Shane. "Let's grab a bite to eat. My treat."

Shane, his eyebrows scrunched, stood up straight. "What just happened here? A minute ago, I thought you were going to slit your wrists. Now you're beaming like you've just won the lottery. Did you take a happy pill when I wasn't looking?"

"God, you can be so dramatic. It's just … time to move on." Malachi chugged his coffee until it was gone. "Now, do you want me to buy you lunch or not?"

"Absolutely." Shane took a step forward and wrapped his arm around Malachi's shoulder. "You know I'm here for you. Always."

"I know. And thanks."

They headed into the foyer to put on their coats and shoes. A short time later, the front door banged shut.

As the cold wind hit Malachi's face, he felt … different. He felt as though he could move on and, perhaps even more importantly, let go of the past. It wouldn't be easy, but he would try. This was his moment when reaching back into the past and rushing forward to the future meant unearthing a new creation. A sort of rebirth. The feeling, surprisingly shocking, instilled a calm. He was ready, ready to free himself from a world where love was conditional and wildly savage. It required hope, and faith. But he could do it, free himself. And ending up alone didn't scare him the way it used to. Maybe being on his own for a while would be his saving force.

Maybe, when the time was right, he and his heart would be open to love.

Acknowledgements

I am deeply indebted to the people who helped me bring *Everything He Thought He Knew* to life. Dave Taylor, of thEditors, who edited this book. His insights proved invaluable and always on the mark. Dave, you're the best. Much gratitude to the team at Frostbite Publishing. Heather-Anne Gillis, Myrtle Gillis and Adrienne Ascah for your unwavering friendship, encouragement and support. And, John, for simply being you.

About the Author

MARCUS LOPÉS is the author of *The Flowers Need Watering*. An avid runner and amateur chef/baker, he lives in Toronto, Ontario. For more information, you can visit his website at marcuslopes.ca. You can also follow him on Facebook and Twitter.

Made in the
USA
Middletown, DE